★ "[H]ighlights the inconsistencies between the beliefs a country projects to the world at large and the realities experienced by immigrants.... **An excellent choice.**"—*SLJ*, starred

★ "With **riveting, lyrical prose,** Gibney's accomplished novel explores universal themes of home, family, power struggles, and endurance while demonstrating the liberating power of storytelling."
—*PUBLISHERS WEEKLY*, starred

★ "**Historically grand and intimately detailed.**"—*BCCB*, starred

"**[A]n illumination** of how humans end up treating each other cruelly and how they resist." —*THE HORN BOOK*

"*Dream Country* **asks big questions and exposes new histories** as it digs into the complexities of what Gibney calls 'the ongoing, spiraling history of the African–African American encounter'."
—*MINNEAPOLIS STAR TRIBUNE*

"A smart, many layered, and sometimes challenging book for smart people."—*ST. PAUL PIONEER PRESS*

"Ever-present is the tension between one kind of African and another, the destructive power of white colonization and the unending struggle to build a secure home and future."—*MINNESOTA PUBLIC RADIO*

"A vast and epic tale that explores racism, slavery, war, refugees, immigration, and what it means to be African-American as a whole."—*BUSTLE*

BULLETIN OF THE CENTER FOR CHILDREN'S BOOKS BLUE RIBBON BOOK
KIRKUS REVIEWS BEST YA HISTORICAL FICTION
NEW YORK PUBLIC LIBRARY BEST BOOK
FINALIST FOR THE MINNESOTA BOOK AWARD

DREAM COUNTRY

SHANNON GIBNEY

PENGUIN BOOKS

PENGUIN BOOKS

An imprint of Penguin Random House LLC, New York

First published in the United States of America by Dutton Books,
an imprint of Penguin Random House LLC, 2018
Published by Penguin Books, an imprint of Penguin Random House LLC, 2019
Copyright © 2018 by Shannon Gibney

VISIT US ONLINE AT PENGUINRANDOMHOUSE.COM

THE LIBRARY OF CONGRESS HAS CATALOGED THE DUTTON EDITION AS FOLLOWS

Names: Gibney, Shannon, author.
Title: Dream Country / by Shannon Gibney.
Description: New York, NY : Dutton, [2018]. | Summary: "Spanning two centuries and two continents, Dream Country is the story of five generations of young people caught in a spiral of death and exile between Liberia and the United States"— Provided by publisher.
Identifiers: LCCN 2017055923| ISBN 9780735231672 (hardback) | ISBN 9780735231696 (ebook)
Subjects: | CYAC: Family life—Liberia—Fiction. | Family life—Minnesota—Fiction. | Slavery—Fiction. | Refugees—Fiction. | Liberian Americans—Fiction. | African Americans—Fiction. | Americans—Liberia—Fiction. | Liberia—History—To 1847—Fiction. | Liberia—History—1847-1944—Fiction. | Minneapolis (Minn.)—Fiction. | BISAC: JUVENILE FICTION / People & Places / United States / African American. | JUVENILE FICTION / Historical / Africa. | JUVENILE FICTION / Social Issues / Prejudice & Racism.
Classification: LCC PZ7.1.G5 Dre 2018 | DDC [Fic]—dc23 LC record available at https://lccn.loc.gov/2017055923

Penguin Books ISBN 9780735231689

Printed in the United States of America

1 3 5 7 9 10 8 6 4 2

Design by Lindsey Andrews
Text set in Sabon LT Std

A condensed version of the first section of this book appeared as the short story "Lonestar," in the anthology *Sky Blue Water: Great Stories for Young Readers* (University of Minnesota Press, 2016).

A condensed version of the third section of this book appeared as the short story "Norfolk, 1827," in the anthology *Fiction on a Stick: New Stories by Minnesota Writers* (Milkweed, 2009).

*For Boisey, Sianneh, and Marwein, children made by
and living in the chasm, but not swallowed by it.*

For me, the rupture was the story.

—Saidiya Hartman

Let an ocean divide the white man from the man of color.

—Thomas Jefferson

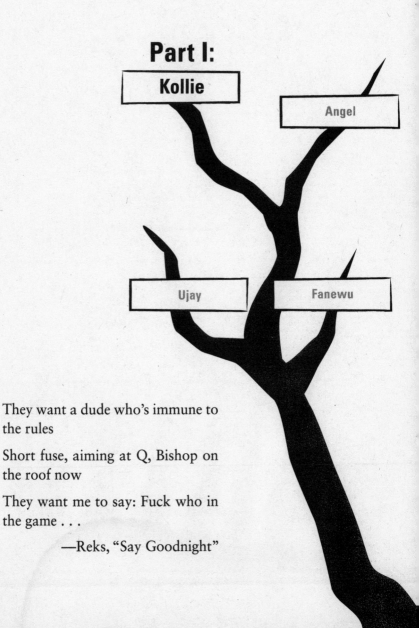

Part I:

Kollie

Angel

Ujay

Fanewu

They want a dude who's immune to
the rules

Short fuse, aiming at Q, Bishop on
the roof now

They want me to say: Fuck who in
the game . . .

—Reks, "Say Goodnight"

CHAPTER ONE

2008, Brooklyn Center, Minnesota

KOLLIE FLOMO WAS *DONE*. All he wanted was a moment's peace and quiet.

"Fucking motherfuckers. No fucking culture-menh." He echoed his mother's words under his breath as he wiped the spit from the back of his neck. He searched the hallway for the spitter—probably the same person who'd cough-shouted, "Jungle nigger." When he saw no obvious culprit, he gave up, walked into geometry, and found his place beside Abraham. His younger sister, Angel, sat in the back of the room, her textbook already open to the appropriate chapter, her pencil resting on a blank notebook page. Kollie grimaced. It was annoying to be in the same class, but they had a tacit agreement to ignore each other. So far, she was holding up her end of the bargain, scanning the room with a bored look on her face, pretending not to see him.

"Ya hello," he said to Abraham absently.

"Good morning, Comrade," Abraham replied, far too brightly. "You exactly seven minutes late-oh."

The two of them had lived three houses down from each other since the sixth grade. Some days, though, Kollie wondered if he even liked Abraham.

"Six. I had to urinate-oh," Kollie said. He took out his phone. No new texts. He threw his book on the table and then slouched down in his chair.

At the front of the room, Mrs. Walker turned around from the blackboard, startled by the noise. Kollie knew that she wouldn't do anything. She smiled at him nervously. Kollie nodded at her, then pulled his ball cap down over his eyes, how he liked it. She faced the blackboard again and continued writing some theorem that was basically illegible to him and probably made perfect sense to Fake-Ass Angel. He didn't know why he even bothered with this class. His daddy was buying him a basement club in Crystal, where he and his friends could spin the latest tracks for their friends and relatives, and make plenty of cash. He could almost hear Big Boi's dope lyrics skipping over the beat like a stone across cracked sidewalk.

"Sonja say she finished with Clark now," whispered Abraham, his pencil diligently moving across the paper.

Kollie pretended not to care, but his palms began to sweat. "Eh?"

Sonja was the flyest girl in school, and she was into both black and African guys, which was pretty rare for a black girl. Kollie had heard that her father was Kenyan.

2

"Definitely," whispered Abraham.

There was something about Sonja—maybe the way she smelled like clean soap, or the way her medium-sized, perky breasts peeked out of her T-shirts, or maybe even her loud laugh—but Kollie had a huge crush on her. He had been trying to get up the nerve to talk to her for weeks, but she always seemed to be surrounded by so many people. His own girlfriend, Lovie, was always around, too.

"Yes," said Abraham. "You should get her-oh. That big jue not be free for long now."

"Just like that?"

Abraham looked at him sideways. "Just like that, Comrade. Why not?"

Kollie thought about it for a moment: *Why not?* He grimaced. For starters, Clark, Sonja's now ex-boyfriend, had recently beat the shit out of Hassan Mohammed, who had four inches and thirty pounds on Kollie.

Why y'all jungle animals here, anyway? (Hassan wiped the blood from his nose with the back of his hand while Clark stared down at him.) *Minnesota's too cold for y'all. Can't run around here butt naked, like, Ow-wwwoooo!* (Accompanied by monkey-like gestures and noises.) *Admit it: It'd be better to get back to that one tree y'all got in your little African village, the one that throws enough shade to cover your small little dicks. Oh yeah, I heard about that—your secret's out. They took all the big-dicked dudes outta Africa and brought them here . . . and left all you small-dicked niggers to satisfy your poor-ass women there. Which would be why the la-dies love us.* (The black guys were whooping and holler-ing by this point.) *And why they steady running from you fake-ass Negroes.* (Jake Evans, the varsity quarterback, was clapping and laughing with his friends, like they were watching the Super Bowl or something. And all the teach-ers and lunch monitors were pretending that nothing was going on, like usual. Eventually someone handed Hassan a wad of napkins to clean himself up.)

"Let me think about it-oh," Kollie said, as casually as he could muster.

Abraham laughed. "Think all you want-menh. Just don't be surprised if someone else gets her while you do-ing all that thinking."

Kollie pounded the controller as fast as he could, but his zombie's bazooka refused to fire.

Sitting to his right, Gabriel laughed. "Team Plants 'bout to eat you alive, my brother." He snickered.

"Eeh-menh! What the fuck is wrong with your con-sole?" Kollie whined. What he really wanted to do was throw it across the room, but he didn't want Gabriel's parents to come down from their Bible study group. They had already threatened to throw away the PlayStation last week after a five-hour, seven-player odyssey of *Dark Souls II* got a little too rowdy. And before that, the boys' gaming sessions had earned them exile in the basement. The steady stream of profanity did not go well with the Kamara family living room's fifty-five-inch 4K OLED TV, with its clear-plastic-covered leather love seat and recliner, or with the framed poster of a white Jesus smiling down on it all.

"Gabe, you so corny, man," Tetee said, perched atop the back of an old couch. He stuffed a handful of Doritos in his mouth.

"Yeah, but at least I don't suck," Gabe said, firing a round into Kollie's staggering masses and blowing off most of their heads.

"Fuck you, asshole," Kollie said. "The fact is, this bitch-ass *game* is some motherfucking bullshit." Sometimes he marveled at how easily swear words rolled off his tongue now. When he had first come to America, every time he had even heard a swear word he had jumped. Now he couldn't even imagine speaking English without them. They were like ketchup on a hamburger or pepper in soup—they gave everything flavor.

"Spoken like a true loser," said Gabriel.

"Whatever, bitch." Kollie pounded the X button on his controller until his finger hurt, but still his rocket launcher refused to reload fast enough. "Fuck!"

These words had power when he used them, like little bombs going off all around. When he was ten, he hadn't understood that, hadn't gotten why the black boys used them every other word. But now he was sixteen.

"Yes! Who's a bitch now?" Gabriel threw his hands in the air. Kollie resisted the urge to punch him. He knew

Gabe well enough by now to know that he was only playing, that this was part of the fun of gaming with his crew. Still, his belly felt raw. Things had been bothering him lately that he knew shouldn't, but somehow, he couldn't help it. He dropped the controller into his lap.

"*Plants vs. Zombies*, who comes up with that pussy shit? Just stupid-oh, a flower running around with a peashooter, trying to eliminate zombies. What kind of faggot game is that-menh? Americans can be some stupid-ass people-oh," said Kollie.

Tetee leaned down and put a hand on his shoulder. "Relax, Comrade."

"And then you got to be even stupider to actually *buy* the fucking game," Kollie continued, undaunted. "My man, would you plead temporary insanity was what made you buy this piece of shit?"

Gabe's suppression-fire specialist massacred the last of Kollie's zombies, and the big red game over flashed across the screen. "I wouldn't plead shit, Comrade My-Bitch," said Gabe. He had been in the U.S. since he was four, so it was easy to mistake him for a regular black guy. "What I would do is tell you to get used to getting your ass kicked by a damn *plant*."

Tetee laughed.

Kollie's stomach still hurt, and his fist was now screaming to connect with Gabe's jaw. He knew that Gabe had no idea, that he had really meant nothing by it—this was all part of regular gamer trash talk. But Kollie couldn't shake the idea that it would feel so *good* to hit him, to hit anybody.

Tetee, who had lived next to Kollie in Red Light the year before the war came to Monrovia, squeezed his shoulder again. "Relax, Comrade. It's just a game-menh."

Kollie sighed and closed his eyes. An image of his family and Tetee's huddled together in a small church auditorium while rocket launchers exploded into the night flashed before his eyes, and then he pushed it aside. Instead, he imagined himself kissing Sonja, her soft lips covering his. His breath became deeper, more regular, and he began to feel like himself again. "My man, put down the chips and play this rebel bitch already." Kollie stood up and handed the controller to Tetee. "Motherfucker, you 'bout to get shown how plants are put down in Red Light." Kollie was both surprised and encouraged that he could manage a smile.

Tetee laughed and moved to sit beside Gabe.

Gabe stood too, and then pulled his jeans down below his butt, exaggerating the way the black dudes wore them at Brooklyn Center. Then he started jumping around, making an AK-47 out of his hands. "Try me, bitches. Do it. Niggas call me General Saggy Pants, 'cause my Small Boys kill Big Men in fancy suit-oh," he said. "My AK shoot your zombie dead with my black magic peas!" Gabe said now, prancing around like a pony on amphetamines.

Both Kollie and Tetee collapsed in laughter on the floor. And just like that, everything was fine again.

CHAPTER TWO

"WHAT THE HELL'S WRONG with you, Kollie? I'm only trying to help."

The air was damp and cold the next morning, as Kollie and his sister waited for their bus to school. Angel had asked him if he needed to copy yesterday's geometry homework, and he'd responded by putting on his headphones and pulling up his hood.

The sun was just coming up over the horizon, and languid heat might roll up behind it or maybe it would snow. For the millionth time, Kollie thought that he would never understand the weather in this country. There was no rhyme or reason to it, which was why he always opted to wear jeans and a hoodie. He could be sure to be more comfortable than uncomfortable during the day, no matter what happened.

Angel called the outfit his "uniform"—or his "armor" if she was trying to piss him off. He never bothered to tell her that if anything was armor, it was his headphones.

"Here comes your purse," Angel said as Lovie rounded the corner on the other end of the block.

"Handbag," he said, and then he sighed. Why could Angel never quite get Liberian idioms right? Their mother called anyone, especially children, who hung around someone too much a "handbag," which was how Angel saw Lovie.

"Whatever. Fuck you, Kollie," Angel said, and put in her earbuds. The fact that Lovie was Kollie's girlfriend irritated his sister so much that Kollie actually noticed. Actually Angel had introduced Lovie to Kollie, and the two girls used to be close, until Kollie and Lovie started dating.

"Good morning, Sweetie," Lovie said as she neared the stop. She was wearing tight jeans that showed off her wide hips and substantial butt, and a bright white T-shirt with sparkles. Lip gloss and a new bobbed wig completed the look.

"Good morning-oh." Kollie pushed down his hood and headphones and forced himself to smile at her. They had been together three months and he was tired of her, but didn't know how to tell her. And he knew he couldn't get away with ignoring her like he did Angel. Like the rest of his life, it seemed easier to ride it out until something better came along. Something like Sonja.

"Yeah, hello, ma," Lovie said to his sister. Unlike Angel, Liberian English expressions—like calling all female acquaintances "ma"—came to Lovie without a second thought.

"Yeah, good morning," Angel answered back, then deliberately looked away from her.

Lovie turned back to him. "How everything? What news? You good?"

"Yeah, fine," Kollie said.

Lovie looked at Kollie for a second, like she was going to ask if he was okay again, and he wished more than anything he could put his headphones back on. But then she smiled and dug something out of her backpack. "Lowell said this top-of-the-line-oh." It was a Bose Bluetooth speaker. Her older brother worked at Best Buy, and often got special deals on merchandise. Lovie had a small gap between her front teeth that he had always found endearing, especially when she smiled shyly like she was doing now. "I got it cheap-cheap," she said. "I knew when I saw it, it was perfect for your room-oh."

His other speakers had busted last week, probably from too much use. He had to have his music pumping whenever he was home, no matter what he was doing. It was just that simple.

"You my black diamond-oh," he said, and he almost meant it. He had had two other girlfriends before Lovie, and none of them did half the stuff for him that she did. She cooked him *both* burgers and bean soup with fish and cow, helped him with his homework on occasion, and had even cleaned his room once. Lovie didn't freak out

about sex, either, and was pretty much down for whatever. She was a good church girl, showed up every Sunday
with her family, and memorized line and verse, but the
meaning—especially the dire warnings about the effects
of fornication on the soul—seemed to go in one ear and
out the other. Which Kollie knew he ought to appreciate.

Lovie leaned over to give him a quick kiss on the lips,
and he let her.

Angel snickered beside them. Kollie knew she thought
all of this was nonsense, that Lovie was wasting her time
and energy on him. Angel called herself *a feminist*, which
as far as Kollie could tell meant that she hated men but
wanted a penis. She certainly hated their father enough.

The bus rumbled in the distance. Kollie sighed at the
thought of another day at school. Lovie was texting, so he
put in his headphones and started pumping the P-Square.
The bus stopped, Angel got on, then Lovie, then him.
Lovie expected him to sit by her during the ten-minute
ride to school.

"Hey, bro, wassup?" Saah said as he walked by
the first front seats. He held out his hand, and Kollie
slapped it.

"Yo, wassup, Comrade?" Kollie said back, dropping his headphones to his neck but leaving the P-Square
playing.

"How everything, Comrade?" Mardia asked, seated
next to Saah.

"Yeah, fine," Kollie answered, taking a seat behind

them, next to Lovie. Mardia and Saah lived a few blocks west of him, and played with him on the soccer team. Their mothers also frequently cooked large platters of Liberian food together for community gatherings, either at their houses or at church.

"The weekend good-oh," Mardia said as the bus pulled away from the curb. "I don't know why it need to end with this school shit."

Kollie smiled wryly.

Saah smacked his friend lightly on the arm. "Man, the weekend been done for a whole day now. Today Tuesday, Mardia."

Mardia hit back. "I know that. I just talking about how there never enough time in this country to *relax-oh*. No wonder the people so wack."

Kollie shook his head. Mardia was right, of course. Everyone here worked all the time and went to school when they weren't working. All the adults, anyway. The Liberians threw their own parties on the weekends, which started at ten and lasted until three or four in the morning, but then they had to get up a few hours later for church or work wiping old white people's butts at the nursing home.

Up ahead, the gray institutional face of Brooklyn Center High School got larger and larger in the front windshield. It looked like a prison, with its blank concrete walls and tiny windows.

"Yo, Comrade, how you doing-oh?" A teasing voice boomed from behind them.

Kollie felt his fist tighten.

"Yes, very well, Comrade. 'Cept the shit I got for lunch came out of my mother's asshole-oh before she put it in my lunchbox," the voice continued.

Someone snickered.

This was how it was most mornings, riding in with the black kids who sat in the very back of the bus, smacking their gum and talking shit about everyone, like they owned the whole fucking vehicle. The guys had do-rags covering their heads, and the sickest Nikes on their feet—Kollie had even seen a few of them with the new LeBron Soldier Xs. *Don't concern yourself with them,* his mother had told him since the very first day they had seen the black Americans in the neighborhood. *They are not serious, and they don't have culture. That is why they act that way.*

"Seriously, did y'all smell that rank green shit Saah brought out at lunch yesterday? I swear I saw a fish head in it. A fucking fish head, y'all! Isn't that, like, a violation of state health laws or something?"

More laughing. One of them was almost on the floor, he was laughing so hard. The old white dude who drove the bus was watching them in his mirror, smiling.

"Nigga, you wrong for that. You just wrong."

Saah looked from Kollie to Mardia and shook his head. *It's not worth it,* is what that meant.

The bus pulled into the school parking lot, behind a row of others. Kollie felt sick. He couldn't wait to get off.

"I'm serious, man. That shit was *disgusting*. Take that African shit back, 'cause we eat *real* food that ain't been taken from the dumpster here. For real."

The bus driver pulled the brakes and then opened the doors. Everyone stood up and started filing out.

Kollie closed his eyes. *They have no culture-oh*, he could hear his mom saying again.

Clark slapped Kollie lightly on the back of his head as he walked past him. Kollie jumped.

"Seriously, though. What the fuck is wrong with y'all? How can you eat that greasy, stank soup every day? Don't it make you wanna vomit?" he said, turning to look straight at Kollie.

Beside him, Lovie grabbed his arm. Kollie looked back at her, and she gave him a muted smile. He knew what she was trying to do. Even though he resented it, he relaxed his fist, which had been steadily rising to his chest.

"Pussy," Clark said as he walked away.

Kollie's backpack slammed against the back of his locker so hard that the rattle reverberated down the hall. People turned around to look at him, which pleased him. The hall monitors were not really awake and moving in full force yet, so he was still relatively safe from what he and his friends referred to as the Agents of Discipline. He looked sideways and saw Sonja walking down the hall with her girl Aisha. Aisha was Sonja's best friend, and she was Kenyan, although she had lived in America since fourth grade. Sonja was wearing a thin purple dress, which somehow managed to look fly and casual at the same time. The dress wasn't tight or so short that she'd get a dress-code referral, but somehow still she made Kollie's testicles ache. Sonja was like that, though—a chameleon who didn't seem to be governed by the same laws as everyone else.

He caught her eye and nodded at her as she passed. He tried to look as nonchalant as possible. She nodded back, training her gold-flecked, dark brown eyes on him. He thought he also detected a small smile, but he could have imagined it. Then the moment was gone, and he was staring at the back of her legs, listening to the faint *swish* of her skirt as she passed. He felt his penis harden and turned back into his locker as calmly as he could, so as not to draw any attention. *The dead bird by the side of the road this morning. The growing crack in the sidewalk outside the house. The dirty dishes Ma was too tired to wash last night.* Thinking of these things, which were the dullest he could conjure, always seemed to bring his body down a notch and back to normal. Today was no different, and after a moment, he slammed his locker door shut and began walking to room 237. He held the tilapia and red sauce with rice his mother had packed for him in his right hand, and at the garbage can in front of room 235, he threw it in.

CHAPTER THREE

"I DON'T KNOW WHY they think this is some MLK Day march-oh," Haji said as he prepared to enter the room for his midday prayers. He was looking at a group of black kids putting up posters on the column the administration had set aside for student organizations. Kollie saw one of them advertised an upcoming die-in to protest a police shooting. "What they need to do is clear out and get over it. Allah got no time for such lazy men-oh. No wonder they can't graduate, and white man got no job for them." Kollie and Tetee cracked up and patted Haji on the back. Although he was Liberian, he was also Muslim and floated between the Somalis and Liberians, no problem.

The prayer room itself, however, *was* a problem.

It was a makeshift space, set up on the second floor beside the school's new atrium. The principal had brought in movable walls to be placed around a small set of prayer rugs, at the request of Somali students, so that they could complete their salat during the school day. There had, of course, been "concerns from the community" about the partitions spoiling the new atrium, and certain parents grumbled about "special treatment." A white father even spent a morning in the atrium to "see for himself" what was going on. And one afternoon, everyone found an "Ugly Truths about Sharia" flyer on the windshield of their car. But none of it had escalated. And this was before some Somali parents made contact with the ACLU, just in case.

The real tension was with the black kids, anyway. They had previously used the space now occupied by the prayer room as an informal lounge. "It was *our* place. Our one space where we could chill and be us in this whole raggedy school," the black student union president said in an editorial in the school paper. "So, of course, you had to take it away from us." Some of them would still loiter around the prayer room, trading the dozens, laughing loudly, or even talking about how the space was really theirs. The Somali students mostly ignored them, although lately, nerves had been frayed on both sides.

Haji saluted good-bye to his friends and then walked toward the prayer room. He smiled easily at the black guys in front of him and nodded. They did not respond, except to grimace. Kollie watched, his stomach beginning to churn, as they crossed their arms and blocked Haji's way. Their faces were covered in disgust, and when they pushed Haji, Kollie couldn't say he was surprised. He felt a scalding fury bubble up, and before he knew it, he was rushing toward them. It was Abraham who came out of nowhere and saved him, who grabbed his shoulders and turned him around. "It's not worth it," he hissed in Kollie's ear. "They're not worth our futures-oh." Kollie could not stop himself from lunging in their direction again, but this time, Haji lodged his small frame between them.

"Eh-menh," he said, so that only the three of them could hear, "listen to your brother, Kollie. Don't let this be the thing that ruins your life in America."

The black guys were looking at them perplexed, wondering what was going on. Abraham had caught Kollie before he could make his move, so it just looked like he had stumbled toward them, his true intent still unknown.

Kollie would still have grabbed for them, but Abraham, Tetee, and Haji were holding him back.

The bubble of fury found a way to burst. "Motherfuckers! Don't think this is over! You goddamn motherfuckers!" Kollie shrieked. "Motherfuckers!" echoed through the atrium silencing all other conversations in the adjacent hallways.

"We're counting on it, jungle nigger," a black guy threw back at him. "Best watch your back."

Before he even had time to think, Abraham, Tetee, and Haji moved him around the corner, out of their sight line.

"Get off me, man," Kollie told his friends, and shrugged off their hands.

Tetee held up his palms. "Easy. Easy, Comrade."

Kollie scowled. Then he put his hands on his head and kicked the nearest wall.

CHAPTER FOUR

"WHO CAN TELL ME about the Great Migration north?" said Yasmine Jackson—Ms. Jackson to her students. Ms. Jackson taught American History and was the only black teacher in the whole school, and as a result, her classes tended to be filled with black and African students. The white kids had plenty of other choices.

Tetee groaned. "What the fuck," he said to their entire table. "Again?"

Kollie laughed openly.

Ms. Jackson whipped around and eyed him icily. She crossed her arms and kept on staring. Her bright brown eyes seemed to see everything in the room, but there was a familiar weariness in them too. Kollie had begun to notice it more often, not just in Ms. Jackson or his mother, but in the other black and Liberian women he knew.

Kollie sat up in his seat, a bit chagrined despite himself. He had spent his first nine years in Liberia, and it was drilled into his very marrow that teachers were not to be disrespected—at least not outwardly. That reverence was a liability in this new context, in which it was clear to all of Kollie's friends that American teachers were out to destroy them, rather than raise them up. It was far easier to ignore them, like they did Mrs. Walker, and pretend that they were not even there. But Ms. Jackson had a hardness in her, like so many of these black women, and wouldn't allow that.

"Sorry," he said softly.

Apparently satisfied, Ms. Jackson finally broke from his glance and addressed the entire class. "Now then, let's begin, people. I want to start with what might sound like an obvious question to guide our discussion: Why would anyone ever want to leave their home?"

Because they have to, Kollie said in his mind, before he could stop himself. Because there is no food, no work, no school, and they have no choice. Or because General Butt Naked or Colonel Do-or-Die will make their Small Boys kill you for a cassava leaf—or for no reason at all.

As the Second Liberian Civil War geared up, Kollie and his family had fled such rebels and ended up stranded in Ghana in the Gomoa Buduburam refugee camp outside of Accra. They waited three years for whatever papers the people in charge said were needed in order to come to the West. If he tried hard enough, he could still see a dusty orange road in his memory, the compound in the village in Lofa County where he was born and lived the first five years of his life. The goats who lay lazily in the road and would not get up, the mist that covered the tips of Mount Wuteve at dawn. The sound of an AK-47. His mother carrying water on her head and baby Angel, ever-present and watchful, on her back. But these memories were all a patchwork of faded images now; there was no narrative to hold them together and give them meaning.

"Like, war?" a white kid said.

"People leave their homes when they're being treated like second-class citizens," said a black girl.

"Because the white man is a crafty devil and drives them to it," said Henry, a black kid. Henry was Clark's best friend, and his father was an assistant principal. Some people said he got special treatment because of it.

An audible cackle passed through the room, as the black kids reacted to his comment.

"That's racist," said the same white kid. "And stupid."

"Is that right?" Henry said, and began to stand up. "You got anything else you wanna say, you ignorant—"

"Enough!" Ms. Jackson exclaimed. She walked over to Henry. "Sit down."

Henry looked back at the white kid, who was cowering in his seat.

"Sit. Down," Ms. Jackson said again, this time getting up in his face.

Tetee looked from Kollie to Abraham, his eyebrows raised. Things at Brooklyn Center High School had never seemed calm, but lately, it was like something was rising to the surface. And there only seemed to be a few adults in the building—Ms. Jackson among them—who actually wanted to deal with it.

She gestured back at Henry's chair, demanding that he take it, and he finally did grudgingly. Then she slowly walked back to the front of the room.

"We talk about these things because we have to," she said, "not because we want to."

Kollie sucked his teeth. How many things a day did he *have to* do, anyway? Was this the way to spend the precious few years of youth?

"You all think you hate one another precisely because we *don't* talk about this stuff." She sighed. "You don't realize it yet, but that is the real tragedy. Not a name somebody got called."

It was strange, almost like she had forgotten that they were there, and was talking to herself, rather than the class.

Ms. Jackson shook her head, as if waking herself up from a dream. "But we will have these discussions in my class, and when we do, we will conduct them respect-fully." She looked meaningfully at Henry, who was still defiant, and then at the white kid, who was still shrinking. "Understood?"

They both nodded. Henry rolled his eyes.

"Good," she said, her voice returning to its nor-mal, conversational tone. "Now then. Back to the topic of leaving home. During the Great Migration, African

Americans relocated at a rate and number so high that it changed the entire face of the country. To them, Jim Crow was something no one should suffer through if they had the choice, so they made the decision to leave for what they hoped would be better, more welcoming communities up north. Unfortunately that wasn't always—or even often—the case."

Kollie let her voice become background noise, as he worked out the beats to a new track he was putting together. He closed his eyes and wondered what it would feel like to have his own music blasting through the speakers of his own club, while he and Sonja danced, their hips grinding together.

"I heard you flunked the test in geometry. Again."

No matter how high he turned up his music, it was never enough to drown out Angel. Especially not when it was just the two of them at their mom's house.

She leaned into him, pulled one of his headphones, and whispered in his ear. "Mom said this was your last chance, and you messed it up. So that's it—you're going back to Liberia."

Kollie snickered and turned up the Kanye.

This was the threat parents always lobbed against Liberian and Somali boys in Minnesota: Shape up, or we will send you home. And there, they don't love their children too much to teach them respect. There, you will learn the value of everything you just junk away here.

His mother, who worked nights as an LPN at Abbott Northwestern Hospital and was finishing up her coursework to be an RN at St. Mary's during the day, often told him the very same thing, late at night, when she'd stumble in after her shift to find him on the couch playing games on her iPad, another suspension warning letter in her hand. But he knew she would never actually do it. He was her only son, and she had hid him from Small Boy rebel soldiers, fed him her own rations, and taught him to read and write throughout the war and its aftermath. All her hopes were with him.

Angel put a hand on her hip and wagged her finger at him. "Hear me? You're gonna be on a plane to sad little Africa this summer."

Kollie sneered but decided not to give her the satisfaction of acknowledgment. She wasn't worth his time.

She sighed, then turned around. "Don't know why I bother anyway."

Kollie didn't know why either. He had no idea who she hung around with or what she did in school, and he didn't want to. He knew she was an academic superstar, because she dangled it in his face every chance she got. The brilliant younger daughter who everyone liked, and the disappointing older son who just wouldn't try. Those had been their identities and their relationship to each other as long as he could remember. He didn't hate her; he just found her irrelevant.

Angel threw herself down on the opposite end of the couch and began to scribble something on a page in one of her many notebooks. She was two years younger than him, in the ninth grade, but sometimes it felt like two decades. Everything was easier for her, and he didn't know why. Maybe it was because she was a girl. Maybe it was because she didn't care what the black guys—or maybe any guys—thought of her. Or maybe because she had left Liberia before it had begun to mean something to her.

She stood up and shoved the notebook in his face. *"DAD CANNOT SAVE YOU FROM EVERYTHING. ESPECIALLY YOURSELF"* was scrawled across the page.

He turned off his music finally and then slowly, deliberately, tore out the page and ripped the paper into long shreds.

Right hand on her hip again, she stuck out her tongue and then ran from the room.

CHAPTER FIVE

VIVIAN PLACED A HOT bowl of fufu in front of Kollie and his father. She took the steamed, pounded yam delicately from the plastic platter, which also held two cold waters and a bowl of okra soup. After everything had been carefully laid before them, his father's girlfriend left her apartment's small dining room and retreated back to the kitchen. His father lifted the lid from the bowl of fufu, scooped out a piece, dipped it in the okra, and then sucked it down in one gulp. The years at Buduburam had sweetened his father's palate to Ghanaian dishes like fufu and kenkey—fermented, pounded, and steamed white corn.

In Liberia, Ujay Flomo had been a sociology professor at the university. Here, however, he was just another home health aide, making sure crazy white people didn't harm themselves or others in the special houses where they were forced to live. He worked an average of sixty-five hours a week, splitting the hours between two jobs.

Kollie and his father did not speak while they ate. They simply scooped, dipped, and swallowed until the fufu was all gone. Then, each gulped his bottle of water and dried his hands on a towel. Kollie's father burped, excused himself, and then snapped his fingers. Vivian appeared and carefully cleared the table so that it was spotless.

"I believe I have found a suitable space for the club-oh," his father said quietly. "In the basement of Brother Johnson's establishment." Brother Johnson ran a small travel agency in Crystal, specializing in buying large numbers of seats on flights from Minnesota to Monrovia from airlines that could not sell them at full price, and then selling these bundled seats to Liberians locally. "He said that you and your friends could use it on the weekends, as long as you make sure to leave it better than you found it each night. I am sure that Angel and Lovie can help you-ya."

Kollie winced at his sister's name—a brief sour note in the otherwise good news. He wasn't sure if his father didn't see the tension between him and his sister, or wouldn't see it. Whatever the reason, Kollie's father still believed that he and his sister were friends. Kollie did not plan to disabuse him of this idea anytime soon though, especially since he was finally getting everything together for the club.

Kollie nodded. Inside he was jumping up and down, but outwardly he tried to show no emotion.

His father looked him straight in the eyes. "Do not embarrass me-oh," he said evenly. "Or the ma." The last part was said under his breath.

Kollie sat up straight in his seat and folded his hands in front of him on the table. "I will make you proud, Papi."

His father studied him up and down, like he was inspecting a car to see if it was drivable. "I expect nothing less-menh," he said. "I don't want to hear nothing about no liquor there, or nothing else bad-oh. I am trusting you to have control over the people who will come on that side and don't have good ma and pa. You pekins don't have no good place in the community to be. I hoping this spot can be positive, with your guidance-ya."

Kollie nodded. "Thank you, sir."

His father took a small envelope from his bag and slid it toward him.

Kollie eyed him incredulously. "What this-menh?"

His father shrugged impatiently.

Kollie grabbed it before he could stop himself. He felt wide-awake in a way he hadn't in weeks. Inside the envelope he found five crisp hundred dollar bills. "Sir?" he whispered. He couldn't quite believe it. Loma men were known to be particularly tight-fisted with their money, so he knew how hard it must be for his father to part with it.

His father surprised him with a muted smile—something no one saw regularly. "Show me you got good pa," he said. "You are my son. Make me proud-oh."

Kollie was startled by the tears he felt gathering at the corners of his eyes.

"I will do it, Papi," he said. "I will do it-oh." He meant it too.

His father sat back in his seat and crossed his arms across his chest. "Good."

CHAPTER SIX

KOLLIE WALKED INTO THE locker room, his soccer duffel slung over his shoulder. It was finally Friday, but he had practice before he could go home and relax. He sat down on the metal bench and held his head in his hands. He had arrived early so he could be alone for a moment. He just needed some fucking peace and quiet. His eyelids felt heavy, like he could close them now and never have the strength to open them again. Like he could sleep forever and not have to worry about anything again: school, the club, Sonja, his mother. He could finally let it all go. Everything could become whatever it was meant to be, and he wouldn't be required to exert any energy on its development or dissolution. Everything he had done, everything he had failed to do, everything he might or might not do, would fade into one, comforting blackness behind his eyes. And he could rest.

"Man, I told you! It ain't me who you're looking for!"

Kollie jerked his head up, awakened, at the unexpected sound of someone's voice—it sounded like Clark's. Kollie was pretty sure he played football or ran cross-country.

"I just got here, man," the voice continued, almost pleadingly. It was definitely Clark.

Kollie followed the sound of Clark's voice, careful not to make any noise. It sounded like he was around the corner, toward the east side of the locker room.

"Then who the hell wrote it?"

The other voice was Eddie's. The old white dude was one of Brooklyn Center High School's three security guards. Eddie was universally hated for his love of the very little power he could wield against students in the hallways.

Kollie peered around the corner and saw that Eddie had Clark backed against a row of lockers. Clark looked angry, but Kollie could see the fear in his posture too.

"Man, how the fuck would I know?" Clark answered. "Isn't that what they got you pussy pigs for, to figure out these little mysteries?" Clark snarled back and then spit at Eddie's feet.

Perhaps Eddie thought he would beat the bravado out of him, because the next thing he did was punch Clark in the stomach. Hard.

Kollie gasped before he could stop himself. He clasped his hand over his mouth and yanked his head back around the corner, praying that they hadn't heard him.

Clark's coughing masked the sound.

Eddie laughed. "Who's the fucking pussy now, you little nigger?"

Kollie didn't want to hear this, didn't want the additional weight of witness on his shoulders.

Clark gasped. "Wha-what did you call me?"

Eddie laughed again. "You heard me. Think you're something special 'cause you can talk back to a man in a uniform?"

"A fat *white* man in a rent-a-cop uniform," Clark corrected him.

Kollie heard the sound of metal connecting with flesh, and he closed his eyes and willed himself to find some courage. Then he peered around the corner once more and saw that Eddie had lifted Clark's wiry frame from the ground, pinned him against a locker.

"You don't seem to understand how this works, Clark," Eddie was saying, his pudgy white finger stabbing at Clark's face. "I'm the one in charge here, the one who you can either talk to respectfully or beg for your goddamn life. *You're* the tiresome little degenerate who will flunk out of here with all your little hood friends and who I'll see on the corner smoking and selling weed in a year or two, with no prospects, no money, no self-respect, while I'll still be patrolling these halls collecting a paycheck." Eddie leaned into him, the spit from his words hitting Clark's face.

Clark was coughing and wheezing. It looked like he was panicking, as Eddie slowly twisted his collar so that it began to cut off his windpipe. Violence didn't seem to explode from Eddie like it did from Kollie. The beating was almost orderly. It seemed to Kollie that, for Eddie, hitting Clark restored some kind of balance to his universe.

Kollie wiped a drop of sweat from his eye. He knew he had to do something, but it was like his body could no longer process commands from his brain—nothing was moving, even though every part of him was screaming.

"Clean up the goddamn wall. The sooner you do it, the better things will be for you and your bitch-ass friends, trust me."

Kollie saw the rebels running through the streets of Congo Town with AKs, shooting them randomly at passersby. He felt his right hand seize up, and his legs begin to buckle the same way they did during what Liberians called World War II, the second siege on Monrovia, all those years ago. His mother had grabbed him then and carried him to safety, but right now, he only had himself. He felt his left hand grab the rough concrete wall, steadied his balance before he fell down and revealed his position.

Eddie let go of Clark, and he sank to the floor and collapsed.

"Yeah, that's what I thought. Not so tough now, are you?"

Clark wheezed on the floor, clutching his throat. Kollie wanted to go to him, but didn't dare.

Eddie scowled and began to walk away toward the

locker room entryway that led back into the school. When he was a few feet away, he turned back to Clark and said, "You know, when I first started here I couldn't figure out why they wanted us to spend so much time, so many resources on policing you all. I mean, you have big nigger mouths, but at the end of the day, you're kids, you know? That's what I thought, anyway. But now I see they were right: You are some destructive little assholes. It's like there's something in you that absolutely *has to* destroy order and everything good around you. I don't understand it. Really, I don't. When you have so much handed to you, so much at your fingertips. You have to spray-paint 'fuck you pigs!' across the hall walls. You could be learning geometry, splicing cells, writing computer code. But no. You really think we're the enemy."

Kollie was surprised to see that Eddie's face actually looked pained throughout this whole speech.

Eddie pointed at Clark, who had pulled himself up to sitting position against the locker, breathing normally again. "*You're* the fucking enemy, bro. To yourself, to the rest of us. You remember that." Then he turned around and walked out.

Kollie closed his eyes, wishing again that he was someplace—any place—else. Gabe's basement. His own living room. Vivian's dining room. His fingers involuntarily found a crack in the concrete wall, and he was forced to confront the fact that he was still here, had witnessed one of his schoolmates being beaten by a security guard.

Even if he didn't like Clark, there was no denying that he didn't deserve that. Then all at once, the silence was punctuated by the sound of weeping. Clear, unabashed sobs ricocheted through the locker room. Kollie stepped from around the corner and saw Clark holding his head in his hands, crying. He obviously had no idea he was not alone, as he made no attempt to conceal it, and just let it take over. It wasn't until Kollie was basically standing over him that he realized with a start that he had a witness. Kollie reached out to him, but Clark recoiled in disgust.

"Man, what the fuck you looking at?" Clark yelled at him. He pulled himself up, so that he was inches from Kollie's face.

Kollie could still smell the fear of the encounter all over him, saw a long pink welt spreading across his right cheek.

Clark cocked his head to the side. "What? You think you're better than me now? You think you something other than the same kind of nigger we be?" He laughed bitterly. "Yeah, I know how you African niggers think. You probably think you coulda stopped him with one of your spears or something, right?"

Kollie was surprised to discover that he felt no anger about anything Clark was saying. What he felt most was sadness and regret, and he wanted to tell him that.

"No, I just—"

"You shut the fuck up! Shut up, already, everyone!"

Clark's spit was flying into Kollie's face as he yelled, and his eyes flashed with intense anger. He stepped away from Kollie, then put his hands over his ears. "Why can't everybody just shut the fuck up, already? I need some fucking peace and quiet." His voice broke on this last sentence, and he turned away from him.

Kollie wondered if he was about to cry again.

"Look. I wasn't trying to—"

Clark whipped around and pinned Kollie against the wall in a choke hold. "You tell anyone what happened here, I will personally break your ass off in so many disparate parts, it will fucking crumble into dirt. You hear? Into fucking dirt. *Comrade*."

Kollie wheezed under the weight of Clark's strong arm. He could still breathe, but not easily. "Please," he choked. Looking into Clark's eyes, he saw the anguish in their depths, and the tears he wasn't even trying to conceal.

With a yelp that sounded like the cry of an animal caught in a trap, Clark backed away from him and let him go. Kollie crumpled to the floor, exactly where Clark had been only moments before.

"You ain't shit, you hear? Motherfucker, you ain't shit!" Words exploded from Clark until finally his voice broke. "Not shit!" Then he turned and slowly walked away.

When he heard the thick metal door slam, Kollie knew he was alone. The concrete floor felt good against his face, and he lay there for some time, curled in the fetal position. He didn't blame Clark for what had transpired; he had his pride. How else would a man react to the witness of his brokenness? Kollie rubbed his throat and tried to breathe normally. He was relieved to see that this was easy; he was fine.

Kollie sat up. He had to get himself together. He had to get ready for practice; the guys would be pouring into the locker room in the next five minutes. He sighed, and began counting to twenty slowly in Loma in his mind. It was something he did while hiding out in various homes and even the bush once during the war, to try to calm his mind. *Eala, faylay, sawah, nanni, dolu, dozita, dafala, dosawa, pu, ou-kao-eala, pu-kai-faylay, pu-kai-sawah, pu-kai-nanni, pu-kai-lolu, pu-kai-lozita, pukai-lofala, pukai-llosawa, pukai-tawu, pufay-laygboh.* He stood up.

The boys gathered in the center of the field to discuss the last drill, which had ended in a perfectly executed goal, assisted by Kollie.

Coach Morris, a white guy in his early thirties who also taught PE, had been called to a mandatory all-staff meeting—about "emerging discipline issues," rumor had it—so X, the team's goalkeeper and captain, was running the practice.

"Listen, we can't let our defense go down like that." X lit into his fullbacks. He was out of breath, but he still had their attention. "I know it's hard, but we have to stay in formation. You gotta stick to your man. That's how these teams be killing our defense in games."

X broke the huddle, and as they headed back to their positions, he slapped Kollie's shoulder and said, "Great pass, man. Great pass."

Like most boys his age, Kollie had grown up playing soccer in the dirt with whatever balls could be found. He had always been mediocre until those three years at the refugee camp, when there was absolutely nothing else to occupy his time, unless he wanted to sit with the men on the stoops of the shacks the UNHCR had the gall to call "houses," playing draughts and talking about the exploits they would achieve once they finally made it to the West. In America, Kollie, Gabe, Tetee, and a few others had played pickup games in the park by their house on weekends. Kollie had always been the most swift and agile of his peers, but it had never occurred to him to join the high school team until X had begged him to at the end of last year. "We need you, man," X had said, after leaving his black friends in the middle of lunch late last spring and sitting down with a table of Liberian freshmen and sophomores. This definitely raised a few eyebrows, but X was like that: He was a senior now and his family had moved to Minnesota from Chicago two years earlier. He really didn't give two fucks what other people thought about him, but was too good-natured about it for this fact to get to anyone. People accepted that he had everyone's best interests at heart and didn't ride him for things they would crucify anyone else for.

"Okay!" X clapped his hands, startling Kollie out of his reverie. "Let's run it again. Except this time, Gabe, you switch with Vince and make a run up on the left. Watch how Vince defends you. Kollie, you go center."

It was an unseasonably cool October day, and the wind was at Kollie's back, pushing him forward as he found the ball at his feet. He didn't really remember X starting the drill, but soccer was like music: Finding the flow was effortless. He moved the ball forward, running and tapping with the tips of his shoes. Sometimes it felt almost like he was dancing, he and the ball, each one taking its cue from the other, spinning in or out of control endlessly downfield. This was why he played, for this feeling. He would never be tired, would never have to stop or think. It was pure freedom, and therefore so fleeting that he could not even describe it.

In the bleachers, both Angel and Lovie sat waiting for Kollie to finish practice. Books on their laps, they were separated by several rows, but they both wanted something from him.

On the field Kollie deftly pulled the ball backward as Gabe came sliding in to try to gain possession. Someone called for Kollie to pass as he spun away from another defender. No one was taking this from him.

The first frost had not come yet, so the ground was still soft. Kollie felt his cleats bite as he changed direction and juked another defender. This was not part of X's drill. He could do whatever he wanted now, and the goalposts were becoming larger and larger in his view.

X clapped his padded goalkeeper gloves together and then crouched down, elbows on his knees. He looked straight at Kollie. Kollie grinned. This was what he'd wanted.

But the angle he'd taken on his run downfield had been slightly off—and X had positioned himself accordingly. Kollie was too far left—his weaker foot—and since he'd chosen to go one-on-one and ignored all the cries to pass, no one had bothered to get in position to receive a cross or even a back pass.

Kollie managed to beat one more defender before he was forced into a weak, left-foot shot X easily saved while managing to give him a disappointed look at the same time.

CHAPTER SEVEN

AT DINNER THAT NIGHT, Kollie picked at his fish and rice. His mother sat across from him at their modest kitchen table, almost inhaling the food she had cooked the weekend before. After working a double shift at the hospital, she had raced to St. Mary's to take a biochemistry test. She was only three classes and a board exam away from her RN degree. Most of this was noise to Kollie, who just knew that she was always working. His mother eyed him wearily. "How was school today?"

Kollie sighed. He wished she knew how much he wanted to be the son she could rely on, not the one she had to worry about constantly after making herself sick through too much work. He wished he could tell her something good. "It fine-oh," he said softly, chewing his meat.

The garish clock his parents had purchased in the dollar store ticked in the silence between them, but did not fill it. Angel was at a yearbook meeting, and his father was working late (they all knew he was at Vivian's place, but "working late" was what they always said), so it was only the two of them.

His mother glanced at his barely touched dinner. "You want something else? Or you just not hungry-menh?"

When he had first come to America, all he had ever wanted to eat was soup and rice like every other Liberian he knew, but in the past few years his palate had become decidedly more American and he preferred a hamburger and fries to a bowl of torbogee any night. But that wasn't why he wasn't eating now. He had actually lost his appetite. "I fine-oh," he said.

If his mother didn't believe him, she didn't let on. She shrugged and scooped up the last few bites on her plate. "A boy need to eat-oh." Her blue hospital scrubs clung too tightly to her stomach, which was becoming thicker rapidly, it seemed to him. In Africa, fatness was seen as a sign of prosperity and even status, but here you were thought to be lazy or even a bad person if you were big. He knew she ate because she was sad, and also lonely. A devout Baptist, it was the one vice she allowed herself.

"I ate at school," he said, seeing the image of the lunch his mother had meticulously prepared for him poured into the garbage. Then he stood up and grabbed his plate. The dishes from the last few days were stacked in the kitchen sink, almost overflowing onto the counter. If he couldn't be the son she needed, then the least he could do was the dishes. He began to run the water, then grabbed the scrubber. His father would have laughed at him for doing women's work if he were there. But he was not there.

"Eh-menh, I almost forgot!" his mother exclaimed suddenly. She sat up in her seat and raised her right index finger, punctuating the important words for emphasis. "Your teacher, Ms. Jackson, called me this afternoon-ya."

Kollie felt his arm stiffen. The dishwashing soap he was squirting onto the scrubber landed on the side of the sink, instead. "She . . ." He swallowed. "She called you?"

"Yes," she said brightly. "The two of us had a nice, long conversation, all about you-oh."

He tapped his toe on the tiles. This was not going the way that most talks about school did—she seemed genuinely excited about something. "Really?" he asked cautiously.

"Yes, really," she said, laughing. "Don't look so surprised, Kollie. I always knew you were capable of reaching your dreams. All you need is correct instruction and correct environment."

Dreams? Now he was absolutely perplexed.

She stood up, pushed in her chair, and brought her plate to him. "She said she wanted to tell me herself about a beautiful essay you wrote about Bigazi, and the people who lived there before and during the wars. She said it was one of the best in the class, and that she is going to ask you to read it at the academic excellence assembly at the end of the month. She said that when you described the children in church, planting and harvesting ground-nuts and cassava leaves, the beauty of the rivers, the quiet at dusk, and the aimless bullets that tore through compounds in the dead of night, it almost brought her to tears-oh." She was standing close to him now, but her eyes had a faraway look to them. She took his hand. "I know I don't know how hard it has really been for you here, to adjust to the new culture. They say that America is the Land of Opportunity, and I suppose that it is. If you want to better yourself, they will give you the opportunity to do so. But if you want to destroy yourself, they will give you that opportunity too."

The energy coming from her eyes was too strong for him. He looked at the floor.

"And I know for black boys, they will convince you that it's in your best interest to destroy yourself." She sighed. "I don't know why the whole world over, the worst thing to be is a black, but that is how it is. Especially in this country."

He wanted to leave so badly then. That feeling he had had all week, of a scream eating his gut inside out, was bubbling in his belly again, and he didn't know how much longer he could control it.

She grabbed his other arm, more forcefully than before. Then she brought his chin up, so he had no choice but to meet her eyes. "I am just so glad you are now making the choice to better yourself," she said quietly. "Your father and I, the whole family, really, we have always had such high hopes for you. Angel is smart, and she works so hard . . . but she doesn't *feel* like you do." She placed a hand on his chest, and his heart pounded even faster. "You feel everything, which is why it is so hard for you, I know. But it is also why you are meant for great things. And it makes me so happy that you have not forgotten home. You are our black diamond, Kollie. And you are just beginning to shine."

She was crying now. He swallowed the lump in his throat and wrapped his arms around his mother. He wanted so badly to tell her about everything, but he wanted her to be proud of him more. Let her have one thing in her life, for a moment at least, that made her happy.

"I love you, Ma," he said as he rubbed her back.

★

CHAPTER EIGHT

KOLLIE THREW THE FIRST PUNCH.

Midway through the academic excellence assembly, while Kollie was seated on the stage waiting his turn at the mic to read the essay Ms. Jackson loved so much, he saw Clark push Sonja off the fourth row of the bleachers. She landed with an unceremonious thud and screamed, interrupting the principal's long monotone speech on the importance of focus and integrity in classwork.

"What the hell is *wrong* with you niggas?" Aisha yelled, leaping down two aisles of the bleachers to help her friend.

"You stupid jungle bitch," Henry snapped back.

Sonja was moaning on the gym floor, holding her right thigh in pain. Several teachers were looking on in confusion, barely masking their fear.

Before he could think about it, Kollie was off the stage, on the ground, and running toward Sonja. When he got to her, he saw that her face was stained with tears, and that her left shoe had fallen off.

"I'm okay," she said to him as he leaned into her. "I'm okay." She was wearing a spotless white cropped shirt and tight blue jeans, and she smelled of flowers.

"Hey, ma. Are you sure?" he asked.

"Yes." She nodded. "I just . . . need some help getting up, that's all."

It was the longest private exchange they had ever had.

He nodded and held out his hand. She smiled at him and was moving her hand to meet his when Clark shouted, "Keep your hands off her, you sick monkey nigger."

Kollie flinched and then grasped Sonja's hand.

"I said hands off! Or I will beat you and your tiny black dick all the way back to—"

Kollie dropped Sonja's hand, stood up, and lunged at Clark with all his might. He found that his fist was endowed with a kind of terrible force that stunned everyone around him. In his mind, he saw white hands pummeling Clark in the stomach, heard him wheezing in pain, then crumpling down the locker room wall, defeated. His ears rang with the bitter twang of Eddie's voice: *I'm the one in charge here, the one who you can either talk to respectfully or beg for your goddamn life.* He shook his head, to shoo it away. *Who's the fucking pussy now, you little nigger?* the voice said louder. It was Eddie's voice. It was his voice.

———

Kollie sat alone in the living room later that night, the glare of the television his only companion in the house. His parents were both working, and Angel was at a friend's place, working on some project.

"Yes, Bill, we're reporting live here from Brooklyn Center High School tonight, from the scene of a brutal fight that broke out between students at an all-school assembly this afternoon," said a young white woman dressed in a button-up white dress shirt and gray blazer. She was standing in front of the main doors to the school, which you could barely see, it was so dark now.

Kollie leaned over and turned up the volume.

The newscast cut back to the middle-aged white anchor in the studio, speaking to the television monitor behind him.

"Liz, I understand that the school's director of security was wounded in the altercation, as well, is that right?"

The young woman pressed the hearing device in her right ear and scrunched her face, ostensibly listening to the anchor's question as it traveled through the digital ether. "Yes, that's right, Bill," she said after a moment. "He was trying to break things up and restore the assembly to some kind of normalcy, when he got caught up in the fight. I'm actually standing right here with him now, as he has agreed to tell us a little bit about what happened."

Kollie gripped his right hand with his left as the camera panned to the woman's right to bring the image of

Eddie into focus. That motherfucker found a way to wea-sel himself into everything.

Eddie leaned into the microphone. A blue bar on the screen read, EDWARD VAZER, DIRECTOR OF SECURITY, BROOKLYN CENTER HIGH, below him. "Yeah, well, the disruption started out as one between two students, but unfortunately evolved into a melee with more than ten. We had to take one student away on a stretcher, and three more were hospitalized. The student who started the incident has been suspended—"

Kollie sucked his teeth. He didn't know that Eddie was even capable of using words like *melee* and *disruption*. Maybe someone had coached him before his big on-screen debut. He laughed at the thought, despite himself. These white people were crazy; he wouldn't put it past them.

"And you were injured as well, is that right?" the reporter was asking him.

The camera pulled back to show Eddie's right arm in a sling.

"Yeah, I'm all right," he said, bravado rolling off him. "I had a few injuries that needed tending to at the hospital, nothing serious. I should be all healed up in a few days. The main thing is that we effectively stopped the fight and prevented further injury to students—most of whom were simply gathered for a regular assembly at the school and had no interest in participating in or witnessing violence." Eddie looked directly at the camera then, carefully enunciating each word. "We take student safety very seriously here at Brooklyn Center High School. In fact, it is our top—"

Kollie leapt up off the chair and screamed at the screen, "Bullshit!" He brought his face so close to Eddie's, spit was flying on the image of the other man's face. "You lying piece of dog shit! Don't give a fuck about me, Clark, or nobody in that fucking school!" He could still feel Eddie's hands on him, strong-arming him to the ground away from Clark, twisting his arm so hard he feared it would break. And then finally, when things had calmed, being handcuffed, and dragged up again to standing, whipped around to see Eddie's self-satisfied face staring into his, saying, "That's enough, now, son." *I'm not your goddamn son!* his brain had screamed, but his mouth and body were too wracked with pain and exhaustion to say it.

Bill the anchorman was now talking to Eddie. "We talked to some students there tonight who preferred to remain anonymous and did not want to appear on camera, who said that the atmosphere at the school has been very tense there for some time now—especially between the African American and African immigrant students."

Eddie's mouth pinched into a thin line, which caused Kollie to snort. "Oh, you don't like that, do you, you little pussy? Somebody talking truth on your employer, shitting on your paycheck-oh?" He took a step back from the TV and crossed his arms.

"No, I wouldn't characterize it that way at all," he said quietly.

"Eh-menh!" Kollie exclaimed.

"There have been some tensions at the school, certainly, but I would say no more than what you might find at any other, normal school."

"Bullshit," Kollie said again.

"Okay," said Bill back in the studio. "Okay."

"Look, we've got kids with all kinds of issues, with difficult family lives, poverty and violence, and they don't know the best way to deal with their problems. Which is why a limited few resort to violence, and have ruined it for everyone, on this occasion. But the principal is working hard on her new zero-tolerance-of-violence platform, and these disruptive elements will be dealt with, are being dealt with." Eddie focused his needlelike green eyes outward, and Kollie swore he could feel them pressing on him, pushing on his skin for blood. "They have been removed, so that they can no longer endanger innocent bystanders, who are here to learn and positively contribute to our community."

Kollie shivered involuntarily. His parents had not heard yet about the suspension, or his phone would already be blowing up with more than texts from Lovie and Tetee. From Angel, who was hiding out at a friend's house. The school had surely left messages for his parents, but they could only check their phones on the rare breaks at work. There would be hell to pay when they did, however. Especially since he had sent Clark to the hospital.

"And I want all your viewers to hear me clearly when I say this, Bill: Brooklyn Center High is a safe place for *all*. This was an isolated incident, which we have now contained. We never have and never will condone violence here. Our number one concern is creating a safe, welcoming, and engaging learning environment for our students," said Eddie.

Kollie couldn't listen anymore. He leaned over and turned off the television. Then he massaged his right knuckles, which he had bruised from punching Clark so hard and so many times, and closed his eyes.

CHAPTER NINE

THE AIR WAS FRIGID, hefty with the coming frost. It was a little after five in the afternoon, and the daylight would not last much longer.

Kollie walked steadily westward, the thought of his destination moving his feet forward. The team would be preparing for the state tournament they had recently qualified for—the first time in more than twelve years. Coach and X (mostly X) would be running them hard, he knew, with speed and endurance drills, zone simulations, passing and defense moves. They would all be tired, but exhilarated about the prospect of winning against some of the best teams in the state. Of being better than they, or anyone else, ever thought they could be. A team of black boys who no one thought would really amount to much. *And now look at us!* Kollie thought proudly. Then he frowned, spit on the ground, and revised the sentence. *And now look at them.*

As the hard November earth crunched under the weight of his Timberlands, he saw Brooklyn Center High School looming to his right. He grimaced before he could think about it. He was coming through the back way, appraising the school from behind. Its windows looked on at him dimly, holding little light. The gray walls seemed taller, more imposing than he remembered. A cold gust of wind kicked up and blew in his eyes; he shielded his face with his hand and pushed on.

He had been condemned to sit at home in his room for the past two weeks, on strict orders of no video games from his parents. This was to be part of his punishment. It was ridiculous, though, because his parents worked all the time, and his father pretty much lived at Vivian's anyway. So, he stayed in his room playing *Plants vs. Zombies* and *Star Wars: The Old Republic*. Last Thursday afternoon, he had even managed to sneak in Gabe and Tetee through the back door, for a lively three-hour game of *Dark Souls II*. No one—not even Fake-Ass Angel, who had been at one of her frequent study sessions—had been the wiser.

Off in the distance, little black dots darted back and forth over brown grass, pursuing a small, white, spinning ball. Kollie began to jog, and he could almost feel the light *thunk* of the ball from foot to foot as he dribbled it down the field. His teammates were getting bigger now, growing into normal-sized human beings as he came closer. They had stopped running and were walking slowly toward the center of the field, hands on their hips in that familiar stance you took when you were trying to catch your breath. Kollie smiled in spite of himself. He had missed this—had missed them. It was wrong that he hadn't come sooner. His team needed him.

"Kollie, man!" Jamil was the first to spot him and ran up. "Where you been, brother?" He grabbed his right hand and shook it, then pulled him in for a bro hug and back slap with the other.

"Yo, man, it been too long, man! It been too long."

Then X stepped forward, interrupting him. "Kollie. Sorry, man, but you can't be here now. You just can't."

Kollie turned to him sharply, really looking at X maybe for the first time. Despite his imposing presence on the field and in the goal, X was not tall or particularly large. For the first time, he wondered what it would be like to hit him, perhaps the one black kid in the school he would have ever ventured to call a friend. He was a pretty boy, after all, with a chiseled jaw and equally well-defined cheekbones. It would feel good to sully all that.

"You're suspended and not supposed to be on school grounds. You know that." X's tone was level, not accusatory. So then why did Kollie feel like he was taunting him, trying to get him to react?

"I'm still part of this team-oh," he said, trying to regain control, to mask the anger he felt overflowing every pore. "I might not be able to play in the finals, but I can still help. I *want* to help." He hoped his voice didn't sound as desperate to them as it did to him. He had not allowed himself to feel how much he missed the game, how he needed to be a part of something until this moment.

X sighed and hung his head. "But you're not," he said. "You're not part of the team anymore, Kollie. Not after what you did to Clark. You put him in the hospital, man."

Kollie could feel the energy of his teammates changing around him. As usual, they were considering the logic of X's words, responding to their moral demands. *Fuck you!* Kollie screamed in his head. *Fuck you, X!*

"That motherfucker came at me swinging," Kollie said, stepping toward X. He couldn't stop the anger spewing out of him now; it had been building for more than two weeks. "He came for me, bro, and he was going to fuck me up good. So I had no choice—it was either me or him, man. You would have done the same."

X simply blinked at him, apparently not intimidated. It was just that kind of confidence that made Kollie want to pummel the hell out of him. "I would not," X said evenly. "I don't care how much static I might have with a dude, and I know some of you don't like Clark one bit— not even a little." He was speaking not only to Kollie now, but to the whole team. "I know a little of your history and everything, so I wasn't entirely surprised, but I was really, really disappointed. And that's the God's honest truth."

His history?

Kendall, Jamil, even Gabe, they were turning away from him now, he could feel it. All because of X.

An unreasonable heat coursed through his body, and

Kollie felt his fist tighten. If he did not let it out, it would consume him. So, he let his fist fly toward X's perfect jawline.

X ducked, and Kollie spun around, his momentum carrying him.

A sharp intake of breath reverberated around the small circle.

"You seriously need to get the fuck outta here, dude."

Kollie could not tell who had said this, but judging from the incredulous stares, it could have been any of them.

X had recovered from the attempted punch and was now standing firmly, regarding Kollie with disdain. "It's past time for you to leave, *Comrade*." He uttered this last word with derision. "That worthless piece of shit Eddie is headed over here right now." He pointed to the right.

Kollie looked and saw a thick figure walking briskly in their direction. He turned and ran.

A small wooded area buffered the fields and the sidewalk, and he thought that if he could make it there, he might be able to lose Eddie. He pumped his arms harder and willed his legs to speed up. He dove under the cover of tree branches and hoped they would mask him somehow. He had just extracted himself from a patch of burrs when Eddie turned him around.

"You. Are. Not. Supposed to be here." As he said each word, he pushed a fat, gloved index finger into Kollie's chest.

"I'm sorry. I—" Kollie was startled, and struggled to respond.

"Save it," Eddie said. "I don't give a fuck."

Kollie heard Clark's skull scrape against the lockers again in his mind, and shuddered. They were far enough into the woods that Eddie could probably mess him up good, and no one would see. And he had put the one person who could corroborate any story of abuse in the hospital.

To his surprise, Eddie took a step back. "Just stay away from the school, the grounds, okay? I personally don't have a problem with what you did to that little cunt, but once you have a notice, I am obligated to report to the police if you step foot on the premises." He smiled. "Are we clear?"

Kollie felt bile collecting in his stomach. "Yes, sir," he said softly.

Eddie squinted at him, like he couldn't quite see him clearly. "What?"

Kollie swallowed the bile, then cleared his throat. "I said, 'Yes, sir.'"

"Well, all right then." Eddie smacked his arm lightly, like they were buds. "Glad we understand each other." He laughed to himself before turning to go. "But then, it's so much easier to come to an understanding with you people. You're just so much more reasonable."

Kollie didn't know why he was frozen in time and space, why he couldn't move. He felt like he was standing outside himself, watching the scene unfold.

Eddie winked at him, which brought the bile back up his throat. Then the security guard turned to go and walked slowly back toward the school.

Kollie watched Eddie's back recede into the mess of tree branches that marked the entry into the woods and did not move until he was sure that he would not turn back. Then he flexed the fingers of his right hand. He was relieved to realize that he could still move of his own volition. "Motherfucker," he said, first in a whisper. He glanced around him furtively, making sure that he really was alone this time. Then he took one step, then another, and another, until he fell into the rhythm of his own gait, and forgot he was walking at all. "Motherfucker," he said again, this time louder. And then it became a mantra he uttered as he walked, stomping through weeds and dry grass and branches on his way back through his neighborhood, back home.

Later that night, he sat out on the deck, letting the cold air make him shiver. With his hands in his armpits, he collapsed into himself, daring winter to make him smaller. It was comforting in a way he never could have imagined in Liberia, the all-encompassing nature of the cold here. If you surrendered to it.

Of course, the rest of his family didn't see it that way. "What you *doing* out there?" Angel shouted at him, when she got home. "Are you okay?" She had opened the sliding glass door perhaps an inch and projected her voice outward through the small space.

Kollie scowled. He leaned forward and wrapped his arms around his legs. This was his whole problem: There was no place where he could find some peace. When he was at school, he had to listen to a steady stream of irrelevant information and endure all kinds of ridicule. When he was at home, people who were intent on causing him disquiet took every opportunity to throw him off. Which wasn't that hard, given everything coming at him at school.

He needed to clear his mind. He stood up and walked off the deck. He took one look behind him as he left the backyard and saw the strange image of his sister's face in the glass, reflected and refracted by the glare of the living room light against the dark night. He expected her to look smug, having run him off the premises again. But instead, she seemed sad. He looked away, before he might ask himself why.

The suburban night enveloped him, and he was grateful. His mother wouldn't be home from her shift for hours, and when his father called him in an hour to "check up" on him, he could tell him anything regarding his whereabouts and activities. This was the extent of their hold on him.

As he rounded the corner of the street that connected

to his, he bumped into something. "Shit," the something said, and they both fell to the ground.

Kollie jumped back, his fists up, ready to fight whoever it was. "Who that?"

"Easy! Easy, my man!"

Kollie could see the outline of a figure, maybe an inch or two taller than him, standing back up.

"Why you hurry, suh?" the figure said. "You got somewhere to be, at eight thirty on a Monday night on Danberry Street?" Low, easy laughter followed.

Despite himself, Kollie began to relax. He lowered his fists.

"That better, my man. That better."

Kollie's eyes were adjusting to the night now, and he could see that it was only William, the twenty-something good-for-nothing who everyone's parents said to steer clear of. You could usually find him at or near the Super-America, hanging out with whoever stopped by to fuel up or to buy a gallon of milk and did not imagine themselves sufficiently above him to engage in small talk.

"Eh, man," Kollie said. "Sorry-oh. I didn't see you."

William laughed and brushed off his arm. "Yeah, man. I know." He took a step closer to Kollie, and Kollie could see his NY Giants cap cocked to the side, his mouth full of smiling teeth, his slightly crooked nose. For some reason, the fact of this obvious, visible imperfection made Kollie feel more at ease with him, like he wasn't trying to hide his defects like everyone else. His nose was busted, this was something that had happened. There was nothing pretty or nefarious about it—it was just a fact.

"They call you 'Kollie,' right?" William held out his hand, and Kollie shook it.

"Yeah."

"William."

Kollie nodded. "I know."

William eyed him sideways. "You know, eh?" He sucked his teeth. "Liberian people like to talk-oh. I know they talk about your expelled ass too."

Kollie couldn't mask his surprise. "Expelled!? I'm only suspended, man! I'm not expelled!"

William laughed. "Suspended, expelled. Word about a delinquent gets around-oh. Especially from people who think they better."

Kollie grinned, although he knew he shouldn't. Although he knew that the last thing he should be doing was talking to this person, who his mother would describe as "de-gen-er-ate," enunciating each syllable. Perversely, the thought of this made him want to talk to William even more.

CHAPTER TEN

YOU JUST STAND HERE, and the people, they come to you-oh. You don't even have to do nothing. Easiest money you ever make, bro. William had given him the instructions the night before, dropping a bag of product in his hand before he had even asked for it. He had been to parties where weed was available, had even tried it twice but didn't like it; it didn't take or something. But he had never seen someone make a sale, much less ever considered getting into the business himself. But talking to William these past few nights, seeing the vast stash of cash that kept growing in his pocket with each passing car, he had to admit it was something that merited further exploration.

Before, it had never made any sense to him why anyone would get into a business as potentially risky as this. Cops, guns, permanent records—it was all the stuff of the *CSI* shows his mother loved to watch, with the sorrowful-looking young black and Latino dudes who were doomed to get caught and, eventually, incarcerated. But as a dirty white Lexus drove up and a young white guy in a freshly pressed dress shirt rolled down his window, Kollie understood something that the shows never seemed to get right: the ease, the essential *logic* of the business. How it actually made perfect sense to sell something to folks who wanted it, even in some cases, medically *needed*. Shit, the stuff was even legal now in some states! And with money to be made like this, who wouldn't get involved and make themselves something more?

Kollie hunched over and walked briskly to the car, a small bag of product slid between his middle and index fingers, exactly like he had seen William do, ready to make the exchange in less than a second.

"You'd better get up. Mom wants to talk to you before her shift." Kollie hadn't been able to find a pillow to cover his head and drown out his sister early that morning, but he had nearly managed to fall back asleep before Ma entered his room minutes later.

Ma asked him to please stop by Tetee's family's house that night—even if for just a little while. It would mean so much to Tetee's father, who had recently completed the master's program in computer science at the University of Minnesota and received word that he had secured a good-paying job downtown at Oracle. Tetee's family and a bunch of their friends were throwing him a full Liberian party to celebrate his achievement, and Ma had been baking pans of sweet bread and spicy Liberian meatballs the past three days for the occasion. Kollie was lying facedown on his bed, his clothes still on from the night before—the roll of cash for William still in his pocket—when she popped her head in. She leaned over and touched his leg lightly as she spoke, and his fuzzy brain was lucid enough to hope there was not even the slightest smell of weed lingering on him. He would need to learn to be much more careful.

"Well?" she asked expectantly.

Kollie groaned and turned his face away from her, not ready to face the day, much less the night after it. The last thing he wanted to do was think about seeing Tetee and Gabe and Haji and who knows who else from school there, plus family and community members who had undoubtedly heard about his suspension and the "unfortunate incident" at the assembly. He didn't know why his mother would want him there anyway, with all the questions and embarrassment his presence would bring up. No, it was better to stay away as long as possible, until memories of the event had faded from people's minds and he was back in school doing well. But he couldn't say any of that to Ma, so he said instead, "I'll think about it."

Now, after spending the day wandering around the neighborhood and the evening selling a bit of product for William, his stomach was growling. The thought of platters of delicious, fresh Liberian food made him ache with hunger. Maybe he could sneak into Tetee's, grab a couple of plates of food. It was nine o'clock, and the party would be in full swing. Liberians from Brooklyn Park, Brooklyn Center, and Crystal would be descending upon the house to celebrate Tetee's father's degree, greet family and friends, and eat until they were beyond full. He could squeeze his lanky frame against the wide bellies and ample bosoms of the decked-out men and women who would be pushing through the door of the house, and no one would see him. There were probably eighty people packed into the modest ranch house already. That was how Liberians lived on this side: Work hard, play hard. This much, at least, they had learned from the Americans.

Kollie walked this way and that, down this neighborhood street and another, until he heard the steady beat of Liberian gospel music. He was almost there. When he turned the corner, he saw cars parked all the way down the street, women in too-high heels and shiny low-cut dresses holding on to elbows of men in brightly colored button-down shirts and suede shoes. Kollie laughed in spite of himself. He remembered one night after another such gathering, when his parents were still together, his father commenting on the *hordes of Christian women dressed like tramps.*

These people work all day, all night breaking their backs, making their pressure go off for these old sick white people-oh, his mother had snapped back. *This the one time, the one place they have to show themselves off and be something. Let them have it, Ujay. Just let them have that.* Kollie remembered that his mother's rare verbal challenge to their father had shocked them all.

He pulled his hood up over his head and thrust his hands in his pockets. Then he fell in behind a large family bringing gifts and pans of food through the front door of Tetee's house. This way, he could almost look like he was one of them, the teenage son bringing up the rear. The tween girl of the family, wearing tight jeans and an equally tight T-shirt, gave him an odd look as he neared her, but he pretended not to see. She shrugged, then looked away.

"Siraj! Edwin!" Tetee's mother exclaimed as they entered. "Welcome to the family-oh!" She glanced over the group quickly, but Kollie was fairly certain she didn't see him.

"Congratulations, my sister," the man said, hugging her warmly, and Kollie used the moment to slip past them, fighting through the crowded living room toward the kitchen where he knew the food would be.

"—A man's achievements are never just his own. His whole family, his whole community are what make everything he has, everything he enjoys in his life, possible. So, I need to thank my wife for making sure I had the space and time to complete my lessons, and the food to give me the energy to do it. I also need to thank my children, for listening to their mother when she told them to leave me alone-oh." The room laughed appreciatively. Tetee's father was standing in the middle of the living room, giving the formal speech that was always expected on such occasions.

When he was younger, the content and length of the speeches had seemed normal to him, but as he got older, Kollie found them over-the-top, too long, and self-important. They evoked a sense of Africanness that he found embarrassing now.

Out of the corner of his eye, Kollie saw his own father standing to the right of Tetee's. Ujay looked proud of his friend from his university days, and Kollie was aware that he wished his father would look at him that same way someday. His breath caught when he saw his mother seated on a couch partition beside his father, her hand reaching up to touch his elbow. He couldn't remember the last time they had been out in public together, much less touched. Kollie frowned. He wondered where Vivian was, and how his father had persuaded her not to come. As concerned as his father was with how people in the community saw him, he rarely if ever came out for any events besides weekly outings to church, where he was the last one in and the first one out of services, where he barely spoke to anyone. Liberians here hardly knew Ujay Flomo at all. And if he was honest, Kollie was beginning to see that he probably didn't either.

Kollie made himself turn away from the spectacle of his parents and carefully pushed between sweaty, over-dressed bodies toward the kitchen table. He stuffed a plastic fork and knife in his pocket. Then he grabbed two paper plates and tried to balance them flat between his fingers on his left hand. It would be tricky, but he would try to fill them both high with the spicy Liberian meatballs and sweet bread his ma had made; the tor-bogee and rice, fried tilapia, Liberian potato salad and rice, ribs, and gravy the other women had brought. His mouth watered.

At the far end of the table, he saw a sheet cake, al-ready halfway eaten, with the remnants of the words, CONGRATULATIONS, JOSIAH! written across it. He would see how many pieces of that one he could fit on the plates, as well. He made himself focus on serving up the most food he could, quickly and efficiently, ignoring everything around him. If he could get out of here without anyone recognizing him, it would be a miracle.

When he was done, he turned around and tried to carefully walk back across the packed living room the same way he came—but now with two overflowing plates of food. Someone jostled his elbow and almost made him drop everything. He sucked his teeth. "Sorry-oh!" said an older man in a blue-and-white country shirt, and Kollie nodded at him absently to let him know it was okay.

A group of four men in their twenties stood right in front of the door. "The Old Ma wan eat da money even more than the wicked Papi," one young man said, the spit flying out of his mouth and punctuating each syllable. Kollie knew they were arguing about Liberian president Ellen Johnson Sirleaf.

One of the others shook his head and laughed. "Hey-menh! Give Ellen shot-oh. You can't say her name in same breath as Taylor."

The first man sucked his teeth. "She appointing her one son to the ministry of health, and the other to the ministry of finance, I hear? Or something like dat. What she think, we just her pekins, don't know what happening?"

A third young man, who couldn't have been much older than Kollie, laughed bitterly. "We live through the war for this? Just more corruption? This is why we can't ever develop-menh. Why I glad I on this continent and not the other one. Man, that place still going nowhere!"

The fourth man's eyes lit up suddenly, and he came alive. "It still too early to judge, Comrades. Ellen may still be great-oh. Liberia may still be great, if we finally challenge the West and their neocolonial economic and political slavery." Two of his friends rolled their eyes, and the other looked like he was stifling a laugh. "You mock me, but mark my words: Africa will rise again!" Two of his friends patted him on the shoulder, looking like they had heard this Pan-African fervor all before.

Kollie felt a grin leaking out the side of his mouth, despite his best attempts to contain it. It wouldn't be a Liberian party without fiery political debate about the state, fate, and future of the homeland. But then came the inevitable next wave—the shame that came with knowing this was an old and useless debate.

He was three steps from the door when he sensed someone at his left trying to get his attention. He told himself to ignore it, but his curiosity got the best of him, and when he looked he saw Angel, seated in the corner alone. Her eyes were lit up, and she actually looked pleased to see him. He had no desire to see what all that was about, so he took a huge step through the middle of the would-be political reformers who he knew were really just future home health care aides, and then Kollie was out, free of the party, free of his family, free of Liberia, walking briskly away from the laughter and the noise. When he was a block beyond the last of the cars parked for the party, he sat on the curb under a streetlamp to eat the food, which had grown cold and flavorless.

★

CHAPTER ELEVEN

A WEEK LATER, the fake flowers in the center of the modest dining room table looked even more pathetic than usual. Their waxy stems were peeling in the cheap plastic vase his mother had bought from Target years ago. Kollie sat sullenly in his halfway-broken chair, staring at the vase and flowers in a kind of rage meditation. His mother and father sat directly across from him, for once appearing unified—if only in opposition to their son, whom they regarded with equal parts disdain and disappointment. Kollie knew that Angel had stationed herself on the other side of the wall and was anxiously absorbing every word.

"You will go to Aunt Garmai's, in Atlanta," Kollie's father said quietly. "You will stay there for the next term, completing a business class at her college." Aunt Garmai was his mother's older sister and was doing the best of all the family, having earned an MBA at the University of

Georgia, and then securing an instructor's position at a local community college in the city.

Kollie's hands balled up on his lap, and he looked down at the scarred tabletop, so his parents could not see the hot tears pooling in his eyes. He had known this talk was coming for weeks, had anticipated everything that would be said, but somehow hearing what had been felt for so long, but never spoken, brought about a surprising turn in him.

"Now that your cousin is away at college, she has room for you there," said his mother. Gone was the vibrant and energetic face he had seen at the party last weekend. She looked more exhausted than he had ever seen her. Each word seemed to drain her of more life. "This is a kind offer, one we will not get again." She sighed. "We must take it up-oh."

"Yes, a kind offer to ship off your only son and be rid of the problem you created." The words spilled out of him before he had time to think. He was almost whispering, but bitterness punctuated every utterance.

His mother promptly burst into tears. He was pleased to see that his words had had the desired effect, that he still had the power to hurt them. That he still meant something to them.

His father stood up, anger pulsating through his biceps and shoulders, streaming from his eyes. He was not a big man, but he had an intimidating kind of presence when he stood to his full, commanding stature. "Don't," he said, pointing at Kollie. "You don't talk to the Old Ma that way."

Kollie tried not to cower, but it was impossible.

"*You* have disgraced this family. *You* have blemished the Flomo name in the community. I never thought I would have a child so wicked-oh." He was yelling now. Kollie could not remember the last time he had heard him yell. His father was never around when discipline was to be doled out to the children, leaving his mother the unenviable task. But circumstances were different now.

"Papi, I didn't—"

"Silence!" his father boomed.

Kollie sunk into his chair further. He wanted to break the plastic vase into a million, sharp little pieces, and then tear the sad flowers to shreds. Instead, he began his ritual: *eala, faylay, sawah, nanni, dolu, dozita, dafala* . . .

"You can no longer take decision to speak for yourself-oh. You cannot handle it-menh." His father was shaking with anger. Angel must be beside herself with happiness on the other side of the wall, he thought. Soon he would be as irrelevant to the Papi as she was.

"Look what you have done to the Old Ma! Look!"

Kollie lifted his head slowly and felt a few warm tears run down his face. His mother was bent over, her face in her hands, weeping openly. He wanted to rush over to her, to embrace her and tell her he would change. That he would not cause her any more pain, that he would make her suffering mercifully stop. But he knew he couldn't do that.

"We brought you here for a better life, and you just chaclar the whole thing! This is not why we fought those government officials to let us come to this side-oh. This is not why we work from dawn to dusk to care for you pekins."

Kollie smiled. "The thing already broken, naw," he said quietly. "The white people already made it so we can't get *nothing* on either side. You not working for nothing good anyway. It was just a stupid dream." This was something William often told him, something that made more sense the more he heard it. It felt good to say the truth, even if he could only whisper it.

His father whipped around and slapped him on the cheek, hard. The sting of it woke Kollie up, made him sit up straighter.

"Ujay!" his mother yelled, standing suddenly. The sound of his father's name in her mouth was as foreign to Kollie as the idea of them trying to run a household together, to raise children together. He had not heard his father's Loma name spoken aloud in years. At work, he told the white bosses and coworkers to "just call me James," because it was "easier."

Kollie looked on his father now with a new kind of hatred and shame, a deeper understanding of what he could do.

His father took a step back from him, as if he didn't

trust himself so close to his son. "You think you a Big Man now, hunh? You think you going to run things now?" His tone was icy, pulsating with anger.

Kollie looked away, out the window. There was nothing to see, had never been anything to see in their quiet, boring neighborhood. A woman walking her dog. A car driving by. He wiped his face clean of tears.

"But you just like them. In the end you come here to be another *nigger*, hunh? You want to junk the whole thing." His father put his face inches from Kollie's, then sneered. He shook his head woefully. "No. No. I can't watch you do it-menh. You must go."

His mother had sat back down in her chair again and was drying her face with a tissue. Kollie could see she was trying to pull herself together.

"Papi, I beg. I can take better decision-oh." He didn't know where things would end with his father like this and needed to find a way to diffuse the situation. His cheek still rang from the impact of his father's palm. He leaned forward and clapped his hands in the familiar West African gesture. "I can work with you on the club. That one could make a positive difference in the community, like we talked about." He was pleading now, but he couldn't stop himself. Saving face was everything in his father's culture, and he knew that finding a way to do so would be the surest path to changing his father's mind. He could not go to Atlanta, or anywhere else, for that matter. Half of him wondered if Angel was not right and if the real plan was to send him back to Liberia. He wasn't stupid; he'd heard plenty of stories of parents who told their "problem" kids they were going on a family vacation or to visit a relative in another state or something, only to find themselves halfway around the world on a one-way trip to Monrovia. It had happened to a distant family friend some years ago, when their youngest son fell in with the wrong crowd. He had never heard anything else about the boy, once he was gone.

Kollie snapped back to the present abruptly. The shock of his father's deep baritone laughter brought him to.

"Do you really think I would ever trust you with that kind of project now, the *rebel* you've become-menh?"

Kollie squinted at his father, trying to grasp the true meaning in his words.

His father laughed again. "Yes, well, now you start to see that we are maybe not as stupid as you think," he said. "That maybe we old, useless people know a thing or two-oh. Especially about your recent evening activities."

Kollie's chest contracted. How could they know? He and William had been very careful, had taken every precaution. And besides, he had only made twelve, maybe fifteen sales so far—nothing at all in the grand scheme of things. There was no way they could have . . . Kollie turned his attention to the other side of the wall and could almost see Angel crouched there, gleefully taking in every word.

"Oh yes, we know all about that. Your new commitment to criminal activities," he said. He sucked his teeth. "You are truly no longer my son, Kollie Flomo. No more. That is why you must go-ya."

With this, his mother stood up and walked quickly to him, embracing him in a wide, full-bodied hug. "God will be with you, my son. And so will I. This journey will not be in vain-oh."

Just as he lifted his hand to embrace her back, she released him and walked out the door without another word. Kollie watched her leave, confused. What was happening here? Another minute later, he heard the car start.

"Get packing," his father said evenly. "You leave tomorrow."

CHAPTER TWELVE

TWELVE HOURS LATER, they pulled into Departures at the Minneapolis–St. Paul International Airport. Kollie had been here many times, dropping off this or that relative or friend who was flying to Liberia or to Rhode Island or Philly, places where other Liberians had relocated. But he hadn't been on a plane since he was nine and they flew as a family from Accra to Brussels, to Chicago, to Minneapolis. He hadn't liked all the planes, all the transit and sitting then, and he wasn't looking forward to it now. Plus, in the rush of everything, he hadn't had time to even say good-bye to anyone. His father had taken his phone right after their "discussion" the night before, so he couldn't text Gabe or Abraham or Tetee and ask them to tell everyone else that he was being condemned to Atlanta for the spring, on order of his despotic parents. Still, he knew they would hear about it before the day was out, one way or another.

"Here is your ticket," his father said, handing him a slim envelope, with the Delta Air Lines logo across the front. "Safe journey-menh."

Kollie felt the heat of anger rising in him again. Liberians loved meaningless platitudes like that, especially when they were doing things that were distasteful, and his family was no different. He flung the door of the Jeep open and jumped out, his carry-on slung over his shoulder. He opened the back and grabbed his large suitcase, which contained everything he had been able to fit in during his frenzied packing session only hours earlier. On the other side of the car, Angel jumped out and was beside him now, her hand on his suitcase.

"I got it," he said, shaking her off.

"It's too heavy. I can help," she said.

"Hey, ma! I got it," he said again, and successfully flung her hand away. He had no idea why she had insisted on coming to drop him off. They had not spoken since his parents informed him of his fate.

"Let me help!"

He used all his strength to pull the suitcase down to him. It must have weighed at least fifty pounds. He had no idea if the airline would let him check it. In fact, he'd been so exhausted by rage and fear when he packed it, he had no idea what was in it. Even now, the possibility that this could be a dream—a nightmare—tugged at the edges of Kollie's mind.

His sister continued to pull on the handle. "Let me, please!"

"You've helped enough," he said evenly. He would not look at her.

She burst into tears then, something he had not seen in years. She was always careful around him, not wanting to reveal any weakness and give him any chance to get one-up on her. She tried to grab his arm, but he shrugged it off.

"I'm sorry," she said. "I was worried about you! I had to tell them, K!"

The hardness he always cultivated around her cracked a little, with the mention of the nickname she had called him when they were little, when they were closer. But he was determined not to let her see this.

"You not sorry at all." He mustered all his strength and pulled the suitcase to the curb. Inside the car, his father looked straight ahead, as if the sight of the two white men saying good-bye to each other with a hug and a kiss was the most fascinating thing he had ever seen. Kollie sucked his teeth. It would be good to be rid of them, all of them.

Angel took two steps toward him. "Look," she whispered in his ear. "You flying to Atlanta, but not to Aunt Garmai's. You flying *through* Atlanta, K."

Her words stopped him, brought the feeling of the cold November nights he had been spending walking, and waiting, back to his body. He shivered. "What now?"

She took both his hands, looked into his eyes deeply for the first time in years. "They sending you to Liberia, K.

You going to Aunt Mawu's, to the Riggs School. You not be back here for long time-oh."

It was the first time he had heard her speak Liberian English in a long time. She was crying openly now. "They not telling you 'cause they scared you won't go. Aunt Garmai gonna meet you at the airport in Atlanta. She going to tell you the whole plan then."

Kollie shook his head. "No," he said. "They won't. They wouldn't."

They were standing in his father's blind spot, so he couldn't see them talking, but they could see him. Plus, his window was rolled up, and as far as Kollie could tell, he was trying as hard as he could to not admit that what was happening was happening.

Angel wiped away some tears with her hand. "They will. You know they will."

Kollie kicked at his suitcase. "Motherfuckers!"

Angel grabbed his shoulders and steered him back to their secluded spot. "Stop it! He'll hear you," she hissed.

Kollie pressed his eyelids together, tried to regulate his breathing. *I'm going to Atlanta. I'm going to Atlanta.* But deep inside him, in the quietest part of his mind, he knew that he wasn't going to Atlanta. He was terrified. "I won't go. I won't do it." He paced in front of the suitcase.

"Listen! We only have a second now," said Angel. "He's going to tell you that if you don't get on that plane to Monrovia, you will stay there four years instead of three. That he will send you no money. Even that he will make sure you never come back here."

"He can't do that!" But as he spit out the words, he knew they were not true. His father could do it, and would.

Angel looked at him. Her pity was overwhelming, and he wanted to hit her. Even in the midst of this small kindness she was offering him, her last gift to him made her better than him.

And then, before he could say anything else, the Papi was beside them. Kollie did not even have time to wonder how much of the exchange he had heard. "Angel, get in the car," he said quietly.

Angel looked from Kollie to her father back to Kollie again. "But—"

"I said, get in the car!"

She hung her head in defeat and turned on her heel to go. Then, she thought better and ran up to her brother, giving him a hug and a kiss on the cheek before he had time to react. "Good luck," she whispered. She ran back to the car.

Kollie and his father were alone, for a moment, before an airport security officer shouted that he should get back in his car, that he was blocking traffic and would be given a ticket if he did not move promptly.

"You were always a good boy, back home," his father said. "You will be a good boy there again."

Kollie shook his head. "I won't go. I won't."

"You will go," the Papi said simply. "And you will be fine-oh." Then he turned and began to walk back to the Jeep, as security approached him.

"Yeah, fuck you then! Fuck you, *James*!" Kollie yelled at his back desperately.

The Papi didn't respond, only held up his right hand, in an officious "good-bye" gesture.

"I'm not going!"

The Papi turned back just once, the last time he would see his only son for five years. "We will talk on the other side. You will be fine-oh." Then he got in the Jeep and started the car.

Angel leaned across the seat, pressing her hands against the left-side window. *I love you*, she mouthed.

Kollie lost all sense of propriety then and pressed his hands, his face against the driver-side window. "Don't do this! You can't do this!" he screamed.

"You will be fine," his father seemed to say through the window. Kollie couldn't hear anything, though, over the siren burst from the airport cop telling them all to move along.

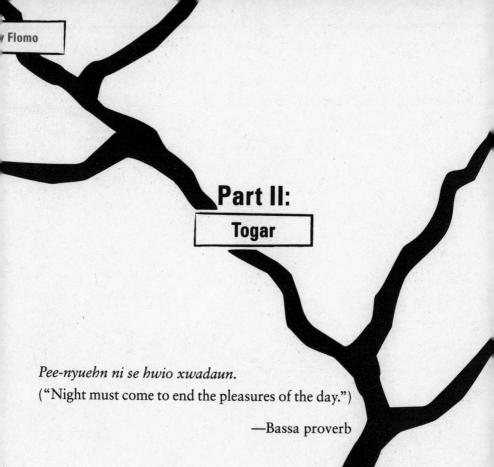

Flomo

Part II:
Togar

Pee-nyuehn ni se hwio xwadaun.
("Night must come to end the pleasures of the day.")

—Bassa proverb

Lani Wright

★

CHAPTER THIRTEEN

1926, Grand Bassa County, Liberia

AM I STILL A MAN, then? If he was doomed to live a life of banishment from all he knew and held dear, fleeing the Frontier Force infantrymen at every turn, subsisting on roots and leaves and the occasional kindness of strangers, then his father, his grandfather, and their fathers would regard him with shame and embarrassment. He would be no man at all, really. He would be only a shadow, spreading out at dusk, and alighting each morning, not attached to any body, place, or feeling; just moving, being, escaping.

How could this be? He was no longer a rightful citizen of Giakpee and would therefore be thrown out of the clan if the soldiers' claim was sound. Then he could never return to Jorgbor and their son. That all of this had come to pass in the space of three days was incredible. His whole world, gone. Everything that mattered to him cleaved open, dried out like so much cassava.

And, however much he swatted it away, the question always returned like a tsetse fly, biting until the disease fully bloomed in the blood. The longer he was in the bush, the weightier the question became, taking more shape until it finally broke in on itself and echoed in the dull space of his skull: *Am I still a man?*

Togar Somah, son of Baccus Somah and grandson of Aku Mawolo, leaned down into the creek and cradled a cupful of its cool, clear water. He knew that the soldiers were probably less than a half day from him, but he hadn't stopped to drink in hours and was on the verge of collapse. He brought the liquid to his parched lips and sucked it down hungrily, dipping back in the creek several more times before pushing himself down on to the rich dark clay of the bank. How soothing the mud was on his overheated, sweaty skin, chafed from days of running in the bush without bathing. *How strangely easy it is to become nothing,* he thought. *To be unknown to everyone but your pursuer, and to disappear into this land.*

He couldn't remember the last time he had set out on his own alone, as his family had constant need of him. Besides, with the recent raids in neighboring villages, it was no longer safe. Still, Togar mused, admiring the green abundance of the ironwood trees, the palm fronds that reached around his every turn, no one ever really took the time to actually *see* this land, their home, unless they were alone. And this was the first time he had been so in years. He heard the shrill call of a monkey somewhere high in the tree branches above him and the steady beat of a woodpecker nearby. A flock of guinea fowl walked to the edge of the creek, about five feet from him, to drink. They did not seem bothered at all by his presence, though a few fluttered their gray feathers, speckled with white dots, and after drinking, raised their curved bills to the sun. Togar watched the perfect, pear-shaped birds strut and gather around one another, and for those few minutes he was glad to be there with them, simply *being* in the harsh afternoon sun. At least there was this one moment that he could honestly say the wicked ones had given him.

Of course, he hated them too—hated the Congo people for snatching his newly won manhood from him. Just eighteen and a husband and father, where would he go and who would he become, now that his future had been uprooted from its rightful soil? Who *could* he become? He didn't want to be another beast of burden for their plantations, would rather die than be shipped off to Fernando Pó, that home of the devil where so many Kru men met their final resting place.

Togar shivered and the water churned in his otherwise empty belly. There were not enough curses for the Congo men. *Don't think they ain't kill you for a scrap of land*, his great-grandmother Lani used to warn him and the other children who gathered round her. *Congo people evil-oh*, she would say, gravely wagging a gnarled old finger in their faces. *You forget at your own peril.* Even now Togar laughed, at the memory. She used words like that, *peril*, on occasion, white words that none of them quite knew what to do with. And she even had a small stack of books she kept in the corner of her compound, a gift, it was rumored, from her own Congo mother, who was apparently one of the first to come over on the big ships, full of dreams of taming the wild forests and building a country out of mud and mosquitoes. Grandma Lani had never talked about it, but there were whispers that her mother banished her for marrying a heathen Bassa man, great-grandfather Gartee. And that Grandma Lani had never looked back, even though she had kept some of her Congo ways through all the years, her book learning and her Congo English. She had even given Togar a talisman of sorts when he reached manhood: The remnants of a leopard skin pouch with a metal clasp at the top. *It belong to my poor brother-oh*, Grandma Lani had told him. He remembered that he had been surprised to see tears in her eyes. *Before the fever take him. His Bassa love give it to him to ward off evil spirits and keep him safe in this world and the next. After he gone, it keep me safe too.* She closed his small fingers over the cool metal clasp—the only part of the trinket that was still intact. Then she focused her runny, yellowed eyes on his own youthful ones. *Keep it on your body, and it will do the same for you.* So, he had taken a piece of twine and hooked it through the clasp. Then he had tied the whole thing around his neck and had never taken it off since, not even for bathing. And he had to admit, it had brought him Jorgbor and Sundaygar, the luckiest things in his life.

He fingered the talisman absently now, as he often did when he was thinking. It calmed him, somehow, knowing that it linked him to another history and people he had never known, but who were nevertheless, part of him.

A loud rustling behind a tangled knot of vines threw Togar out of his daydreaming. He sat up abruptly and cursed himself for taking too long to rest. He raised himself up on his haunches and peered into the dense underbrush. Even if they were this close, he still might be able to run. He had always been the most swift and agile of his peers, able to dodge the most tenacious pursuer. And even if it truly was over, if they did try to subdue him, he would resist till the end. He reached down and grabbed a handful of silt from the creek bed. It was a fool's plan, he knew, with little chance of success, but it was all he had. Togar's muscles tensed as another vine cracked. Whatever was coming was coming *now*, and he would have one chance to escape and maybe not even that if they had fresh munitions.

He realized in that split second that although he wanted to live, needed to kiss Jorgbor and Sundaygar one more time before leaving this earth, he was prepared to die if it came to that or imprisonment. Yes, his fathers, his ancestors were surely with him. Togar smiled: Even in death, he would still be a man. Grandma Lani's laughter flooded his ears, deriding the Congo people as it brought him stories of their cruelty and the Bassa ability to resist it. *We always been here, eh?* she would tell pekin gathered at her feet. *And we always be here. That why they hate us.* And then the great laughter would come from her small body, giving them all the feeling of daggers being thrown into the soft earth.

Togar leapt up now, as a loud crash echoed through the bush. Cradling the mud in his right hand, he took five long strides before he heard the petulant oinks of three wild pigs break into the small space of the creek bank. The guinea fowl scattered immediately, heading as far away from the offending animals as possible.

Togar fell down in the dirt and roared a deep belly laugh. It was a sound out of a man's body, but if the pigs had known how to listen, they would have heard echoes of the joy of a child at play. "You wicked, wicked beasts!" he scolded. The pigs regarded him for the first time and took several steps back. Togar's stomach growled at the thought of roasting one of them, and then he forced the image out of his head. God had given him another chance for freedom, another opportunity to reunite with his family, and he shouldn't be distracted by something as base as meat. No, he needed to get moving again. His luck was holding so far, all thanks to the ancestors, but he knew it would not always be so.

He stood up and began running in the direction of

what he thought was north. The only things waiting for him to the south were more Congo plantations run by slave labor and the ports that led to Fernando Pó, and death.

★

CHAPTER FOURTEEN

THE AIR HAD BEEN cool and wet the morning the soldiers came to raid the village, the morning Togar fled into the bush. He'd risen at dawn as usual, in order to walk the short distance to the small plot of land where they grew their crops. He smiled at Jorgbor and Sundaygar, both snoring lightly on the pallet, before he slipped out of the compound. *You should take a second wife now*, his father told him since they had been married for more than a year by then. Jorgbor had taken longer than the family wanted to get pregnant, and Baccus Somah was impatient to see his son's seed spread and his children cover the earth. Baccus himself had three wives and sixteen children, and he wanted to see his son and the family fields blessed with the same good fortune. But Togar could not imagine it—taking another woman so soon after he and Jorgbor were joined. He could not tell anyone, of course, but he had grown to love her over the course of their short marriage and could not fathom lying with another woman. *Soon, soon*, he would wave off Baccus whenever he whispered in his ear about it and then would rush off to work the fields.

It was early November, and Togar wanted to pull a few cassava tubers out of the ground to see if the whole crop should be harvested yet. His brother-in-law, Gardiah, had been telling him for months that he should leave the plant in the ground for a year or more, so that it would grow huge enough to feed the family for weeks, but that seemed far too risky to Togar. Almost no one in Giak-pee or any of the neighboring villages kept cassava in the ground that long. What if the soil turned it rotten after so much time? Gardiah, who had a mind for farming and botany, laughed outright when Togar voiced these concerns. "There is nothing to suggest that that is a risk," he told him. Togar rolled his eyes. Gardiah was one of very few men in the village who had made it to senior secondary school, and he frequently made sure everyone knew it. As a small boy, he had worked at an uncle's house in Buchanan and attended school there until his parents ran out of money for his fees, and he had to return, deject-edly. So, instead of focusing all his energies on his studies, Gardiah now used his talents to cultivate the finest crops in the area.

Togar was another story. He had been helping his father plant, tend to, and harvest the crop on his own plot for years, but paying attention to minute details and noticing patterns had never been Togar's strong point. Consequently, many of the intricacies of successful culti- vation still eluded him. Now that he had his own family to provide for, though, Togar knew he had to do better and make his crops support all of them. This demanded a new commitment to consistency and detail. Every morn- ing, he would need to be at the farm, ensuring his small family's livelihood. Like a man.

When he got to his plot, he immediately grabbed the cutlass and headed to a cassava plant that had grown wild with branches and narrow green leaves. Togar bent down and pushed the blade below the orange-and-brown tuber peeking out of the soft, pliable soil. Pushing Gardiah's voice from his mind, he pressed down on the handle and heaved up a midsize tuber, its brown skin shielding the meaty white interior. He took the vegetable in his hand and held it up, thinking of all the soups over boiled cas- sava, dunboy, and gari they would soon enjoy.

Boom!

Togar jumped and dropped his prize.

Boom! Boom! Boom!

He stood and peered in the direction of the noise. It sounded like gunshots, and when he realized it was com- ing from the village, he broke into a run. Gede Pa and Kpa Dyi, the next two villages over, each had men taken by the soldiers some months ago. Togar heard they even threatened to rape some of the women and burned down a few compounds as a warning and retribution for the taxes they had not paid. But the chief of Togar's village had been on good terms with the paramount chief and the district commissioner for some time, so everyone in Giakpee believed they were out of danger, for now.

As the village came into view, Togar saw a line of men, including Gardiah, standing before five Frontier Force soldiers, each of whom held a rifle. Togar dove behind a tree before they saw him. As the pounding of his heart eased slightly, he strained to hear what the soldiers said.

"—has decreed that ten of you are to come with us now, for the duration of the dry season, for the honor and the privilege of cultivating the rice farm of the vice president of the republic!" one of the soldiers shouted. His boots crunched the hard ground as he paced.

Behind the tree, Togar closed his eyes. He wondered where Jorgbor and Sundaygar were and then decided that they were either safe in the compound or hiding in the bush with the other women and children. *Why God? Why must you make us suffer these demons over and over again?* This land belonged to Togar's people, after all. It was their country. The Congo people only had what they had because they had taken it. The bastards claimed that their Frontier Force brought peace and security in the lawless, Godless interior, but every man, woman, and child from every tribe in the countryside knew this to be a baseless lie. The Frontier Force was the wrathful hand of the Congo government and its private interests, clearing away any obstacle, including the very lives of the indigenous inhabitants of the countryside. There was a terrible price to pay for civilization, and someone had to bear it.

"Chief Thomas does not agree to this!" a woman yelled, running out of her compound. Togar trembled at the voice's familiarity.

He peeked around the tree and saw that the woman was indeed Fortee, Gardiah's third wife and Togar's only sister. Her faded lappa was tied awkwardly at her side, and her shirt looked like it would fall down her shoulder at any minute. Togar's stomach fell. Fortee and Gardiah were well matched, both having forceful personalities, though often lacking restraint. This was especially true when they felt threatened.

"You're wrong!" the soldier sneered in Fortee's face. His pants and shirt were stained with dirt and sweat, and Togar could smell alcohol even from where he hid. "Your benevolent Chief Thomas is now in a holding cell at Edina, being flogged for treason against the state for withholding food, taxes, munitions, and other resources. Yes, your paramount chief finally confided the whole thing to Commissioner Franklin yesterday, which forced his hand and is why we are here."

"Lies!" Fortee shouted. Then she took another few steps toward him and spit at the man's feet. "You are ruining all of us up and down the St. John with your wicked, wicked taxes! They too much-oh."

Togar turned away from the scene, fully hidden again

by the tree. His sister had gone too far this time. And Gardiah would not be able to save her.

Togar heard the unmistakable sound of a slap. It echoed across the wide expanse of the village center, silencing even the hornbills whining in the forest. Togar forced himself to look from behind the tree again.

"Heathen bitch!" another soldier shouted down at Fortee, who was now cowering at their feet. "Forget your place again, and we'll take you with the men. After we have our fun with you."

Togar pressed his eyelids together and felt a tear squeeze out the side of his eye. Inside his chest, his heart thumped like the loudest drum on the longest night of the harvest celebration. *Find the strength. She is your sister.*

From his place in the line of men, Gardiah fell forward on his knees, brought his hands together in prayer, and appealed to the soldiers in a voice that made Togar's skin prickle. "Please," he said, "I beg. She is my wife."

The soldier who had called her a "heathen bitch" smiled ruefully and approached Gardiah. "You have the misfortune of wedding this beast?" He leaned forward and cupped Gardiah's chin, then gestured back to Fortee. "How can you get any joy from plunging your feeble little cock into her foul hole every night?"

Fortee appeared to have finally come to her senses and crawled back from the soldier who had slapped her. Togar saw the fear in her eyes, and for once he was grateful for it. It might save her life and preserve her womanhood.

But the soldier was not going to let her go that easily. He took a long step toward her, grabbed her by the hair, and whispered something only she could hear into her ear. Togar could imagine well enough what it was. Fortee writhed under his grip and shook her head.

As Gardiah looked on in horror, the other soldiers began to laugh.

There had been many times that Togar had imagined a moment like this, had fantasized about, really: The accomplished and arrogant Gardiah, finally taken down a notch, forced to face his own impotence. Growing up under Gardiah's shadow, it had been hard for most boys in the village not to feel resentful. But now that the moment was here, Togar was both ashamed and irate. These pekins were nothing but a bunch of thugs from the lowliest of the Congo people, puffed up by the little power granted to them by their superiors. Togar tightened his right fist, wanting more than anything to pummel each of them to a bloody pulp.

Another soldier walked to Fortee, stuck his face in hers. "A woman like this could never obey her husband," he said. "It must be like a piece of bush meat you can never really chew. But still, you keep on chomping and chomping, hoping your belly will fill somehow." The man, who was stumpy and even a bit fat, looked around at his companions for their agreement. The bastards let their laughter ring out across the savannah.

The fat soldier walked back to Gardiah. "I feel sorry

for you, my friend. So sorry that someone has apparently sold you a false bill of goods. You thought you were getting a nice, fat, juicy swine, but instead you got the sickly grasshopper." He made an exaggerated sad face. "This world is so unfair, isn't it?"

Gardiah met the soldier's eyes, but Togar could see that he didn't know what to do.

"Isn't it?" the bastard demanded again, sneering at Gardiah.

This might have been the first time in his life when Gardiah felt completely powerless over someone else. Everyone knew he had a soft spot in his heart for his fiery, ever-loyal third wife. And then there was also the matter of Fortee's new pregnancy. Gardiah and Fortee had only told Togar and their parents of it—until the baby grew, they said, and they knew it was really coming. Fortee had already lost two babies, one a miscarriage and the other in childbirth, so caution was called for. And if these men did what they threatened, it could not only harm Fortee, but the life taking root inside her, as well. Gardiah hadn't said so, of course, but Togar knew him well enough to know that such a thing would kill him if it came to pass— to know that his baby had been wiped out by some idiot Congo men, that they had violated his wife's womanhood, and that he had not been able to do anything to stop it.

Gardiah hung his head. "Ye-yes," he said.

"Yes, what?" the soldier demanded, prodding Gardiah with his rifle.

"Yes—" Gardiah stammered.

"And you will look at me when I am addressing you, boy!"

Gardiah's face flashed with anger and then, just as quickly, fell back to its docile state.

This is what the demons teach us to survive: to become two people at once. To hide ourselves in plain sight. What kind of sick learning is this? If Togar had had a gun in that moment, he would have shot the bastards dead—all of them, without remorse. A bullet in each of their foul heads. For making them learn the terrible necessity of two faces. Right between each of their eyes as they begged—

"Yes," Gardiah said, looking the evil man in the eyes.

"Yes, what?"

There was a long moment, as Gardiah discerned what the man was truly asking of him. "Yes, sir," he said slowly. "I get no joy from plunging my cock—"

"Your *what*?"

"My feeble little cock into her."

The bastard looked surprised then, that he actually had the power to persuade a man to publicly destroy his wife and himself this way. He pointed to Gardiah, looked at his friends, and began to laugh.

"I knew it!" he exclaimed, jumping up and down in a kind of happy dance. "I knew he believed deep down that his wife was a beast! It's as the commissioner always says: The country people only need some encouragement toward the correct path." He patted Gardiah on the back, while his friends laughed along with him.

Gardiah hung his head farther.

Togar felt like he would vomit.

All the fire had gone out of Fortee, and she sagged under the soldier's grip.

"Stand up!" the soldier yelled.

And then she started crying.

"Stop it! You will stop this embarrassment now, you monkey bitch!" The soldier grabbed her and dragged her across the earth to Gardiah. "You brought this embarrass-ment upon yourself, upon your husband, did you not?"

Fortee shook her head, weeping louder, almost un-controllably now.

"Yes, you did! You did! Because you are not a good monkey bitch. You are not a good wife. You do not lis-ten to your husband. And besides that, your hole is dirtier than a latrine pit. Which is why this man wants to vomit each time he enters you. What kind of life is that for a man to lead? What kind of happiness can you provide him, besides the stirring of piss and shit in what should be his home?" The bastard shook Fortee with each vile word, and she seemed to disintegrate more, her wails became more urgent and higher-pitched by the minute. Togar had never seen her this way, so clearly undone, and it scared him.

Gardiah delicately moved to take her hand. His head was still down, staring at the ground and his fingers grasped, slowly, precariously, her own.

"What? What are you—" the soldier began, and then didn't bother to finish his sentence. He noticed Gardiah's quiet attempt to connect with his wife, and it spread rage across his pinched, doglike face. With a roar, he batted Gardiah's hand away with his rifle butt and kicked dirt in his eyes.

Gardiah howled and dropped to the ground in pain.

Togar yelled before he could stop himself, and a few of the soldiers and some of the villagers turned toward the sound. He yanked the upper half of his body back around the tree, cursing in his mind. He was no help to anyone if he got caught. In fact, his parents' pressure might go off if that came to pass. Both their children and son-in-law abused in one day would be far too much for their elderly bodies to bear.

"Enough of this!" a soldier yelled. "We don't have the time."

The man sounded forceful, like he was a commanding officer, perhaps. If such beasts could even *be* commanded.

Fortee's cries still punctuated the dry air. And now, they were accompanied by Gardiah's sad moaning.

"Oh, calm down, Ross!" said another one. "The commissioner doesn't pay us enough to forgo our amusements." He laughed, and a bunch of soldiers roared in agreement.

"He hardly pays us at all. We need our refreshment to keep us going," another soldier said, and Togar could hear the lascivious undertones of every word. If there was anything on this earth that disgusted him more than they did, he didn't know what it was.

The soldiers made lewd sounds, and Togar could imagine far too well how they were approaching Fortee. *If I were a true brother, I would stop them. If I had the strength of my father, my grandfather, all my ancestors, I would kill them now, without remorse or hesitation.* Togar could feel his breath thinning, and he looked down at the cutlass he had carried all the way from the farm. *Gut them each like pigs. If I die fighting, at least it will be an honorable death. My son and the child that grows in Fortee's belly will sing songs of my bravery. As will the griots.* He moved the cutlass stealthily from left hand to right and crouched. He would slit the throat of whichever one came nearer, and he would enjoy doing it. His family would be avenged, and the Frontier Force would think twice about bringing their foul, polluted stench into their village again.

"We make for Edina at half past the hour," the apparent commander said again. "I don't care what you do before then or how you enjoy yourselves. Just be ready to go and free of complaints."

A soldier laughed. "More than enough time to partake in this backward hellhole's most potent natural resources."

Another roar erupted from the soldiers.

Togar could hear one of them not more than ten feet away, and drifting nearer by the minute. A drop of sweat fell into his eye and burned. He gripped the cutlass tighter.

"No!" Fortee screamed. "You cannot do this! You cannot!"

The sound of another slap. Then Fortee's whimpering.

"We're doing you a favor. We're going to make you clean again. We're going to wipe out the jungle fungus and malaria your monkey man here has been shoving up your hole all this time and give you the gift of Christian cock," a soldier said. "The light of civilization will enter you, and you will be redeemed by the Light and the Word. You will be saved by the coming of Jesus Christ our Lord, Amen."

The sound of the bastards' raucous laughter screamed through the lonely village, mixing with Fortee's hysterical cries and the sound of her kicking feet being dragged along the ground. She wouldn't go easily, that much was clear. He hoped she somehow managed to claw out one or two of their eyes before they were through with her.

"I was last at Gede Pa," one of them said. "Let me be first now!" Then the sound of a belt unbuckling.

Togar shuddered. How many Bassa women had they ruined like this? How many men had they pushed to madness?

More laughter.

Out of the corner of his eye he saw two of the soldiers pull Fortee roughly into the bush. Abandoning his former plan, Togar thought now that he would charge them and slice them open as they prepared to take her womanhood. The element of surprise would be in his favor, and he was sure he could take down at least one of them. Though he may be killed by the others, it would be worth it to know the bastards would think twice about attacking other villages. And his family, his ancestors, would sing songs of him. He readied his heart, calmed his mind. *It is almost the moment—*

"I will give you everything!"

The sound of Gardiah's voice, strong but trembling, interrupted the rustling of the grasses.

"What now?" A bastard's voice again.

Togar peeked around the tree and saw his brother-in-law standing and addressing the men holding Fortee, his face and eyes covered in dirt.

"Let her go, and I will give you all of my rice and cassava crop as well as my fowls and goats. I have one hundred dollars in taxes for you too." Gardiah's voice broke. "And I will go with you and work your rice plantation all year. I will make sure it makes the highest yields of anyone in Bassa—maybe even the country. I am well-known in these parts for my abilities with crops."

Fortee shook her head, obviously taking in the full meaning of his words.

"No," said the soldier who had insisted on being first with Fortee. "That is still not enough."

But the other soldiers had stopped to consider Gardiah's offer.

The man who seemed to be commander—the one they had called "Ross"—stepped toward Gardiah. "Now, that," he said, "is the most reasonable thing I've heard any of you apes say all day." He pressed a long, thin finger into Gardiah's chest. Oh, how Togar wished he were close enough to chop off the sad, strident digit!

Ross turned around toward the rest of his men. "Sadly, my distinguished Unit Five, I think we must take this extraordinary boy up on his offer and enjoy the fruits of conquest another time."

The men protested, but it didn't seem to affect their commander. He simply held up a hand to them and turned back to Gardiah. "Yes," he said. "I have been hearing about such a one as you described in these parts. Someone who has a magic touch with the crops and can make them grow like bush weeds." He walked around Gardiah slowly, eyeing him up and down as you would a woman. It made Togar want to kill him all over again. "Yes, you'll do fine, I think." He cupped Gardiah's chin like he was a child. "And who knows? We may even be able to return you to your insolent wife here for a few months out of every year." Then he laughed. "Go collect the beasts and all the rice and cassava you can carry," he told the village men, who had been standing in line all this time. They looked at the commander in confusion.

"Am I speaking Greek? Do you not even understand English now, you backward country people? Go now!" Ross yelled, his face reddening with anger. The men scattered and headed to Gardiah's compound and the granary.

Once they were gone, Ross turned back to his men. "And you, go help them."

The men stared back at him, not comprehending.

"Now!" the commander screamed. If it was possible, his face reddened even more.

The soldiers finally complied and shuffled after the villagers dejectedly, all the while muttering under their breath.

"Ingrates!" the commander yelled at their backs, as they took the longest possible time to walk to the granary. Then he addressed Gardiah again: "I hope you know how much the nation needs a boy like you, with your talents. We appreciate your sacrifice for the greater good. From this day forward, you will be considered a true nationalist."

Gardiah uttered a barely audible, "Thank you, sir." Then he looked at his wife, who was still his wife now, not the violated shell his wife would have been had he not acted. Togar knew that, for Gardiah, it would all be worth it to avoid that catastrophe. And Togar would take care of Fortee and the baby like they were his own. They would be safe and well cared for.

"No," Fortee cried as she fell to the ground. She reached her long, thin arms toward Gardiah in a pleading gesture, but he shook his head. "No," she cried again, and buried her head in her arms. Soon, he would comfort her. She would see—

"You behind there! You can come out now!" Ross yelled in Togar's direction.

Togar shivered. He saw the future he had created in his mind of he and Jorgbor and Sundaygar caring for Fortee and her baby rapidly disappearing.

"I say, you there!" the commander yelled again. "Make yourself known. I know you are there. I know you are strong, but not strong enough to evade me. We need you on Commissioner Franklin's plantation, serving your country like the rest of your brothers. You will not be harmed if you come out right now."

The edge of the bush where the soldiers had dragged Fortee was maybe five strides away from him. If he could launch himself from behind the tree, he could make it there before the vile man could catch him, and from there the forest would conceal him. He knew every branch, every fern, every kind of beast for miles. These bastards knew none of it, and even worse—they hated it. But this was Togar's home, and he loved it. The land in turn loved him back, and that could make all the difference between survival and death, freedom and capture.

Togar heard the man's strides on the dirt, rapidly approaching. If the bastard had his gun drawn now, he was a dead man for running, but Togar was ready to take that chance. He thought of Sundaygar kicking him during his baby dreams the night before, when Jorgbor had taken him to her breast to suck. Of how the light from the almost full moon had streamed in from a small crack in the thatch roof, making a bright beam across their faces. They hadn't seen him watching them, hadn't had to account for the weight of his love from his eyes.

"Van-an se m bada hweh oh gbehn ke m bada de," he said under his breath. *A billy goat has beaten me, but its horns cannot beat me again.* Then he pushed off the redwood trunk and pumped his arms and legs as fast as he could.

"Stop, I say!" he heard someone yell behind him, and then felt something small and fast whip by his shoulder. He dashed into the bush and didn't stop running till nightfall.

CHAPTER FIFTEEN

THE SMALL FIRE MADE strange shadows in the dark forest around him. Its flames greedily devoured the small sticks and dry leaves he had been able to gather. He would have to put it out soon or risk sacrificing all the miles he had put between him and the soldiers; but Togar was willing to take that chance in order to warm up and eat. A small lizard he had caught cooked on the stick he held in the flames. It wasn't much meat and it would be tough, but it would do. Togar knew well enough what would happen if he didn't keep up his energy: The soldiers, who would be well fed, would catch up to him quickly. No, he needed to maintain his energy in order to keep a quick pace. He would eat and then rest his legs for a few hours before starting again.

After the lizard carcass had been licked clean, Togar gathered the palm fronds he had collected at dusk, placed a few on the ground, and gently tried to pull the balance over him as he lay down. Togar closed his eyes and shivered. The mosquitoes were ravenous and bit his legs, feet, stomach, and arms. One even had the audacity to bite his eyelid. Still, exhaustion claimed him after a few minutes.

His eye was swollen and puffy at dawn, and Togar awoke to its incessant itching. He had never relaxed enough on the hard earth to truly dream, but he did remember for a few minutes before waking, and the sweetness of the memory was almost unbearable.

Jorgbor had asked him to hold the baby for a few moments, while she tended a cut one of their neighbors had gotten while collecting firewood. Despite her youth, Jorgbor was a talented healer—not as strong as the medicine man, of course—but she had skill with the plants and knew how to tend to the sick and wounded. Sundaygar was fussy that morning and resisted being tied on his mother's back, as was their custom. The boy was getting over some kind of digestive sickness and had vomited all over her several times while on her back the day before. "Just for a moment," Jorgbor had assured him, handing over their son. Togar was irritated and didn't bother to conceal it. It was a woman's duty to care for her children, not a man's. A discussion about the storage capacity of the granary was starting in Uncle William's compound in a few minutes, and he wanted to make sure he got a seat closest to the elders.

Sundaygar fussed in his arms, reaching for his father's nose. "Be still now!" Togar commanded, but this only made the baby more distressed. He began to cry and squirm out of his arms. Togar looked to his wife for assistance, but she was completely focused on tending to the shallow laceration on their neighbor's forearm. Togar sucked his teeth. "Be calm, I say!" he yelled at the child, his voice rising. Sundaygar burst into tears then, and Togar wanted more than anything to be done with him. But when he gently nudged Jorgbor, she looked at him strangely and gestured toward the odd mixture of leaves, roots, water, and herbs she was pounding into a paste. "One minute-oh," she said, and smiled in that way that women always smiled at men when they were fully in control of a situation that their men didn't like. It made Togar unreasonably angry every time he saw it. In his arms, Sundaygar squirmed and almost fell. *Why won't you listen? Don't you know your father knows nothing of tending to women's things?* Jorgbor looked over at him, alarmed, and pressed the baby against his chest. "Soothe him," she said. "Rock him." Togar frowned but followed his wife's instruction. Once the child was on his chest, he rubbed his back with his right hand, jiggling him gently back and forth. Sundaygar responded to the motions and quieted. He nestled deeper into his father's chest and even cooed once. Togar laughed, despite himself, at his son's going so easily from a feeling of deep distress to comfort. "Yes, you are with Daddy now," he whispered in his ear.

"You are fine." Jorgbor was carefully wiping the healing paste on Alice's wound, but she looked over then and smiled at both of them. He met her eyes, and he allowed his former resentment to fall away. He was lucky he had them both, even if he was forced to act like a woman from time to time. It was worth it if it meant they would be a healthy, happy family.

And then a strange thing happened: Togar felt a warm wetness spread across his chest. Before he could even register what was happening, Sundaygar issued a loud fart and with it an explosion of soft, runny excrement. The smell was overwhelming—Togar wanted to vomit. He held the child toward Jorgbor. "Take him! Take him now!" Pried from the sheltered warmth of his father's arms, Sundaygar began to scream again. Alice had turned away from him, but it was impossible not to see her laughing. Togar's face reddened. He had put on his best shirt for the men's meeting, and now it was ruined. He had just bathed, and now he would have to do it all over again. "I'm sorry. He urinated a few minutes ago. I don't know what happened," said Jorgbor. But she wouldn't look at him straight on, either. Togar knew why: because she was laughing at him too. She wasn't even making that much of an effort to hide it. All of it was too much. He had to get out of the compound. Jorgbor took their sick son in her hands, and Togar burst out the door. He ran to the river as fast as he could, fervently hoping that no one saw him along the way. Once at its edge, he took off everything and dove in.

The memory ended there, and Togar opened his eyes reluctantly. The sun was peeking out over the small hills all around him, and an elephant trumpeted far in the distance. Togar sighed. That was Monday. Now it was Thursday, and he would give anything for the stench of Sundaygar's feces. To hold his baby son once more and feel the shock of warm urine across his chest.

Togar began to lose track of the days. He knew when it was daylight, because he could move more easily through the dense bush, and when dusk came, he would cook whatever he had been able to find and rest for a few hours before getting up and running again. These things were all he needed to know: daytime, nighttime, food, rest, move. Everything else—the soldiers; longer units of time like days, weeks, months; even Jorgbor and Sundaygar—was more than he could focus on. He concentrated on weaving a small net from palm fronds to catch tilapia in the river, which he had decided he would follow as far as Yela, in Bong County. As his fingers worked, Togar willed himself not to see the beautiful scars from Jorgbor's Sande ceremony he loved to trace along the small of her back when he lay down at night. Suddenly he felt driver ants feasting on his bare flesh, and he focused again on his task and recited his new nightly prayer: *For a time I will forget you. Just for a time. So that I may come back to you.*

Without the distraction of human voices, his ears became remarkably attuned to the sounds of the forest. The braying and strange mooing of the buffalo herds. The bright chirping of the cowbirds. Togar even began to recognize the sound of the snakes moving through the dry grasses late at night. As a child, being bitten had been one of his great fears. . . .

And just like that, she was back. Jorgbor had shown him how to suck out the venom from the bite right after an attack and also what herbs to chew afterward to deaden its effects. She only had to use this particular set of skills twice in all her years, but they successfully saved a small boy and an old man who had strayed into a pit on their way back from the farm. It was one of the reasons why he loved her: all the knowledge she had about healing and so many other things, which she shared freely with anyone who asked. It had made their whole village stronger. Togar's stomach churned as he thought about what would become of their village now, with all the men and so many of the crops taken, the taxes and all the farms abandoned—

No. Making his way through the more than one hundred miles to Zigida was the one goal he could allow himself to entertain. He had to believe that Jorgbor's brother would help him form a plan to save his family when he arrived. He had no idea what that might be, but they had to come up with something. It was what the ancestors demanded.

Togar was headed due north, maybe a bit northeast, to Yela. Once he crossed the border into Bong County, he would skew northwest a bit, and from Yela move through Palala, to Belefuanai near the Nianda River, over the border to Lofa County, into Zorzor, Yella, and then finally, Zigida. Sometimes as he was running, one foot tromping the tall, green grasses, the other midway through the next stride, he would string the names together in a kind of pekin song that matched the rhythm of his movements: *Yela, Palala, Belefuanai, Zorzor, Yella, Zigida.* The song was a comfort to him, a familiar thing in his mouth and limbs, in places where he was the most unfamiliar thing for miles. But he would still be alive, he reminded himself, and he would still be free.

After what felt like weeks and weeks of running, Togar came upon a well-beaten path in what he believed was Bong County. He hesitated for a moment. *It could lead me into trouble, but it could also lead me to rest and some decent food.* He was well outside of land he had ever walked on. He had some kind of inkling of where he might be, but still no concrete evidence. Though he doubted it, he reluctantly had to admit that for all he knew he could be running in circles around Giakpee. Togar took a step as quietly as he could, then another, and then another.

Not long after, he spotted a stand of papaya trees to his right. He stepped off the path, picked one of the succulent yellowish-orange fruits from a cluster of six near the top of the trunk, and sat down to cut it open with a wooden knife he had fashioned some days ago. He clawed at the fruit. Sweet juice ran down his chin, and he wiped it away with the back of his hand.

"You there!" someone shouted.

Togar jumped. The sound of a human voice was sharp, almost piercing after so much time alone in the bush.

"Whose papaya you think you eating? You pay me for this papaya, boy."

It was an older man's voice, and though he couldn't understand every word, he could make out enough to glean their basic meaning. If he was where he thought he was, the man was speaking Kpelle. Togar did what he was beginning to think was his greatest talent in life: He hid behind a large mahogany tree.

"I say, you there! You think I can't see you? I see you, boy. I see you eating my money-oh."

Togar began to chuckle, in spite of himself.

"Oh, now you think me funny, boy?" The man's voice was getting closer and closer, more and more agitated by the minute.

Togar wondered how the man could see him so clearly. He was well hidden. He looked to his right and left for an opening in the bush where he could dash off and be concealed.

The man walked faster, his every step rapidly encroaching on his hiding place.

Togar wanted to move, but there was another part of him that wanted to stay and talk to the first real human being he had come across in far too long—even if it would probably not be an amenable discussion.

"Poor old country man got nothing to eat way out in the bush 'cause rich, rich man come and steal it," the man said. "Enjoy all his papaya so he can't feed his family after Congo soldiers take all his crop money for taxes. You, boy. You probably work for Congo soldiers, eh? You show them where to come, how to take the most from us poor country people. Oh yes! That's what Bassa man do to Kpelle man, Loma do to Vai man, Mandigo man do to Mano man. That's what we learn best from Congo people: how to destroy each other-oh."

Togar could not stand to listen to these lies any longer. He stepped out from behind the tree.

The man was short but solidly built, with muscles that strained his once-white shirt and ripped trousers. A cutlass dangled from his right hand, although not menacingly. He simply held it in the way that so many farmers in the village did—as an extension of his arm.

"You don't know me," said Togar. "So I will forgive the suggestion that I would ever have anything to do with those brutes. Much less inform on my brothers."

The man cocked his head at him, sizing him up. "You speak Bassa, but not the same Bassa round here-oh."

Togar stared right back at him. He thought that fear was making the man posture, when his true nature was kindness. Togar could see a speck of mirth on his face, although it was gone as quickly as it came.

"You from down-down, maybe," the man said, gesturing ahead of them. "South Bassa country."

Togar said nothing. He was still deciding about this man.

"Oh, now you can't talk, eh? Worried that Bassa gonna tell too much, eh?" He walked around Togar slowly, inspecting him.

Togar bristled under his gaze. He dropped what was left of the papaya.

"Maybe you a criminal, stealing rice and cassava and papaya village to village. Maybe you raid the farms in the night, when everyone is sleeping and never see a thief grabbing their hard-grown food from their mouths." His voice was thin and raspy, and it got under Togar's skin. "Or maybe you trying to make haste from the authorities. Maybe you hate them as much as we. Won't let them take all your crop money or steal you to their farm to work for nothing. Maybe they after you for that, been running for days and weeks now. So far from home you forgot which was up, which way was down." He laughed. By this time, the man was a hairbreadth from Togar's ear. "Maybe you been in the bush so long, speech even left your lips. Maybe you forgot how to talk, how to tell your story. Maybe you even forgot your own name, boy," he whispered in Togar's ear.

Togar pushed the man back. "I am Togar Somah, son

of Baccus Somah and grandson of Aku Mawolo, father of Sundaygar Somah," he said. He felt his back straighten at the sound of his family's names. "I live in Giakpee with my family, or I did, until the soldiers chased me from there because I am a man and would not submit. Do not call me boy again."

The man's whole bearing changed then. His eyes lit up, and his torso lengthened. "Submit to what?"

Togar frowned, the vivid and painful memory resurfacing. Fortee, Gardiah, the soldiers, his near miss with the bullet. "To work their farms while mine goes to ruin. To leave my newborn son and wife. To allow them to take my sister's womanhood." His voice broke unexpectedly in the middle of this last sentence.

The man sucked his teeth, looked down at his feet, which were rough and cut up like most villagers'. He exhaled slowly, then looked up again to meet Togar's eyes. "You a friend, man. I can see now. I was just vexed 'cause you stole my papaya-oh. Give me hard time." Then he reached out his right hand and grasped his shoulder. The man smiled, and though he was missing almost as many teeth as he had, it was a warm welcoming smile that made Togar instantly at ease.

"I no criminal. I ate papaya fresh off the tree 'cause I thought it belonged to the forest. If I knew it belonged to a brother, I would have left it to rot on the branch."

The man sucked his teeth, apparently agreeing to go along with Togar's explanation. "I am Manhtee," he said,

"Son of Togba Kpangbah; grandson of Yarkpawolo; father of Zaowolo, Siakoh, Toimu, and Sianeh; and grandfather of Cammue, Kpakelah, Kollie, Konah, Lurpu, Kortolo, and Kehper."

Togar felt his eyes widen. The man was older than he thought, and had a formidable lineage that came with all the duties and responsibilities of being an elder.

The man laughed. "Oh yes! I am a potent old man-oh! My seed has nourished not only the soils of our village, and of Yela around it, but has grown powerful sons like you who will never submit to the terror of the Congo beasts. And their sons, they will cut down the Congo people all the same and throw them back into the sea from where they came." The man's smile was wide and easy now. He clapped Togar's back. "Come," he said. "You are welcome. Let me take you to our small village. My wives will give you some goat meat and rice, so you may fill your belly before running once more from those devils." The man gestured toward the path in front of them.

Although Togar wanted to trust Manhtee, and though his stomach rumbled at the thought of what would be his first real meal in weeks, he hesitated, just as he had at the start of the path that had taken him to this point. Stories abounded of scoundrels, men who sold their own cousins and friends back into bondage, for a few coins, a few guns, a steady stream of palm wine, and the promise of security. Manhtee had been right about one thing:

The Congo people had turned the country people against one another.

"Ah! Now your belly is full of my sweet papaya, maybe you don't want to go?" said Manhtee.

Togar had to admit that the man was an expert at reading people.

"Maybe you don't have to trust a poor country man now that you have taken what you wanted?" Manhtee continued.

Togar frowned, then looked at the ground. Manhtee's goodwill would not last forever, so he needed to decide now: Take a chance and trust him, or play it safe and endure yet another cold and hungry night alone in the bush? His stomach rumbled, louder this time.

Manhtee took another step on the path, and began walking. "My wives will be expecting me," he said. "If I am gone too long, they will think I have been taken like the others. You know." He looked back at Togar for a moment.

Togar nodded.

Manhtee turned back to the path and continued walking. "Come if you want. Go if you must. But whatever you decide, leave my poor papaya alone-oh."

Togar laughed. Manhtee reminded him of his own father, who had the same sense of humor and the same pride of family. Togar took a step along the path, then another, then another. Before long, he and Manhtee had walked in silence for a few minutes, well behind the stand of papayas and into a small clearing of grass huts, women tending pots over fires, and children chasing one another wildly around them.

"Welcome to Tuma-La," the man said, turning around. "Where we make sure our brothers from the south are well cared for."

CHAPTER SIXTEEN

MUCH TO HIS SURPRISE, Togar ended up staying in Tuma-La for almost three days. Despite his objections, Manhtee gave him his own pallet to sleep on in his compound, insisting that it was the softest he would ever enjoy. One of his sons had apparently been collecting bird feathers for some time and stuffed them all into the mattress as a gift to his aging father. After sleeping on the cold, hard earth for so long, Togar slept like a baby. And Manhtee's three wives, their innumerable children and grandchildren made sure that his every need was met. They carried him water from the river to bathe in; cooked him fish, okra, and goat meat over rice; and even mended some of his clothes, which had been torn from his weeks in the woods. It wasn't like being back home in Giakpee, but it was surely the next best thing. For the first time in weeks, Togar felt he could relax a little bit, and spent his time trading stories of Frontier Force raids with the men, discussing the area around Tuma-La and its proximity to Yela, and debating possible routes through Palala, and on to Belefuanai.

"Very few of the brutes make their way across the Nianda," one man told him. "If you can get to the other side, you may find safety in Lofa." He sucked his teeth and chomped down on a chicken foot from the pot of soup a bunch of them were sharing. "That far north, they don't think it's worth it-oh. To risk the rains and mosquitoes and beasts of the forest for their precious coins."

Togar nodded, taking heed of their words. He was the first Bassa man from that far south that many of them had ever encountered, and they were as eager to compare stories of the local chiefs, paramount chiefs, and district commissioners.

"This Congo government only for the Congo people—everyone knows that. We country people just like the rice we grow for them: They eat it, eat it, eat, then shit us out," a man said, and the rest of them laughed bitterly and nodded in agreement.

Later on, he saw a small, bright boy with straight hair and a thin nose like a crow helping his mother gather firewood. His color was somewhere between the strange, ghostlike hue of the Congo people, and the familiar deep black of the villagers. The man next to him noticed him staring, which made Togar want to stop, but he was somehow compelled. He had never seen anything like the boy, and wondered how he had come to be here, in this small Bassa village deep in the interior. Had his mother been raped by one of the Frontier Force bastards? Was this what they were trying to do to women like Fortee: breed out the blackness, the Bassa, through diluting it with their seed? Togar's pulse raced at the thought.

"He is Henry, our half-caste," the man next to him said. His tone was amiable, as if he were talking about one of his own children. The man nodded toward the boy and his mother. "His father was a Congo man who lived with us for a time, before he fell ill with the fever and died." He shook his head. "A nasty, nasty business-oh. Left the mother and new baby out here on their own, to fend for themselves. The man had left his own people, said they were brutes who could not be reasoned with, and that one day all the violence they conjured on the land would come back for them. Said he didn't want anything to do with them. And then he fell in love with our Monji, and ha!" The man clapped his hands and grinned. "That was it. He packed his things and left those Congo people, never to return."

Togar looked at the man, perplexed. "This really happened?"

The man laughed again, and nodded vigorously. He pointed his chin in Henry's direction. "Where do you think the boy came from-eh?"

Togar looked away. "I thought . . ."

"Ah, yes. That is what they all think at first," said the man. "But if you had known George, you would have slowly come to the conclusion that he was a good man. As good as any in Tuma-La. Better than most, actually." He thought for a moment. "Better than most. Told us once how the Congo people were so wicked to us because they had been unjustly treated back at their home, on the other side, and it had changed them in ways they couldn't see. Made them angry, because they came to a place which was supposed to be their new home, only to find that it didn't want them at all. The land didn't want them. The insects and animals and plants didn't want them." He laughed. "And we surely didn't want them-oh."

Togar studied the man's face to catch any traces of mirth. He didn't seem to be joking, even though he had a jovial way about him. He tried to absorb what the man was saying: The Congo people had been hurt across the ocean, hurt so badly that they had to leave their home—a wound they would never recover from. It made sense as a story . . . but he was finding it very, very hard to accept as fact. The notion that these sheer brutes had feelings at all was impossible to him.

"George say, 'We were slaves in our own home. So, we had to make someone else a slave in their home to feel like somebody,'" the man said. He looked back at Henry, laughing with his mother. "It was a strange story to hear, I admit it. But somehow, it made sense too, ya?" He looked back at Togar, for confirmation.

Togar nodded slowly. He watched Henry's mother direct him to the bush, presumably to gather more firewood. The boy's legs looked like small, delicate twigs themselves, as did his long, spindly arms. Togar wondered if he had inherited them from his Congo father, along with other traits that might weaken him in the bush. Everyone knew that Congo men—former slaves or not—could not survive the harsh life of the interior. Togar frowned and thought that his mother should have considered this before she lay down with a Congo man.

When it was finally time to leave the village, Manhtee and his wives insisted that he take a week's rations. Another family in the village had an extra blanket and cutlass, which they also said he must carry. "You could be gone for months," the man said, "and you will never survive with so few things." Togar had to admit that they were right. It would still be at least fifty miles to Zigida, in the deep bush, quite possibly with militiamen chasing him. He would need every possible resource in order to arrive there safely.

As he stepped on the path that led out of the village, around Yela, and then past Palala, Togar felt a deep sadness that made him almost turn back. He felt even more alone than he had felt his whole time in the bush. Like his mother, father, brother, ancestors had left him to die on some strange land, among the beasts of the forest. Like he belonged to no one and would never find his way back home. He thought of Sundaygar then, and all he would endure in Giakpee with no father and no food or coin from the farm, and he willed the lump in his throat back down again. *For you, I make this journey. With you, I am never alone.* Togar turned back only one time to look at his new friends, and then set off again, letting go of the familiar comforts of human contact with each step into the wild, untamed bush.

CHAPTER SEVENTEEN

TUMA-LA WAS CLOSER to Yela than Togar had realized, and it took him only a day to reach the bustling village. His friends had told him to stay out of the village proper, that soldiers had been spotted there recently, and that there were also informants who always had their eyes open for possible runaways. So, Togar went around the western side of the village, giving it as wide a berth as possible, skulking through the tall grasses and ironwood and mahogany trees. He made what he thought was halfway to Palala by nightfall, thankful that he had a real meal to fill his belly, and a warm blanket to fight off the chill. Now that he knew exactly where he was, he felt calmer and also more hopeful that he would make it to Lofa County. It was far, but others had walked farther alone in the bush; he had heard stories. He knew he could do it.

Togar drifted off to sleep, images of the rolling Wonegizi Range as Jorgbor had described it, flooding his mind.

The thick green hills far off in the distance, touching the sky. The mist of morning covering one side. The sun burning it off quickly, so that the trees of the hills look like they bleed into one another. It is the most beautiful place you can imagine. Jorgbor would tell him these stories of her beloved Lofa, as they lay down together at night, Sundaygar dreaming contentedly beside them. He would ask her then why she ever left such a perfect place, and she would turn to him, her eyes shining, and say, *Because it is not the only beautiful thing in the world, my husband.* And then she would kiss him. And his hands would find their way to the small of her back, lingering there for just a moment before grabbing her buttocks as she softly moaned.

Someone was kicking him now. He felt an insistent boot nudging his ribs. Togar pried his eyes open, reluctantly leaving the warmth of the memory of Jorgbor and the promise of Lofa. The sour smell of alcohol woke him up with a start, as did a raucous laugh.

"That's him all right," someone said. "The beast in the village was not lying after all."

The taut, unforgiving face of Commander Ross came into focus, standing in front of the soldiers who had almost raped Fortee.

Togar jumped back and grabbed his cutlass. He waved it at them, as he crouched and scanned the area for the possibility of escape. It was dawn, and the sun was just beginning to cast shadows and light.

Ross laughed. "Don't do something rash now, boy. So sorry to wake you from your dreaming, but we've just come to fetch what is rightfully ours. There doesn't have to be any trouble about it."

Togar backed up slowly, looking each soldier in their deadened, inebriated eyes. Although he had just woken up, they would be slower and clumsy. And there were only four of them this time.

"I understand your predicament, Togar," said Ross.

Togar winced at the sound of his name, and Ross smiled.

"Yes, Togar Somah, husband of Jorgbor and father of Sundaygar," he said. "I make it my business to know exactly who I'm dealing with, exactly where they're going, and exactly what we may be able to offer each other."

If he ran now, they would probably catch him and maybe maim him, and what of Jorgbor and Sundaygar? Togar's mind couldn't keep up.

And then a Bassa man stepped out of the stand of trees and tall grasses Togar was thinking about running to and shook his head. "It's too late now," he said, and he lifted a rifle.

Togar froze.

Ross laughed again. "Zigida is still miles and months away, through treacherous terrain, and hordes of insects that would delight to feast on flesh as young and succulent as yours. I'm sure you would contract malaria or some other jungle malady if you attempted to journey there so ill prepared. So, you see, we're doing you a favor, returning you to Edina and Vice President Yancy's rice plantation."

"Traitors!" Togar blurted out, his frantic rage alighting on Manhtee and Tuma-La for a moment.

"Oh, I wouldn't be too hard on them," Ross said. "I really didn't give them a choice, your friends. I said they could either tell me where you were, or I would round up all the small boys in the village and take them with us, as well. What would you have done?"

Before this moment, Togar did not know how deeply he could hate a human being, actually *want* to do a man physical harm. That he could take delight in it, even probably laugh while chopping up or pummeling his body. But that was what he wanted to do to Ross, more than anything in the world.

Ross sighed. "This is all well and good, conversing with you. We have a lot to catch up on, don't we? All the time in this unbearable jungle, what rats you ate to stay alive, which magical heathen ceremonies you performed to keep yourself concealed for so long. I mean, I have to hand it to you: You really gave us a chase! You got the farthest that any country boy has. Isn't that right, men?"

Looking bored and drunk, two of the men shrugged at Ross.

"This is quite an accomplishment for an ape man. You should be proud. But now it's over. We have to be getting back to Edina. You have made us quite late, actually." Ross nodded at the Bassa man.

The Bassa man made a move toward him, and Togar waved his cutlass toward him.

"Don't," the man said.

"You are even worse than the dung beetle," Togar sneered at him. "Delivering your own people up to them for coin. I know your ancestors are disgusted, your family humiliated."

The man stepped closer to him and raised the gun. "You don't know me or my family-oh," he said.

"Jaa se behn-indeh bun-wehnin," Togar said. It was something his great-grandmother used to say: *The truth needs no decoration.*

"Dhu kpa sohn dyedeeh sin-in," the Bassa man said. Togar winced at the meaning: *A young child who sticks his hand in the flame is burnt.* How appropriate for this tool of the white man to spit back their people's wisdom, in order to enslave him.

Then the Bassa man knocked the cutlass out of Togar's hand and tackled him. Togar pounded his fists into him with all his might as they both tumbled to the ground, but it was useless. The man was almost twice his size and flipped Togar over his head easily. Togar blinked slowly, the shock of landing on the ground and having the wind knocked out of him temporarily blinding him. Still, he could hear whoops of encouragement from Ross's soldiers, who were finally roused from their boredom by this spectacle. The Bassa man lunged, intending to stomp on him. Togar rolled aside, dodging him easily as he landed awkwardly on the uneven ground. The man groaned and staggered as he tried to turn for another attack. Togar spotted his cutlass lying in the dust a few feet away from him and went for it. He grabbed its handle as the man charged at him again. Togar raised the blade as fast as he could, pointing it at his opponent. Then came the sick sound of metal penetrating flesh, and blood was everywhere. The man looked down at his stomach in horror and at the cutlass blade stuck halfway through him.

"You—you killed me," he said, shocked. "You killed me, brother."

Togar could only look on in shock, his hand still gripping the blade but shaking now. He had never killed or seriously wounded someone before. He hadn't meant to do it; he was only defending himself.

"I'm sorry," he whispered feebly.

The man pushed Togar's hand off the blade and then fell back on to the ground. He writhed there for a little while, blood pooling in every direction, until he died.

Togar could not move, which made it very easy for Ross's men to wrap his hands tightly in rope. Pee-nyuehn ni se hwio xwadaun. The phrase came to him then, for some reason, and he found he could not stop mumbling the proverb: "Pee-nyuehn ni se hwio xwadaun," he said over and over again. *Night must come to end the pleasures of the day.* "It is night now," he said finally. "It is night." Then he collapsed.

Ross walked over to where Togar lay on the ground,

his whole body scrunched together in the fetal position. Togar closed his eyes and tried to get back the feeling of kissing Jorgbor, the image of the Wonegizi Mountains, but they were gone.

"Oh, don't be such a sore loser. You and I both know there was no way you would win anyway," said Ross. "We own this country and always will. The people, the land, it's all ours." He leaned down so that he was mere inches from Togar. "You. Are ours."

Togar refused to look at the brute.

Ross kicked him in the stomach.

Togar wheezed.

"Get up," he said.

Togar curled up tighter.

"Now," Ross said icily. "Need I remind you that we have complete access to your farm, as well as your wife and infant son? Don't make me do things I don't want to do."

Togar sucked his teeth. *Why, God? Must it be like this for the rest of my days? And I am a young man.* He put the pain in his stomach out of his mind and stood up slowly.

Ross patted him on the back, and Togar flinched. "There now. You see how much easier things are when you can be reasonable?" He signaled to his men to gather their things and prepare for the long walk. "Our horses are stationed not far from here, but you of course will be pulled behind us. It will make the trip slower, of course, but far more meaningful, don't you think?"

CHAPTER EIGHTEEN

MUCH TO TOGAR'S SURPRISE, Ross walked beside him, seemingly delighted at the opportunity to make small talk with the man they had pursued through swamps and impenetrable jungle, and mud and overflowing creeks and riverbeds.

The bastard is not well, Togar thought. *He is not sound. Perhaps this is what this work does to their minds. How it eats away their hearts.*

"You really are an outstanding specimen," Ross was saying. He reached out and clapped Togar's shoulder, like they were comrades. "As is your brother-in-law, I might add. Do your families have any white blood in their lineages, I wonder? That would explain things. Your extraordinary abilities, I mean. Word is that Gardiah has been doing visionary work on the plantation. Thinking of crop rotations and soils and cycles we never would have considered. Positively striking, the mind of an ape holding that kind of knowledge and talent, don't you think? I have half a mind to write my cousin in America, to ask him to book passage for such a monkey miracle to the next World's Fair. The journey might soften the blow after he hears what befell his bitch and their—oh, but where are my manners?"

Togar stopped and dropped to his knees.

"My condolences." Then Ross yanked Togar to his feet by his shackles. "Anyway, I'm sure that the Western man would be shocked to see how far a coarse brute can come." And on and on he chattered for miles until they came to their horses.

"Yes, Togar. I think I will send your brother-in-law to America," concluded Ross as he slid into his saddle. "You, though." Ross sucked his teeth and shook his head. "You poor black devil will surely end up on a boat to Fernando Pó."

And they rode all the way to Edina over one week, Togar running behind them the whole way.

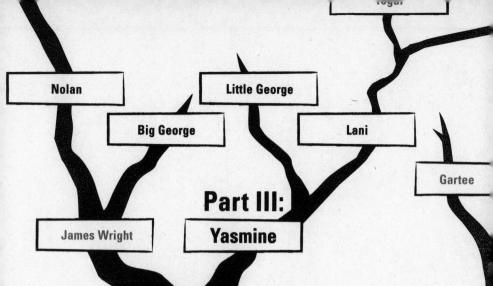

Nolan

Big George

Little George

Lani

Gartee

Part III:
Yasmine

James Wright

What our brethren could have been
thinking about, who have left their
native land and home and gone
away to Africa, I am unable to say.

—David Walker

CHAPTER NINETEEN

1827, the Scott Plantation,
75 Miles from Norfolk, Virginia

"IF I AM GOING to die, it's going to be my own kind of death," Yasmine Wright said, standing up. Lani cooed in the red oak cradle James had carved for her. "It ain't going to be no white man's work killed me. It's going to be God's work."

If there was no other way to leave, she would still leave. She had been tiptoeing around the Scotts all her life, and as she sat down on her bed to pull on James's old boots, she delighted in the thought that she would stomp the entire fifty miles to Norfolk, thrashing through brush, kicking away burrs and pinecones. She would get on that boat, no doubt about it, and Little George, Nolan, Big George, and Lani would too.

She had been to Norfolk only once before, as a child, when Daddy was sick. There had been an outbreak of the yellow fever, and Old Master Scott (then Young Master Scott) had sent for the best doctor in the county.

She was only eight at the time, but she had been sent to fetch Doc Lawrence, while the master himself sat over Daddy day and night, feeding him liquids and keeping a steady stream of cold cloths on his forehead until finally he slept. "I ain't never seen no white man hang over one of us like that," James told her on the carriage ride into town, which seemed interminable. She hushed him—even though he was ten years older—and he grimaced and turned away out into the night. She had known even then that she would marry him. She also knew that Daddy would die. Even if she and the family were set up with the nicest white man in six counties, their bodies were still broken by work and time.

Baby Lani looked on as her mother smoothed her skirt and gazed down at the worn, checkered pattern. "It's going to be *my* work, *my* time." She smiled and stepped toward the small table by the window, on which she had set the bushels of tobacco, yards of dyed cotton, beads, and fine hand tools that she hoped to be able to carry with her on the boat, over the ocean, and into the motherland, where they would build their new home. Big George had also managed to steal cheese, sausage, apples, and several bread loaves out from under Old Master Scott's careful and increasingly greedy eye in the kitchen. All this bounty was assembled on the modest table, and it was more treasure than she had ever seen in one place.

She walked over to Lani, crouched down, and began

rocking the cradle. She looked at her chestnut-brown hand resting on the cradle's edge, and was shot six years back in an instant, when Nolan was inside an ordinary tub that Mrs. Barnes had scavenged for them, and James's hand was on top of hers, resting easily, and they both knew—she knew that they both knew—that this day would come, the day when they would choose their own destinies, when they alone would be responsible for any act they did or did not engage in, when a black God's vengeance would trump anything a white could mete out. She had never considered, however, that James might not be here with her now. And then she was shot back into her body just as quickly, and the pain came back, the sharp jab in her chest, the physical presence of his absence, the going on and on and on and on, and she stumbled out of her crouch, onto the floor with a thud. Lani was startled and looked up. The baby opened her eyes wider. Yasmine stared back at her daughter, the last person James had acknowledged before he passed on. She was disturbed and about to cry. Yasmine gathered her weight and regained her balance, then reached out and wrapped Lani's small fingers around her index finger.

"Barely six more hours before we gone from this place, forever," she told her. Lani's clouded eyes instantly began to calm at the sound of her mother's voice. "All you need to do is sit pretty like you always do and get ready to see some new country. Just so you don't get to worrying, here's what we going to do: Little George and Big George is going to leave early for church service, like Old Master always wants us to do on Saturdays. But instead of going to church, they gonna hide in the tree stand up by the creek. Nolan'll be with Mrs. Barnes in the kitchen, but soon as she goes out to fetch the linens for washing, he run back here and wait for us. Now, you'll be with Penny in the house, as usual. But soon as I see Mrs. Barnes head out the kitchen toward the backyard for the linen tubs, I grab you and head back here. Soon as we get Nolan and pick up this pouch filled with food and necessaries, we make for the tree stand and Little George and Big George. And then we gone." She snapped her fingers, and Lani caught her breath. It felt good to speak the plan aloud, all the particulars perfectly aligned. It made the dream seem real.

Yasmine leaned into Lani, so that their faces were almost touching. "Be as if we never was here at all," she whispered. "Be like we that river used to run beside Old Master's property, then dried up to a creek, and then just dried up, period." Lani's hold on her finger became lax. "Folks might say they remember the taste of that sweet water, be dreamin' they can almost taste it on their tongues, but they never will taste it again, so they might as well get used to thirst." She could hear the sharp edge in her voice and felt her back stiffen. She saw his old, withered hand on her breast, and she closed her eyes tightly and pulled her hands away from her daughter. "Go 'way," she told her mind. "Ain't got no use for you no more."

Her voice quivered, but the image flew away just as fast as it had come, and she was back in the here and now, reaching toward Lani again, readying her for their own flight, their leaving.

CHAPTER TWENTY

WHEN THE SUN WAS just beginning to fall down from its perch, Yasmine placed her last bushels of wheat in the oxcart and nodded to Mrs. Barnes when she passed her in the kitchen. When she walked to the dining room, Penny was already there, sweeping imperceptible dust from the top of the bureau, the bookshelves, and the table. If there was one thing Old Master insisted on, it was a clean house; he could be like a woman in that way.

Lani lay on a small blanket on the floor, sucking on a piece of apple Penny had given her. Yasmine picked her up, hoping that, somehow, being connected to her daughter would remind her of what she had to do.

Penny looked over her shoulder. "Afternoon, Mrs. Yasmine," she said, a shy grin spreading across her face. Penny was only thirteen, and though her body still resembled a child's, there was something older in her neck and shoulders. Or perhaps it was her back, the way she held herself—upright, but a little bit fatigued. Like she was already tired of this world and eager to step across whatever pain would last an instant into the gentle oblivion of the next. Lani would never grow up to know that feeling and have that wish. Yasmine would make sure of it.

"Afternoon, Penny," Yasmine answered back. She walked over to the girl and kissed her on her forehead, just below her head wrap. Yasmine pursed her lips and tasted the bitter saltiness of Penny's perspiration. She wanted the taste and the sweat itself to be the only things she carried from this place that lasted, save her children.

Penny cocked her head and looked at Yasmine askance. "What you do that for?" She placed her right hand on the same hip. Mirth played at the corners of her mouth.

Yasmine walked past her to the bureau. She pulled out the polished maple case that contained all the silver, which was given to Old Master's father, who was the first Quaker to start a plantation in Virginia. Old Master had told them the story so many times—usually when he was handing out their measly pittance of a salary every month. "He was a man before his time, my father," Old Master would say, his palsied left hand pointing at them and shaking with his madness. "All the other white men wouldn't even call their workers 'workers.' They called them slaves—because they *were* slaves! They didn't pay them anything for their labor, whipped them, mutilated them, even killed some. But my father would have none of that. He insisted on a more humane manner of dealing with his fellow men. He insisted that they have decent quarters, be fed properly, never be whipped or physically harmed in any way, even if they flagrantly disobeyed orders—and he even paid them! Can you imagine what it meant forty years ago, to have coloreds in your possession in the state of Virginia, and to insist upon their humanity?"

At this point, Old Master would invariably set an invasive stare on whoever was unfortunate enough to be next in line for payment, and they would flinch and look away. But Yasmine never did. She just stood there, and met him where he was. Once, when she was fifteen years old, in the middle of the story—the part about the things that the other white men did to their coloreds—she had interrupted him. "They rape their colored women too?" she asked evenly. His eyes screamed, and his left hand stopped shaking for an instant. Behind her, in the full line of hot, sweaty coloreds, someone coughed. Someone else shuffled their shoes, but mostly what she heard was the collective quiet of held breaths. He grunted some kind of affirmation finally and then handed her a small pouch of coins.

"What? I can't give my niece a kiss from time to time?" Yasmine asked now, lifting three spoons from their velvet casings and blinking away the memory. She didn't want to take them either.

Lani cooed in her arms, grabbing at specks of dust in the air illuminated by sunlight.

"No, that ain't it," Penny said, turning to face her. "You know I 'preciate anything you got to give me in the way of love. It's just that you ain't exactly a whole bundle of affection, usually."

Yasmine snickered. It was so easy to be with Penny— she would miss that. "Well, I ain't exactly got a lot to be affectionate about, usually." She shifted Lani to her hip and scrubbed at the first spoon with the coarse rag vigorously. The silver caught a ray of sunlight and reflected it back in her eye, and her pupil smarted. Although it could sometimes hurt like this, she loved the sun and couldn't wait to get out in it, moving with her boys and Lani, day in and day out.

Penny sucked her teeth. "You better watch your language, missus. You know God don't like ugly." She moved her dustrag onto the gold-flecked frame that contained a painting of Old Master's father, enthroned in his study, Bible in hand.

Yasmine snickered again and raised an arm toward the picture. "See now, that's you all's problem—you think *that's* God."

Penny turned around and faced her, presumably to study her and see if she was being serious.

Yasmine picked up the next spoon and let its coldness ripple up her spine. "That ain't God. In fact, neither that man nor his son ever had a conversation with God or *his* son. But yet, they got every colored up in this place thinking that they the very incarnation of all that's holy."

She shook her head. "It's a shame. It's a shame what they done to us." She put down the last spoon and peered out the window. The light was beginning to fade; she had better finish up in here, quick.

Penny looked at her aunt, befuddled. "There be plenty of worse places to make a home," she said. "And you ain't even have to go that far to find them, neither." Penny shook her head. "You heard what Master Kennedy tell Old Master Scott last spring, right?"

Yasmine knew, but she turned her attention to the last few utensils at the bottom of the case.

"He tell Master he whip any of us what wander to his place, even if we family relations. He tell him he don't want to see his coloreds getting any strange ideas in they heads about how they should be getting paid, how they should be having nicer quarters and better food. He say every time one of them come back from visiting us, the whole plantation be agitated for weeks—field hands, house help—complaining 'bout unfair treatment and the like. He tell Old Master were it up to him, he like to round up all the Scott people and shoot them. Say they tampering with nature, the way he running things."

Yasmine set Lani down and then pulled her shawl tighter around her shoulders. She walked over to Penny and enclosed her in her arms. The intensity of the gesture surprised them both.

"Good night," Yasmine said, stepping away from her. She wished she could know, know for sure, that Penny would leave one day. She wished she could ask her to come along, but she knew better.

Penny's eyes were wet, and she searched Yasmine's. "Why you so . . . different tonight?" She took her aunt's hand. "Feel like you got something you keeping tight, right here." She brought her fist to her chest. "Like something got caught there, or caught you."

Yasmine only smiled, scooped up Lani, stepped into the doorway, and with a last look, tried to memorize the way Penny's spine curved deeply when she stretched toward items that were out of reach. The sharp point of her nose in profile, the jut of her upper lip, which sometimes made her look stern, when she wasn't at all. Who would she end up being? Who *could* she end up being? Yasmine's eyes smarted, and she walked out of the doorway, into the living room, and out the front door, Lani ever watchful in her arms.

CHAPTER TWENTY-ONE

IT WAS TOO COLD. The first frost had come a few weeks before, but icicles hung down from tree branches in the night, and when they melted in the morning they made puddles that Yasmine and her children sloshed through during the day, leaving a kind of coldness that seeped into their skin. There was simply no way to get dry. Yasmine was thankful that it was only a five-day journey to Norfolk, and that once they were there, they would have lodging at the home of one of the men she had met at the meeting last month.

"Ouch!"

Yasmine turned to see Little George clutching his left foot. She wiped the sweat from her brow and walked over to him. "Let me see," she said, bending down. "What happened?"

"Don't know," he said, pursing his lips. "Feel like I stepped on something—something with nettles."

Yasmine felt Lani stir on her back and hoped that they hadn't woken her.

Little George wiggled his foot out of a worn-out boot, sucking his teeth. He shivered as the wind bellowed around them.

Yasmine sighed. His big toe was punctured, probably by a stinging nettle. There was an awful lot of blood for a wound so small, which told her that it must have gone deep. She wished they were someplace where they could stop, but it would be two more nights before they reached Norfolk and their lodging. He would have to hold on until then. Yasmine pressed the wound firmly with her thumbs.

Little George flinched at her touch. "Your hands freezing," he said, warming his hands in his armpits.

She ripped a small piece of cloth off from her head wrap and tied the scrap around the cut, tight enough so that it would stop the blood. "We can't stop," she told him. "We got nowhere to stop at."

Little George didn't meet her eyes. He pulled his boot back on without a sound. "I know."

The wind kicked up sharply again, cutting at the tips of their ears. From his place beside Big George, Nolan whimpered and dove under the long brown wool of his oldest brother's overcoat, which hung down to his feet. It had been James's gift to Big George on his fifteenth birthday.

Yasmine stood up and got her bearings. They needed to head northeast for the rest of the day. Lani was moving on her back now, crying loudly. Like Nolan, she had no tolerance for the cold. Yasmine picked up her pack and stepped forward. "You shush now," she told her daughter. "We ain't got no time for such carrying on." This made Lani cry even harder. Yasmine felt her kicking her tiny feet into her back. That child could be so willful! Yasmine took another step. The harder Lani cried, the faster she walked.

The next morning, about a half hour after they set out, Yasmine noticed that she didn't hear the familiar sound of a trio of footfalls behind her. She turned around and saw no one—not Big George, not Little George, not Nolan. Her breath caught in her windpipe. They had them, they finally had them! The last thing she would ever see before she left this earth would be their faces. She tried to remember them: Big George's nascent triceps, his deliberate yet easy gait; Little George's intense stare, the way he could almost run you down with it; and Nolan's blubbery baby cheeks. Yasmine laughed in spite of herself. She picked up her skirts and began to run back the way she had come, boots snapping twigs beneath her as she went. White oak and beech trees blurred in her vision as she sped, and the hard shell of acorns pierced her soles. The sun was beginning to rise above everything, its rays slowly melting the frost that had come the night before. Yasmine could see her breath as she ran, heard Lani's faint cries on her back.

The fear that had shadowed their leaving the Scott plantation had been a shapeless thing for the most part. The Wrights weren't truly runaways, and Master Scott wasn't technically their master. In theory, she should have been able to walk to Norfolk without a second thought. In practice, though, Yasmine was sure the formless "they" of her nightmares would solidify and snatch her children.

Suddenly, the boys appeared, gathered around a big rock. Nolan was sitting on it and pressing his palms into his eyes. There were streaks of tears all the way down his face, and his nose was running. Big George stood beside him, taller than she ever remembered him, his right hand on his little brother's shoulder. Big George's expression was stern, and as he looked up to see her, Yasmine thought she saw something akin to disdain in his eyes, but it disappeared as quickly as she thought it. Off to the right was Little George. He was not facing either of them, but rather, looked out into the deep darkness of the brush. He did not turn around to acknowledge Yasmine's approach.

She felt her heart slow as she came nearer to them, and her breath became more regular. "Boys!" she said. Only Big George met her eyes. "What the hell you doing?"

The top of a pine tree sawed near the sky, as the sky's air made it moan. Lani gurgled on her back, but the boys said nothing.

She reached out and grabbed Big George's forearm, and he flinched. "I asked you all a question, dammit!

Now you best answer me. Here I was, thinking you all was with me, and then when I turn 'round and look, what do I see?" She pressed her face into Big George's, and he backed up unconsciously. Nolan looked up at both of them, crying.

"What you think I see?" The pitch of her voice was rising. If James were here, he would tell her to step away for a moment to breathe, that he would handle it first, and then she could make her appeal, as long as she did it calmly. She had always hated that conversation with him, especially because she saw how much better the boys responded to his voice, his discipline, than hers.

Big George was staring at the ground. Tears kept streaming out of Nolan's baby eyes. Little George still hadn't turned around to even let her know that he was listening or even cared.

Yasmine strode over to him, fastened her hand to his shoulder, and spun him around. "You look at me when I'm talking to you, boy!"

His face was blank, completely empty. It was like the night sky before the stars came out, but more blank, somehow. Slowly he focused his eyes on her face. She tried to see what he was keeping in them, what it was that had drawn them here, so far away from her, and not fearful of this distance at all, but there was still nothing. This enraged her further somehow, and before she knew what she was doing, she had slapped him across the face. Behind her, Big George and Nolan gasped, and the pine tree above kept on sawing back and forth, back and forth.

She had pushed Little George's chin farther from her with the slap, and he brought his palm up to caress his raw cheek, which was red from the stinging wind. When he looked back at her, he was not empty anymore—Yasmine recognized what filled his face, his arms, his pores. It was rage, barely contained below the surface.

Nolan ran up behind her and pulled at her skirt. "Mama, don't be mad at your George, please. It was me, it was my fault we stopped. They didn't have nothing to do with it."

Yasmine turned around slowly to face him. He was wiping away tears and snot with the back of his hand, sniffling all the while. He looked up at his mother, looked down at the ground, then looked back at her. "I . . ." His voice became smaller than she had heard it since he was a toddler. "I don't wanna go there." He began to fiddle with his hands.

Yasmine had always said that she knew that Nolan had been here before; she didn't know whose he had been, she didn't know when, but he was definitely an old soul, and one who had known freedom.

"And . . ." Nolan looked askance, as if he were trying to parse out something far away. "I miss Daddy too." Tears began to fall anew with these last words.

Yasmine sighed and crouched down so that they were eye level. "We all miss Daddy, Nolan." She allowed herself to feel the truth of this statement for a moment, then pushed it back down again because she knew it could overwhelm her. "But that don't mean we don't have to go."

"Go where?" Little George asked suddenly, venom in his words. "What you even know 'bout where we going? Livingston said they all heathens over there anyway; that some jungle fever done killed most of the first settlers, and—"

Yasmine stood up and whipped around to face him. "Since when do Livingston say a thing worth repeating?" Livingston was Little George's age-mate, who lived up the road. He could talk a wild streak about nothing so fast you swore you could feel your mind dulling in your skull.

Little George scowled. "You just mad 'cause his mama caught you and Old Master in—"

Yasmine was on him before she knew it. She would have slapped him again, twice as hard this time, if Big George hadn't come up behind her and held her back. "You *never* talk to me that way, you hear?"

"Easy," Big George told her softly. He was deliberately using his calm voice, she could hear it, and that eased some part of her to know that he, at least, was trying. "Easy, Ma. You know he don't know nothing. He just a kid."

"And that is your saving grace, boy!" she hollered at Little George. "That you only eleven. 'Cause if your father was here, he would be slapping you silly right now, and you know that's God's truth."

Finally she saw some kind of repentance in his face.

Because he knew, she surmised, that she was right. There had not been much that James could do about so many things, but one thing he said that he always would do was raise his children—until, he said, he couldn't.

On her mother's back, Lani had begun to wail. She had new energy to spend on her tantrums, full of Yasmine's milk. Yasmine closed her eyes. *Just breathe, baby. Breathe.* It was times like these that he came to her—never in her dreams, where he might linger. "We got to go," she said, willing her voice to be level. "I ain't gonna lie to you and say it's going to perfect, but we got no other choice. We got to go *now.*"

Little George opened his mouth to say something, but Big George shushed him with one look. Nolan took her hand, and the two older boys set out in front, back the way she had come from.

CHAPTER TWENTY-TWO

1827, Norfolk, Virginia

WHEN THEY ARRIVED IN Norfolk late the next day, the skies were clear and the sun had driven away all traces of the frost. Even Little George perked up when they entered the bustling port city. His eyes widened at the naval yards and timber stores, steam mills, tanneries, hotels, churches, bars, and even residential neighborhoods, dotted with expansive houses. Men with wide-brim hats and wider bellies stood outside their storefronts hawking eastern white pine, passage to exotic places, and everlasting salvation in the pews of their worship halls.

"Mama," Little George whispered shyly in her ear, mindful of sleeping Lani. "How come you never said nothing 'bout so many coloreds here?"

Yasmine wished she could laugh at his excitement, seeing so many of their people in one place. She couldn't deny that it was something to see honey brown, chestnut, sallow yellow everywhere you turned. There was a certain kind of beauty to the way the mass of these bodies moved, sometimes across from other, white bodies, but mostly behind them. There was a certain way that they ruptured the sterile, safe landscape that was so deliberately built and maintained. But in the end, she had to conclude that it wasn't enough. There was still a little girl of no more than six, who walked beside them for a moment and smiled at Nolan, and was knocked down by the older white boy responsible for her for "watching them niggers, when you ought to be watching me." There was still the middle-aged woman who followed behind her madame, carrying her skirts over mud and ice, slipping on the bare soles of her feet as they crossed this unforgiving December ground. Yes, Yasmine mused, you could come to the city all you wanted and expect its busyness, its hustle and bustle, to transform its inhabitants into some higher form of being than could be found back in the countryside. Yes, you could hope all you wanted that somewhere in these United States that God had forsaken, someone knew how to treat their fellow men and women, but hope still wouldn't change what was staring you straight in the face.

Yasmine closed her eyes and willed herself back to the room with all the white men in suits and shiny new boots, all those weeks ago. "We cannot wait for the race problem to solve itself," said the man behind the podium. From where she was, standing way in the back, Yasmine could make out that his hair was blond and that he had a large dimple that appeared whenever he smiled, which he did intermittently during the speech. He could not have been more than thirty. "The so-called freedmen in our state create an unnatural situation, whereby many blacks come to accept the false belief that their destiny is the same as the white man's. They come to the conclusion that their minds have the same capacity for reason and good judgment as ours do, and that they can perform the same tasks that God has bestowed to us for the purposes of building this country in the name of spreading His truth. My brothers, you know the deep and dangerous error in this line of thinking!" The orator threw his hand down on the podium after this declaration, for emphasis. Yasmine remembered feeling Lani startle on her back at the noise.

The thirty or so wealthy plantation owners who had sat in finely carved wooden chairs arranged in a series of straight lines radiating outward from the podium puffed on their pipes and murmured in agreement.

Thus urged onward, the man continued. "Whether you agree with the aims of our venerable organization, commonly known as the American Colonization Society, or whether you subscribe to a more modest set of purposes"—he nodded toward the Quakers in the room, a few of whom looked at one another meaningfully, and a few others who shifted uncomfortably in their seats— "you agree that the situation we currently find ourselves in is neither sustainable nor advisable, for any of the parties involved." Again the men toward the front of the room murmured in appreciation. "The state of degradation that the black race now experiences is the direct result of the centuries he spent in the heathenism that runs rampant in their homeland, that dark place of Canaan we know as Africa. Most of these men, women, and children have only just come to know our Savior and the liberation that awaits us all in His arms. They have also only recently come to know the meaning of hard work, the meaning of toil and labor in order to rise out from under the muck of their previous lives in that spiritual desert so far away." Smatterings of applause lit up around the room. "There comes a time, my friends, when we must ask ourselves: What is to become of our less fortunate brethren—both those here, in this land of peace, salvation, and plenty, and there, in that land of charred earth and wasted human potential?" The man patted his handkerchief across his sweaty brow and paused for emphasis. There was no sound in the room, save for the tiny ticking of a watch, hidden in some unknown breast pocket. "Philosophically, this is a question that must be asked and one that must be answered as well, unless we want to risk everything that we have toiled so hard to build here, in our home. Although there will be no easy answers to such complex and difficult questions, if we have courage, we can face whatever may come to us, and then employ the ingenuity that is so fundamental to our way of life, in order to carry out what we are called to do."

Yasmine could see that even the Quakers were paying

attention now; they were sitting forward in their seats, their hands clenched tightly in their laps. And she had to admit that even her own heart was quickening, being carried forward on the current of his words, waiting to arrive wherever it was he was going. "The Gold Coast," the man said, almost under his breath, so that the listeners had to strain to hear him, so that they wished he would say it again, to make sure they had heard him right. "The Gold Coast of Africa is the balm to this gaping wound that now threatens to overwhelm the entire democratic order of our nation."

The Gold Coast. What a funny set of words they were, and yet, Yasmine mused, words that seemed to shine as they flowed out of her mouth in a whisper.

"The land there, unlike other parts of Africa, is plentiful and fertile. The people there are hungry for the knowledge that will transform their lives of sloth to industry, from damnation to salvation. Why not send the coloreds *back* to the place from which they have traveled so far, to the land of their forefathers, to the place that would have ruined them had they stayed, but which now is hungry for the knowledge, the experience, and the salvation they have gained here? *That* is what the American Colonization Society proposes, and that is why I stand here before you, asking for your support." The man patted his brow again, wiping away the sweat gathered there. "We have a ship scheduled to leave from Norfolk for the port of Monrovia in December. We would like to take no more than one hundred and no less than eighty blacks with us on board."

It was then that the talk on the floor swelled above a dull murmur. The speaker was not disturbed, though, and continued on in a louder voice. "This is not such an unprecedented journey as some might think. In fact, quite a few of our people are on the Gold Coast right now, working with the blacks to set up their living places, build their houses of worship, grow their crops, and prepare everything else that is associated with immigrating to a new land. One shipload of coloreds left last year, also from Norfolk, and another left the year before, from the port of Baltimore." The man fished in his pocket and pulled out a tattered letter. "I have a letter from my good friend, Adulus Barnes, who is protectorate of the new town, right here, if you'd like to read it. He says they are all doing just fine over there, that the coloreds are adjusting famously to their old country, and that he will soon be able to leave them to rule over themselves."

At this point, a man in a navy suit stood up and said, "I know of a whole group of so-called freedmen in Hoke County who would do well to take you up on this kind and excellent offer. Since our fair state doesn't recognize such nonsense as 'freedmen,' they are forced to leave their families in some cases and travel north, which they are loath to do. But with this new option you have brought before us, they could pay out the remainder of the value of various family members—if we masters are inclined, if the slaves are so inclined and if they can afford it—and travel back to their homeland to start an entirely new life, completely devoid of the problems they would have here—north or south."

The blond man behind the podium clapped his hands once and then pointed to the man in the navy suit. "Right you are, my friend," he said. "That is the kind of thinking that will get this next boat out of the port. We need you and other men like you to spread the word, to let others know about this opportunity."

Yasmine's head was swimming. The meeting was disbursing. Lani had begun to squirm on her back, impatient and hungry. Yasmine would have to nurse her soon or risk causing a scene. The blond man at the podium thanked everyone for their attention and stepped down. Some men in front surrounded him, and he was soon engaged in what looked like quite a lively discussion. Other small pockets of conversation between groups of men popped up around the room. And the men beside her started to quietly shuffle out. She knew they expected her to follow them and also to serve them their afternoon teas—it was why they had allowed her into the meeting in the first place. She didn't have much time before someone demanded her labor and attention. The plantation had a reputation for being as efficient as it was hospitable, and Master Scott would throw a fit if any one of his workers jeopardized this standing. She needed to move fast.

Yasmine scanned a group that was slowly moving beside her. They were older gentlemen, and they held their felt hats lazily in their hands, like they knew they had to move, but their bodies did not feel any kind of urgency about it. One man had a stripe of gray that ran all the way up his beard to about halfway up to the crown of his head. She had never seen anything like it before, and wondered if it was the sign of a curse or a blessing. He wore a simple dark gray suit, and his shoes were well shined. He turned toward Yasmine, feeling her eyes, and gave her something like a smile.

"Good afternoon, sir," she said, sensing her opening.

The man nodded. "Good afternoon."

She could see him taking in her gingham dress, which was still red despite years of heavy washing and her leather shoes. It was clear, in so many ways, that she was not a slave.

"Come to hear the good Mr. Richards speak this afternoon, have you?" He stepped toward her, and she instinctively stepped back.

She made her face relax. "Yes. His plan look interesting," she said, trying to find the right words that would show her intelligence. White men truly owned everything—even the English language. "I didn't know such a thing was possible."

The man laughed, and it was a deep and hearty sound. "Neither did I, until a few weeks ago. I'm a Quaker myself and a bit skeptical about the whole thing. But if it's what gets you coloreds your freedom, then it can't be so bad, can it?"

She could hear Master Scott calling to her from the meeting room and decided that she had about thirty seconds to finish making the connection. She smiled and said, "No, it can't be. I be thinking 'bout me and mine's booking passage on one of them ships. You know anything 'bout it?"

The man shook his head. "I don't."

Yasmine's breath ran out; she had picked the wrong man. You never picked the man who looked kind—she knew this—because he would also be the one who held the least sway with the truly powerful.

Still, he took her elbow and guided her into the meeting room. She couldn't remember the last time that a white person had touched her so easily, without a thought. Lani cooed, seeming to sense the remarkable contact. "I can take you to who to talk to, though," he said. "You have the look of a free woman to you, the look of intensity, which is just what they want, as I understand it. I'm sure we can work something out."

They were almost to the guesthouse when they saw it. Walking toward the southeastern part of town, the streets became wider, the cobblestones few and far between. The majestic, cavernous two-story houses that they had seen at the center of town had long given way to the more modest buildings. With the change of weather, the new dirt roads had degenerated to mud, and many a horse and carriage were stopped on the side of the road, drivers working anxiously to clear their wheels. This was the new part of Norfolk, the section that was expanding as the cotton trade spread south, and enterprising folk—white, black, and Indian—came from all around to find their own fortunes or, in the case of the last two, to be dominated by them.

"Mama, what's that?" Nolan said, his voice trembling a bit.

Yasmine had already seen it out of the corner of her eye, no more than fifty feet away. She willed Lani and the boys not to notice, but to no avail. Black bodies in chains were being filed onto the block, where white men smelling of sweat and tobacco breathed over them with lascivious, ambitious eyes. She had seen this once before, when she was sixteen, and she had gone to visit her aunt at a nearby plantation by Magnolia. Her aunt's master, openly disturbed by Old Master Scott's leniency, brought all of them to an auction outside of Portsmouth. Yasmine had never forgotten the sight of a girl, ten years her junior, marched out onto the stage where white men pinched her nipples "to see if they would one day be ripe enough to produce milk" and slapped her buttocks for no particular reason that they felt compelled to utter.

"Slave auction," Big George said now, matter-of-factly. His voice pulled her back, violently, to the present.

He spit on the side of the road, a habit that Yasmine had doggedly tried to break him of. "Look like a big one too. They got least a hundred, hundred fifty of them." He took a step closer to the proceedings.

Yasmine wanted to grab his arm and pull him to them, but she thought better of it.

"That ain't nothing," Little George said, coming up behind his brother. "Papa said he saw one in Savannah with almost five hundred." There was an edge to his voice, an unmistakable bitterness, that worried her. "Had them there for a week beforehand, sleeping with the horses, doing all kind of things you should never see a human do."

Yasmine sucked in her breath. Why did he always have to tell them things that they weren't ready to hear? But then, as soon as the thought entered her mind, she heard his voice, *They ain't really children, Yaz, not the way this slavery thing done them. You don't like it, I don't like it, but that's the way it be. And that's the difference between us and the white folks: We can see things for what they are and not turn away. And that's why we'll make it to the Last Day, and why God, in His Almighty wisdom, will strike them down—all of them with their depraved ways.* James had started to shake then. She remembered that she had taken his hand to steady him. Then he had come back to himself and addressed her once more. "They boys. They going to see things . . ." He shook his head. "We ain't going to help them from shielding them. We ain't no kind of shield for them." She had known then, down deep, that he was right, as she knew now, deep down, that he was right. It was just that there was such a distance between realizing a thing and acting on it.

The two older boys, drawn by the spectacle of the proceedings, and Nolan, drawn, as always, by the movement of his older brothers, moved toward the auction block. Yasmine wanted to tell them to stop, that there was nothing to see, that it was too dangerous, that they could get snatched and sold downriver to some eagerly enterprising slave catchers who were bound to be in the vicinity, but James was still with her, in her, and she knew that they needed to see, that they needed to understand why it was they were leaving, understand with every fiber of their still mostly innocent bodies. So she crept behind them, shushing the suddenly restless Lani and directing the boys to a spot she decided was safest, behind a small shed, close enough to the main road that they could run to safety if they needed to.

"Chattel number twenty-nine!" the slave auctioneer shouted, and rapped a stick on the stage. He was a middle-aged man dressed in clothes that might have looked decent if they had been recently washed. He spit tobacco frequently out of the side of his mouth, constantly churning the wad between his molars.

Nolan pressed his narrow shoulders into her stomach. Yasmine rubbed them reassuringly, glad that he was young enough to still be able to show that he needed her.

"Goddamn," Little George said softly, but not softly enough that she couldn't hear.

Yasmine slapped him lightly on the back, more out of instinct than anything.

The auctioneer's assistant led a gaunt and sickly-looking man onto the stage. The man looked to be in his mid-forties, and he towered over the other men. His shoulders were the broadest Yasmine had ever seen, and his feet absolutely thudded on the pine stage.

"He a giant!" Big George hissed to the rest of them. Something was building in his body, Yasmine could see it. Some kind of malignant response to the horrors he was witnessing. His shoulders squared, and his fists tightened. He wanted to do something, to stop it. It was hard to watch it and *not* want to intervene. His whole body leaned forward, ready to act.

Yasmine's stomach filled with panic. Nothing good would come of this—nothing at all. James had left her; she was now suddenly sure of it. Wordlessly she reached over and grabbed Big George's arm and squeezed it.

Big George flinched in surprise.

Yasmine shook her head slowly, while her eyes screamed, "No!"

Her eldest son frowned, his eyes popping with anger. But then he exhaled, and all of the energy went out of his body. His shoulders sagged, and he looked away from her.

"No, he *was* a giant," Little George hissed, still watching the progress of the sale of the wasted man on the block. "They worked him to death. Now he just a shell of a giant."

Satisfied that Big George had been quelled, Yasmine turned back to take in the terrible spectacle before them. The man's gait looked pained, his every movement impossible. Where a normal man would have had gleaming pectoral muscles, this man had only a dry cavity that heaved up and down with great effort. And where a calf should have been fierce and made the white men tremble in their effort to subdue it, the giant's were so narrow that they almost did not exist. Although Yasmine would never admit this to anyone, the bodies of black men were one of her great pleasures in life—admiring them, watching them work, and, when she'd had James, touching one. Seeing a black body abused in this way seemed an abomination to her. God would never have made something so beautiful in order to have it defiled.

"He's healthy, gentlemen," the auctioneer shouted out into the audience of at least fifty finely dressed white men. The auctioneer got down off his podium and walked around the man, pointing to an emaciated rib cage here, a sunken cheek there. "He may not look it, but he's healthier than most of us standing here today!" He paused to spit, to the side of the stage. The sound of it was almost enough to cover up a few guffaws from the audience. Almost, but not quite. The auctioneer balked and peered into the crowd, trying to spot the offending individuals. "If you don't believe me, believe this: This buck can stem and tie tobacco hands faster than any in the county, *and* can pull in four bushels of cotton. His master is here and will attest to this fact." He pointed his long white cane toward the side of the stage, where a white man with all the trappings of a tobacco aristocrat stood, casually smoking a cigar. The white man nodded toward his brethren, and another snicker flew out of the crowd. The auctioneer faltered; his face was visibly red.

"The only thing that nigger'll be picking is his own skin off his dried-up bones," someone shouted. This outburst was met with a smattering of appreciative laughter, which made the seller's face redden as much as the auctioneer's. The Dead Giant just stood there, if you could call it standing, hunched as he was, chin almost swallowed up by the pit of his throat. Yasmine knew he wasn't really there anyway, that the part of him that was real had been beaten out of him long ago, and that it was already somewhere else, living a new and better life—possibly where they were headed, back home in the motherland. This thought comforted her, and she pulled Nolan closer to her. He sniffled, happy to be deep within her skirts. Big George kicked absently at a stone.

Boom! Boom! Boom! The auctioneer pounded his cane into the stage. "There will be order here, or there will be no further sales this morning!" Sweat was starting to pour down his brow in rivulets, and he blinked rapidly, the salt clearly burning his eyes. Just like that, the men were quiet again, blowing smoke out of their pipes and cigars as if nothing had even happened.

The seller tipped his hat to the auctioneer, and the auctioneer tipped back. "We'll start the bidding at three hundred," said the auctioneer, turning back toward the audience.

A short man with a disheveled wig raised a finger. "Three hundred," he said.

"We have three hundred!" the auctioneer exclaimed, suddenly animated. He almost glided across the stage, the primary actor in this theater of commerce. The cane lifted, he made a wide arc in front of him. "Gentlemen, don't be bested in this contest! This is a fine deal we have for you this morning, a fine specimen! Do I hear three fifty? Three hundred and fifty dollars, gentlemen, for this investment in the future of your empire!"

"Three hundred and fifty dollars for that half-dead thing?" Little George spit out of the side of his mouth. He peered at his older brother. "He ain't worth even a hundred. Shoulda listened to them hecklers." Then he chuckled.

Yasmine would have cuffed him if she were able to reach him.

"Why doesn't he cut all the fancy talk and just sell us our niggers already?" they heard a young white man not far from them tell his older friend. "We didn't come here for no lecture." His friend nodded.

"We have three fifty!" the auctioneer shouted, his

pupils dilated. White foam gathered at the corners of his mouth, a sight which made Yasmine's stomach churn. "Do I hear four hundred?"

"Four hundred," said the same short gentleman at the back.

"Idiot," the young white man told his friend, who nodded again. "He'll get him home just in time for him to die."

The auctioneer paused for dramatic effect, a bit sober in the knowledge that this particular act was coming to an end. "We have four hundred. Do I hear four fifty?" *Boom!* The cane came down with the finality of a shut door. "Sold, for four hundred dollars to the gentleman in the back!"

Yasmine had seen enough. She grabbed the boys and, despite Little George's protestations, pushed them away, back toward the road to the guesthouse. "This ain't our business," she told them. "We got more pressing things to attend to."

★

CHAPTER TWENTY-THREE

A SMALL BRICK HOUSE nestled between two colored churches. I have never been there, but everyone says that it is the most hospitable and clean-looking house in the whole part of town. The white man from the colonization society had laughed when he said that last part, his generous stomach jiggling and threatening to burst his shirt. Yasmine hadn't understood exactly what was so funny about that, but she surmised that it had something to do with the notion that a Negro home could actually be clean. *If you can't find it for some reason, just ask anyone over there for the Medger family, and they will direct you. But I don't think you will have any problems, there or in the voyage back home.*

They had been walking for some time, farther and farther away from the slave auction, until the whole affair became a tiny dot on the horizon and, she hoped, in their collective memory.

They passed the shipyards, where poor white men worked alongside poor, but free, black men. The smell of the wood, oakum, cotton, and putty was overpowering, as was the foul language the men spit at one another.

"You half-witted bitch," a squat man with far too much hair yelled to his humongous counterpart. "I told you that treenail was bad! But like a nigger girl's cunt, you just had to stink up this whole process because you thought you knew better than the rest of us, didn't you, you goddamn piss-for-brains piece of shit."

Yasmine couldn't help it; she stood there gaping at the man with the indecent mouth.

"Mama, when we gonna eat?" Big George asked, yawning. Yasmine broke from her reverie and started walking again, Nolan in tow, fervently hoping that the boys had heard none of it. "I need me some food," Big George said again, the incident at the slave auction, and his overpowering need to act, clearly gone from his mind.

Yasmine felt the few coins in her purse and sighed. She hoped they would be enough to buy them a few items for the journey to the other side and whatever they might need once they arrived. She knew, however, that it would not be nearly enough to feed all of them well in the interim.

"Dinner at the guesthouse," she told him simply, and began to walk faster. The Medger family, while being blessed enough to be free, was obviously not blessed enough to avoid working for the likes of the men in the shipyard. She shook her head; the more she saw of this state, this country, its cities, countryside and plantations, the more convinced she became that there was, in fact, no place for them here. Coloreds were like fish out of water, and she would rather eat refuse than spend a lifetime trying to learn how to swim on land. She could see the logic of the white man at the podium that day last spring, talking about how coloreds and whites were two completely separate beings who could and should never try to live together.

And just like that, they turned the corner, almost running into the African Methodist Church and its colorful cloth sign that read, WELCOME, BRETHREN, ONE AND ALL! SERVICE A HALF HOUR AFTER DAWN AND DUSK, EACH DAY. Indeed, at this hour of the evening the small, square edifice was packed with bodies, some praying and singing up front, others standing quietly in the back. Across the way, a Baptist church also overflowed with the faithful and their music. Yasmine was about to conclude that the Baptist congregation was winning the musical and spiritual battle, when she noticed a modest brick structure wedged between the two churches. It had tiny windows that looked like the eyes of a badger within the entire face of the house, a long, thin chimney, and curiously, a bright red door. They had finally found it!

"Hurrumph," Little George said beside her, and before she even had a moment to process, he had walked up to the door and knocked on it three times.

"Why you do that?" She grabbed his freshly-rapped knuckles, as if to take back the knocks.

Her son looked at her incredulously. "Ma, quit acting. I know you as hungry as we are."

Yasmine sighed, exasperated. "That may be so, but it don't—"

Just then, the door flew open, and a short, middle-aged black woman dressed in a well-worn gingham frock stood before them. She had a kind face and warm eyes. "Good evening," she said evenly. "You must be the folks Edwin and them was telling us about?"

Yasmine nodded.

The woman beamed. "You all look tired and hungry, two things we can change right quick. Come in."

The pungent fragrance of meat coaxed growls from all of their stomachs. Fresh cinnamon and apples made matters worse. Yasmine felt her face color, but the boys just stepped through the door without hesitation.

"We just sitting down to dinner," the woman told them. She gestured to a long table in the next room, where a dozen or more people were gathered. Steaming plates of candied yam, gravy, pig's feet, greens, and boiled beans lined both ends. Plates were half full of the delicious-looking food, and the table's occupants were quickly packing on more. "Won't you join us?"

Nolan nodded vigorously, and Big George licked his lips.

"Where they get all this food?" Little George hissed to Big George. Yasmine gave him a disapproving look.

Big George shrugged. "Probably get the churches to pony it up or something."

"Actually we grow a lot of it in our garden. You wouldn't know it looking at the house, but there is actually a long yard out back. We grow all sorts of things out there: corn, beans, collards. We even raise chickens and hogs," the woman said, leading them to the table. She pulled up a few chairs from the corners.

"Amazing you all can get anything done with all that church noise coming from both directions," said Big George. He sat down a little too quickly, and the delicate chair creaked loudly under his weight.

A graying older man at the head of the table, who Yasmine guessed was the patriarch, raised an eyebrow. She didn't register clear disapproval in the movement, but she saw it in the eyes of the thin, brittle-looking woman beside him—probably his wife. No one lived between two very active churches like these unless they were involved in them in some essential way. *Never speak freely in a house that ain't yours.* How many times had she told that to the boys? Sometimes she really didn't recognize them. She decided that the best course of action would be to change the subject. But before she could get to it, Nolan said, "They let you grow your own food, even being slaves?"

This stopped everyone at the table. It was as if he had picked up the potatoes in their fine china serving bowl and had thrown them against the wall.

Yasmine bit her lip. She had definitely failed them as a mother.

"Ain't no one here no slave, boy," said a sinewy young

man who was sandwiched between two young girls in pigtails. "Everyone here make their way with honest, hard work and regular wages. My parents been owning this house going on fifteen years now."

Nolan's eyes were getting bigger by the moment. "Own your house? But I never heard of no colored owning nothing!"

This dissipated the awkwardness at the table and made a few people chuckle. The massive heaping of food on plates resumed.

"Then you been sadly lacking in education, boy," said a frail man of about forty in workmen's overalls. "We all free peoples here."

This did not faze Nolan in the least, even as Yasmine shoved him into the seat beside her. "Well, we all free people too, but we still got no choice but to work for Master Scott and take his wages. Mama always says how you can call a freedman a freedman, but if he work like a slave, and ain't got the rights of a freedman, he no better *than* a slave."

Yasmine's breath caught in her windpipe, and she pinched Nolan under the table.

The patriarch at the end of the table raised the same eyebrow again, but this time directly at Yasmine. "That so, boy? Your mama does have some fascinating, if not wholly accurate, ideas."

The intensity of his glance was too much for her, and she looked down at the tabletop.

"That why we going far across the water to the new land," Nolan continued, undeterred. "Mama say we can *really* be free there." He reached for a steaming-hot biscuit from the platter in front of him.

Mrs. Medger looked vaguely amused as she filled the boys' plates. Some of the guests around the table nodded their agreement, while others frowned or shook their heads. Mr. Medger even hurrumphed.

"Well, we wish you all the best of luck," said a young man to their right. "You got quite a journey ahead of you. And you all so brave to be taking it on like this."

Yasmine nodded at his kindness. It seemed for a moment that the conversation was successfully redirected, as the only sound in the room was that of utensils clicking against plates and Lani fussing for Yasmine's breast. Yasmine turned her around and faced her toward her plate, spooning small portions of meat in her mouth.

Then Mr. Medger broke the silence. "Either brave or foolhardy," he said. "Hard to tell without more information." He worked a tough piece of meat between his molars.

"That fellow we saw in Boston last month say this whole notion of sending coloreds back to Africa just another way for the white man to shore up his power," said a young man, between bites of greens. He looked to a young woman with two long braids, to his right. "What his name again, Amelia?"

"Walker," she said quietly. "David Walker."

The young man snapped his fingers. "That's it all right! David Walker." He shook his head in admiration. "That's a colored man knows how to *talk,* I tell you! White folks is scared of him for it too. Issuing him death threats left and right. Say he been 'inciting the colored masses toward insurrection,' or some other nonsense." The young man laughed, and the girl beside him, who seemed much more reserved, cracked a smile.

"What's inessection?" Nolan asked, his mouth full of potatoes.

No one paid him any mind, and the conversation took on a life of its own, bouncing from person to person, statement to statement, some of which frankly seemed wild in their implications to Yasmine. She had never seen anything like it: free and educated coloreds debating their futures. It filled her stomach with anxiety, but also something else she had never felt before and therefore could not yet describe. But whatever it was, it felt good, made her sit up and listen.

"That Walker fellow is dangerous, make no mistake about it," said Mr. Medger. "Talking openly and in mixed company about equality between the races. White folks ain't trying to hear 'bout that!"

Several women across from her, they looked like they could even be sisters, scrunched up their faces. "We been trying to only dare to say what white folks want to hear for how long now, and exactly how far has that got us?" said one of them. "Nowhere, no how. Most of us is still in chains, and those of us supposedly 'free' can't get no fair wages, housing, treatment, or other kind of respect from these crackers."

A general murmur of assent went around the table.

Yasmine noted that, between bites, her boys' big eyes followed each speaker around the room. She began to relax in her chair as she realized that they were perhaps taking in their first actual political debate between educated coloreds with different views.

"I say bring on Walker," the woman continued. "And God bless all of you's prepared and ready to risk everything and try to make a new start across the water." She gestured toward Yasmine, who felt herself smile. Just a bit. "But that ain't for everybody. The heat, the sickness, the rocking boat on them rough waters all them weeks."

Yasmine looked up and saw a small placard on the wall to her left. She wondered how she hadn't seen it when they first sat down.

> Not that we are sufficient of ourselves to think anything of ourselves; but our sufficiency is of God.
> —2 Corinthians 3:5.

Father had taught her to read long ago, along with a little bit of writing. She had never had reason to want to write anything down before, but now, she wanted a quill, some ink, and paper to record it.

The woman next to her laughed. "You be spitting up

bile the whole way there, Mildred. That the real reason you so against this whole colonizing Africa thing. Your weak stomach."

And soon the laughter was spreading and growing louder around the table. Beside her, the boys were laughing outright, relieved to find release after the stresses of the past few days. Even Yasmine, who couldn't remember the last time she laughed, felt something strange in her belly bubbling up.

Mildred waved her hand. "All right! All right! I'll admit my constitution ain't exactly suited to seafarin'." Mildred glared at everyone, feigning annoyance. Anyone could see that she loved being at the center of things, even if it meant she was the butt of the joke. "You know what my constitution's suited for? Keeping my black behind here. In my home. Away from diseased mosquitoes and angry savages."

Cries of "Chile . . ." went up, and a few women lifted their hands, like they were in church.

Nolan looked like he was on the verge of saying something, but Yasmine shushed him. On her lap, Lani refused her mother's hands feeding her and instead insisted on grabbing bits of potatoes and meat and gravy herself.

Two of the men leaned back in their chairs, shaking their heads in disagreement with Mildred.

Mildred went on. "Yes, home, where I was born to free folk and intend to stay that way as long as Jesus gives me bullets for that gun over there." She gestured toward

the corner of the room, where Yasmine saw a rifle standing up.

The two women beside her started clapping. "Preach,
Sister!"

"They got more guns than we do. They always had
more guns than we do, more bullets, more men to fire
them. Then they got their laws, their money, their land.
You know how many times coloreds stood up to them
and done got themselves killed?"

Now it was Mildred's turn to frown. She noisily
sipped her water as the man's assertions became more
and more spirited.

"Look here, y'all remember my great-uncle Nestor,
right?"

Nods all around.

"He was a good man," said Mr. Medger.

"A fighting Christian," said Mrs. Medger.

"Yeah, well, his fighting ways done got him strung up."

Mrs. Medger gasped.

The man nodded. "Yeah! Posse of white men rode
onto his farm one night, said they were sick of him 'stealing' their crops, inflating the prices and all. Said they saw
him making eyes at their missus."

Sucked teeth and shaking heads everywhere. They
knew what was coming. It was all too familiar in its
horror.

The man telling the story sighed. "Well, as many of
our venerable politicians have uttered, no good can come

of a smart nigger. And Uncle Nestor was too smart, see? And, just like David Walker, wasn't about to lower himself to make those white boys feel better. No, he was going to be a man. His mother had bought his freedom right before she passed, and his father had saved every cent of his hard-earned money to buy him that plot of land, and by golly, he was gonna farm it and sell the produce *and* feed his family well *and* start a colored school *and* make his little store the smartest thing in two counties . . . And he did. By God, he did it all." The pride in the man's voice was unmistakable. As was his sorrow. "Until the white folks caught wind of what he was up to, all the success he was having with all of it, his flourishing farm, his beautiful wife and three little girls. They couldn't take that, no. A nigger in their midst doing better, *far* better than they, who had started off with so much more? No." The man's voice became small, just a little louder than a whisper, so that everyone had to lean in in order to hear the bitter end that they knew was coming. "They came under cover of darkness, like they always do, and they strung up Nestor on a huge cross in the front of the farm, for everyone to see. Then they lit him up, like Fourth of July, and made his wife and chullin watch."

Gasps. Hands over mouths. Yasmine felt sick. She wanted to tell their guests that she and the boys would be retiring so that they wouldn't have to hear what came next. But she knew they needed to.

The man's voice broke while he told the ending, which

was as much a part of their history and life on this land as the pork and grits and greens they ate. "Then they raped his wife and sold his three daughters downriver. When they was done with his wife, they carved the baby she was carrying out her womb and hung them both beside him. They lit him up, but let her and the baby stay there just so, for everyone to see how they do niggers who get too uppity.

"I don't know why the whole world over, there's nothing like a black man standing up to turn white folks into monsters."

The silence around the table was like the chains they had seen around the necks and ankles of the slaves at the auction block earlier—it bore them down. All of them except Lani, who had quietly crawled out of Yasmine's lap, pulled herself up on the table, and stood on her own two feet for the first time, eyes wide at all she surveyed.

CHAPTER TWENTY-FOUR

THEY STAYED IN THE Medger house for the next three weeks, sleeping in the small living room, the boys on the floor and Lani and Yasmine together on a cot. They spent their waking hours helping with the garden out back, cleaning, cooking, and working as needed in the church. Yasmine was uncomfortable with taking advantage of strangers' hospitality for so long, but she had to admit they had no other options. Their ship, the *Nautilus*, would not be leaving port until early January, and her contacts with the American Colonization Society assured her that she should use the time to prepare themselves for the long journey by sewing some additional clothing for the children, procuring farming tools and "practicing" with them, and stocking up on various other items they would want but that would be hard, if not impossible, to get in the colony—which was basically everything.

Mrs. Medger was kind enough to give them three

extra Bibles from the church, and she helped them stock up on paper, ink, and quills. Yasmine, Mrs. Medger, the boys, and the constant stream of guests at the house canned broccoli, peppers, and cabbage from the garden, and prepared salted pork and pigs' feet. When it came time to go, Mrs. Medger insisted that they take two crates full.

Yasmine shook her head, embarrassed by the older woman's generosity and aware of the fact that she could never repay her. "Take it, dear," Mrs. Medger told her firmly, as Mr. Medger and the men loaded them into the ship's cargo hold. "You've earned it. And besides, I keep on hearing bits and pieces of letters some in the church get from family members who've made the journey. They say the first year is hard, brutal even. Planting and growing there ain't like planting and growing here. It'll take a minute for you and the children to get back on firm footing." She hugged Yasmine and Lani tightly, and held her close. "Do it for the children," she whispered in her ear then. "I know you doing it all for the children."

Yasmine nodded, surprised that saying good-bye to this woman who she had known for less than a month could produce such pain in her heart.

"Mama, I don't want to go no more," said Little George, wiping away the tears that streaked across his cheeks. "Ain't it all right for us to stay here now? This place so much better than Master Scott's. No need for us to get in the ship."

Yasmine pulled him into her side, hugging him as they headed toward the walkway onto the ship. "My George, they so many wonders on the other side—wonders we can't even imagine yet! Plus, we gonna have our own house, our own garden, and we gonna find us some new friends."

Little George nodded reluctantly, clearly trying to get on board with his mother's plan.

"I don't want a new home," Nolan said stubbornly, at her other side. "Besides, Malina says you can only ever have one home, and this is ours."

Yasmine laughed. "You be home when you with your family," she said firmly, the phrase her father had told her so many days of her life solid in her mouth. "And we be with one another. Always." She stopped to kiss the top of Nolan's head, then turned around for one last look at the bustling port of Norfolk, at the men and women selling fish at the docks, at the filthy shipyards and the equally filthy men who built the ships that sailed in and out of port each day, at the haughty whites who knew they were better than the coloreds, and the poor whites who knew they were too. She looked, finally, at the army of coloreds walking behind their masters, walking alone to complete some mundane task, at the colored children who were doomed to follow in their footsteps and whispered, "Good-bye."

CHAPTER TWENTY-FIVE

YASMINE WRIGHT WATCHED HER only daughter take her first steps somewhere in the middle of the Atlantic Ocean, still thousands of miles from the West African shore.

CHAPTER TWENTY-SIX

1828, Monrovia, Liberia

"WELCOME TO THE LAND of liberty!" a thin, hawk-nosed white man barked at them as they stumbled out of the dugout canoe that had carried them from the *Nautilus*, their home for two months.

It was mid-morning, and an army of seagulls descended from the skyline, cawing and howling in their ears. A sweet scent of flowers gullied on the wind, and the morning light was so bright it pierced their eyes and brought on headaches. Yasmine thought the beach looked more like a long bank of body-swallowing mud than the sparkling, sandy beach of rejuvenation she had been imagining.

"Welcome!" the man continued to yell as the savages who'd paddled the canoe now dragged it across the mud and foam. "Welcome to the freedom of your homeland!" Perhaps the man was the chief colonial official of the encampment. Yasmine wasn't sure. The fact that he took her arm, steadied her, and even kissed Lani's sleeping head made her wonder if he had lost both his whiteness and his manhood in the bush. "You came all this way with your family, I see, to make a new life." The man gestured to her children. "A new and better life away from that foul institution, slavery. That godforsaken hole that corrupts babes and boys alike." He grinned at Nolan and the Georges, and Yasmine felt her stomach churn.

"We ain't slaves," she said evenly.

The man laughed too loudly. "Well, sure," he said. "You ain't now."

Yasmine shook her head. "No, we ain't never been slaves." She fought to keep her voice from rising. This man stirred something almost primal in her, and she had to work very hard not to bolt from him completely. He disgusted her—his fawning, especially. He looked like he had certainly become much too accustomed to the life of an untethered bachelor, with unkempt hair and an overgrown beard. And even after over a month without bathing herself, Yasmine could smell the wrongness on the man.

The man laughed an awkward, hiccupping laugh. "Well, you'se lucky then." He paused. "I mean, luckier than most coloreds who make their way all the way to these parts. They a bit more familiar with the sting of the lash, I reckon." He laughed again. "Then again, they got a bit more they running from. Willing to shoulder the hard rock of this place 'cause even through all the struggle and turmoil, it's a mite bit better from where they come." The man whistled, looking them over again, like he was appraising them. "But you ain't look like that at all. No. Even after months of sea, you all look like you mighta come from someplace not so hard as that. Which, come to think of it, in a place like this, might be a disadvantage, really. 'Cause you all come to a new home that'll suck the very marrow out them growing baby bones." He reached for Lani's too-thin stick of a toddler leg and gave her a toothless smile. She responded by squealing in delight. Yasmine grimaced and took a small step away from the man. He had clearly been corrupted by the savagery of this land.

Yasmine took a look around the peninsula that they had abandoned Virginia, the Medger house, and the Scott plantation for. Cape Mesurado was a towering mound of rock, clay, and sand above them, rising higher in the sky than many of the buildings she had seen in Norfolk. The Atlantic Ocean slammed onto the coast with a deafening crash that she wondered if she could ever get used to. There was an enveloping mist that seemed to cover everything, and standing pools of water weaved in between the rocky edges of the coast, with mosquitoes buzzing above them. But it was the ubiquitous and uncontrollable green that unsettled her the most. She couldn't even explain why, which was even more troubling. The sheer audacity of the leaves, branches, mangrove swamps, flora and fauna of all types could not be undone. Houses would be built, roads made, brush cleared, but there was a certain wildness that the land would never yield.

And then there were the savages; the ship captain had called them "Kru." They had come up beside them, in thin dugout canoes of some sort as they entered the harbor. They had the blackest skin she had ever seen and faces permanently marked with blue. ("Mama, we get new faces like that, now that we here?" Big George had asked her excitedly, as they prepared to board the boat.) These Kru wore long tan robes, bracelets, and other jewelry. There was raw power in their command of each stroke, and they looked into the eyes of the colonists fearlessly, shouting to the crewmen in a guttural and clipped language. The hawk-nosed white man saw Yasmine staring and whispered violently in her ear. "Like staring in the face of some terrifying nothingness, some yawning void, isn't it? But then, the real stupefying thing is that you strangely drawn to it. A fearful sensation, ain't it?" Yasmine recoiled and wiped the man's spit from her cheek. Lani began to fuss.

You said you wanted freedom, James whispered in her ear. *But you weren't prepared for this much*. She sucked her teeth and hushed him away. *Listen, you long-dead husband. Unless you fixing to take up a hoe or a pistol in the name of your family, you best go 'way*. Mercifully, he was silent after that.

Yasmine pulled Nolan and Little George to her and glanced behind her, to make sure that Lani was still safe on her back.

"Mama, they black, like us," Nolan said, his eyes growing bigger by the moment.

Little George snickered. "Boy, they ain't coloreds. What you got up in that big head of yours—peanuts?"

Nolan glanced hatefully back at his big brother. Their relationship was changing so rapidly with each passing day that Yasmine couldn't keep up. One moment they were the best of friends, sharing food and jokes, the next they were at each other's throats. The one constant seemed to be their baby sister's unflinching attention.

"They blacker than them blue-black boys Ol' Master Scott got working in the fields back home, and they ain't never seen no Uncle Sam," said Little George.

Nolan pulled back and peered at them more deliberately this time.

"They home is in the jungle, and they live in trees," Little George continued. "Probably got no idea what real civilization is. Just look at them."

So Nolan did just that, slowly taking in the widespread bare feet, long legs, and broad chests. "Mama," he whispered in her ear. "What's wrong with them?"

Yasmine frowned. Nothing on the ship, at the colonization society meetings, or in Norfolk had prepared her to answer questions like this. She shook her head, at a loss for words. "Nothing," she said. "Nothing."

Nolan, being a normal six-year-old, did not let this go. His small brow furrowed. "But . . . ," he sputtered, "I thought you said they'd be black. You said, back home, that where we were going was covered in black people everywhere. You said they were *free* too. But these people ain't black." He crossed his arms over his chest. "Who knows what they are."

Beside them, Little George and Big George leaned farther over the guardrail and exchanged grins. "That kid be more right than he even know," said Big George, and they both laughed.

This angered her for some reason, and she said, "They may live different from we do, but they are still our black brothers . . . and sisters," she added, thinking that wherever there were men, there had to be women, somewhere. "They just got a whole other way of doing things."

The two older boys laughed, still eyeing the Kru men up and down, incredulously. "You got that right," said Little George.

The smallest of the three Kru men looked sharply behind him at that exact moment and gave the two insolent boys a withering look. He glanced at them as if they were dogs, the lowest of the low, and Yasmine wondered for an instant if he thought them as barbaric as they did him. The thought did not linger, however, and in the next moment she remembered that they had neither education nor God here yet. At every colonization society meeting, they had echoed this sentiment, and the Norfolk free blacks had as well. She had had very limited schooling on the plantation, but knew, as her children did—as all black children knew—that their brethren had been taken from the motherland in chains to become slaves and beasts of burden. She knew that, at some point in the distant past, her ancestors and the ancestors of her children had spoken the same doomed language and worshipped the same false gods as these blue-faced apparitions before them today.

There was no way she would ever condone what those crackers had done in the name of profit to get them there, but heaven was a reward they had not counted on. She smiled sometimes, when she thought about how surprised the crackers would be to be surrounded by so many black folks in the hereafter.

And now, they had gone back to the root of it, the abominable trade in human flesh that had destroyed so many lives and was crippling so many more. If nothing else, in sharing the truth of civilization with these people, they could persuade them to stop their participation in the savage trade, and help them secure their own places in heaven. They might not all see reason, but there was hope enough to try. Yasmine smiled tentatively. For the first time since James died, she felt optimistic about her future and that of her children. Maybe being born colored wasn't such a bad thing, after all? Maybe she, they, could use their wretched experiences toward something other than death, something beyond the afterlife.

★

CHAPTER TWENTY-SEVEN

"MAMA! MAMA!" LITTLE GEORGE and Nolan came screaming into the communal house. The society had supplied a small space for them there, in a cavernous room that they shared with fifteen other families.

Yasmine turned around, weary from the endless nursing that Lani still required. "What is it, boys?"

Nolan's eyes were as big as work coat buttons, and his face was flushed. "We ran down by the river, and we saw a hippo drinking! Just like the picture in Mrs. Medger's book, Mama!"

Little George pushed in front of him and began gesticulating widely, punctuating his story. "And then there was this elephant swinging to and fro, to and fro, like this." He put his elbow to his nose and threw his weight side to side. "He was following something, we thought another animal he wanted to eat, we thought, but then he ended up finding his babies again."

Yasmine smiled, in spite of herself. She put her hands on her hips. "And just how did this elephant lose his babies in the first place?"

Nolan shoved his brother aside, so he could corner his mother. "We don't know, Ma. We only followed him a few miles, and—"

"A few miles?" Yasmine gasped. Sometimes she forgot how big her children were getting and how they grew more and more independent each day. It made her proud, but also scared her. There was so much that they still did not understand about this dangerous place. So much that *she* didn't understand. "I don't want you boys traveling that far alone, you hear?" She leaned into both of them, so they couldn't escape the threat embedded in her tone. "These woods just filled with things we ain't never seen, heard, or even dreamed of in Virginia. No telling what could get you when you ain't looking."

"But, Mama," said Little George. "We weren't alone."

Yasmine frowned. "What you mean?"

Little George sighed, as if he was explaining something elementary to Nolan. *That boy gonna be a whole pack of trouble, once he grown.* "Right after we saw the hippo, we happened on a village with the black-black people."

"The *black-black* people," said Yasmine.

"Yes," said Little George.

"But not the ones with the blue faces," said Nolan.

"No, it was other ones," said Little George, as if that

meant something. "They looked more normal, though the women walk around with nothing on."

"Do so! They got a cloth or something round their privates!" said Nolan.

"But nothing on top, so that don't really count, do it, Mama?"

Yasmine's face grew hot and she shushed them, worried that some of the other families might hear. What kind of mother let her children be exposed to this kind of depravity at such a young age? She rubbed her temples.

"They didn't see you, did they?" she asked fearfully.

Nolan looked confused. "Well, of course they did, Ma. They knew we were in their town before we did."

Little George crossed his arms over his chest. "Ain't no such thing as a town way out here, stupid. We in blackest Africa, where they only got huts and dirt paths—and that's if you're lucky. Otherwise, they just got trees and animals for you." He hurrumphed.

Yasmine felt the same way she did when her father had come home from the fields two weeks after her sixteenth birthday and said that she was to be betrothed in a fortnight to a man she had never met: As if she were falling headfirst down a well with no bottom. She had to get control of this now.

"That ain't true," she said, sharply enough that both boys stopped talking or trying to best each other momentarily. "We living in a town right now, if you ain't already noticed."

Little George looked at her incredulously, then flopped down on their worn sleeping pallet. "If this a town, we in more trouble than I thought."

Yasmine knelt down so she was eye to eye with him, fire in her throat. "What you mean, boy?" she asked.

Little George recoiled—just a little, not much—and then met her gaze, steady. "I mean, look around. You see any schools? How 'bout churches, general stores, real roads, a post office, munitions store—anything the civilized world we left got? How 'bout some people, either? What is there, 'bout eighty people living here or something? Them's that's survived the tropical death, anyway."

The anger welling up in Yasmine's belly could have burned a hole through her. Nolan could see it, and he took a good two steps away from her. But Little George just kept staring her straight in the eyes, fearless. *Just like his father.*

"That so?" she said. "You the expert on civilization now, is it?"

Little George broke away from her grasp and looked down. "No."

Yasmine grabbed his chin and spit each word into his face. Families were starting to stare, but she didn't care. "What was that, boy? I didn't hear you."

"I said no," Little George said, a little bit louder this time.

Yasmine stood up. At least he was still a little bit scared of her; she would need to use that to her advantage.

"This town got one school, one church, and one munitions locker. And there be four hundred thirty-two colonists here, for your information," she said, reciting the information that officials had imparted on each family at the meetings in Norfolk before their departure. "Every one of them working their tail off to feed their families, which is what we got to see about doing soon enough. They ain't complaining about how bad they got it, how hard it is, 'cause they too busy making something out of the nothing we all found here."

Little George hung his head, clearly chastised and embarrassed by the attention her voice was garnering.

"You ain't noticed by now, we not just fixing to make our own home here, we trying to save these heathens from themselves—to save the race, and by doing so, prove to those crackers that the children of Ham ain't just base animals after all," she said. She took a breath. "Oh, and by the way, anything you want that you don't see, you have to build with your own two hands," she said. "It's what it means to start from scratch, to carve a country out of its own wildness. That's God's work, and I'm here to tell you that that's what we getting ready to do."

Yasmine stopped then, her words having come to a momentary halt. She sensed the room's eyes were all on her. Little George held his head in his hands.

Nolan pulled at her skirts. "Don't be angry, Mama. Your George be doing his part. He met a girl in the village—a black-black girl—and they made friends."

Little George eyed Nolan hatefully.

Yasmine looked from one boy to the other.

Nolan sighed, afraid to continue, but afraid not to. "Your George met a black-black girl on the way to the village. Actually, it was her who brought us there in the first place. They made friends and even taught us a few of their words." Nolan smiled triumphantly. "So you see, once we learn their tongue, we can ask them here to help make the town. Maybe then they even wanna start coming to church with us—"

Little George sucked his teeth. "That wasn't the way of it at all, you little tattletale."

Nolan stuck out his upper lip, pouting.

The other families around them were starting to look away, as the volume and intensity of their voices died down. They began folding their blankets and gnawing on the dried sausage that the colonial officer had distributed the night before. Yasmine did not want to draw their attention again, and her throat felt suddenly constricted besides, so she simply whispered to Little George, "Tell me. Tell me what happened, boy."

Little George glared at her. "Ain't nothing to tell, Ma." He smiled unexpectedly then, which worried her more than if he were recalling a story of one of the heathen men who had approached him with a machete. This small girl, greeting them with a dangerous kind of innocence, was trouble. "She was sweet, real sweet," said Little George. "Reminded me of Penny, actually."

"He's right," Nolan chimed in. "She wasn't scared of us at all."

"Shut up," said Little George. He turned back to his mother. "She try to talk to us in her language, but when she see we obviously can't hear her, she bring us back to her village, for everyone to greet us."

"That so?" Yasmine asked, still whispering.

Little George nodded. "Because she be so kind, I think the rest of them just accepted us as brothers too. And before we left, she gave me this." He pulled at a bit of twine she hadn't noticed before, that hung from his neck, and out popped a small bag at the end.

"What is it?" asked Yasmine.

"I don't know," said Little George, obviously half with them in the communal house, telling the story, but also halfway back at the wretched little village with the girl, who Yasmine feared had already left an indelible stain on his memory and whatever it was inside him that created longing.

Yasmine could contain herself no longer. She reached down and snatched the pouch from her son's neck. It came off in her hand more easily than she anticipated, and the twine snapped up, whipping Little George's cheek.

He looked at her hatefully, but said nothing.

"*This*," she said simply, "is poison. I don't want to ever see nothing like this around you never again, understand?"

Little George nodded, the hate still spewing from his eyes.

"Black magic is what it is," Yasmine said. "It comes from the bush, and it belongs in the bush."

"But, Mama, you said that we need to teach—" Nolan began.

"I know what I said," she said icily, ending all possibility of continuing the conversation. "And I'm telling you both now you better stay away from that village, you hear?"

Her look demanded an answer, and both boys nodded, mostly out of fear.

"Where is your brother?" she asked them.

Little George shrugged. "Ain't seen him for hours now. He run off, down the road with some of the menfolk."

Yasmine sighed deeply in exasperation. Was there no way to keep track of her children in this forsaken land? "Well, go find him then," she told them.

They blinked at her slowly, as if not comprehending her words fully.

She lost her patience, and gestured out the door. "Get to it! Bring him back now."

Both boys ran off then, happy to finally be free from the increasingly constricting presence of their mother.

She sighed after they were gone and looked down at Lani, now sleeping. That child could sleep through anything. *What am I going to do? What am I going to do?* The question echoed into the wide open of her mind.

★

CHAPTER TWENTY-EIGHT

THE COMMUNAL HOUSE WAS meant to be adequate shelter until they got on their feet enough to eke out a small dwelling and farm of their own. Yasmine couldn't wait to get out on the land and really start to work, but she had been searching out stories from other colonists about where the most fertile soil was, what crops to plant, the best cultivation methods, and the like. The last thing she needed to do was ensure that her children fell victim to an ill-conceived plan. Fortunately, her fellow colonists were generally willing to share their stories, especially if she had Lani in her arms when she went looking.

"My husband say best not to settle in the city proper," a woman told her. They were both lingering outside the town store. Yasmine surmised that the woman beside her had been equally disappointed in the selection, which was why they both found themselves standing together in the mid-morning sun. "My husband say missionaries tell him people die here." She shook her head and frowned—a big, burly light-skinned woman towering over Yasmine. "It's the African illness kills so many." She sucked her teeth, as the wind kicked up again, blowing sand into Yasmine's eyes. "And you think these whites care one whit if any of us die?"

Yasmine was coughing, but the woman either didn't notice or didn't care.

"They just happy they got a bundle more niggers off their hands back home," she said. "Drop 'em off in the middle of the jungle, let the beetles eat their flesh." She finally glanced over at Yasmine, whose cough had disturbed Lani, but offered no help. "Let them die of starvation, choke on the foul water, breed with the natives. It's all the same to white folks, you know, whether we're holding spears or Bibles. Black is black is black."

Yasmine finally cleared her throat and could almost breathe normally again. Unfortunately, in the next moment, a series of powerful shivers jumped up her spine.

"They call that the harmattan wind," said the woman. "Only comes during the dry season. Natives say it's a cold wind come down from the north. I say they only think it's cool 'cause they been living here in hell too long." She laughed at her own joke.

Yasmine decided that she didn't like the woman. "That harmtan wind always coming, then?" she asked, forcing herself to be polite.

The woman snickered. "It's har-mat-*tan*," she said. "And that's why I said it's of the dry season. Dry season last maybe three, four more months."

"Harmattan," Yasmine whispered to herself, but the word felt as foreign and irritating in her mouth as the sand had.

The woman waved at a skinny family dressed in rags and coming out of the stockade. They waved back at her, halfheartedly. "There be too many families—way too many if you ask me—looking like the Kingstons over there." She shook her head. "They a hardworking family too. Mr. Kingston a sailmaker, and his two sons be excellent blacksmiths, but no one can farm, so they might as well be dumb apes, living here. I think that's why they turned to thievery, got so desperate for food made 'em think they could get away with stealing it."

Yasmine tried not to stare at the three bent-over men and one frail woman who shuffled down the road, but it was hard. She thought she could almost see some semblance of herself and the boys in the soft curve of their necks, which made her stomach churn.

"You got a skill? You good with a hoe in the field? Can your husband fish and hunt? Or lay bricks?"

If only she had left the woman earlier, but as it was, a speedy departure would appear to be both rude and awkward. She could not afford to make enemies here. "No," Yasmine said quietly. "I ain't got no husband. Just me and the children."

"No husband?" The woman peered at Yasmine strangely, as one would a curiosity.

Yasmine nodded.

The woman laughed. "Now, that's a new one."

Yasmine's face grew hot, and it took every ounce of self-control to not respond.

The woman continued to examine her. "You look strong, though. And I guess you're young enough. You got two wits in that brain you should be able to do something with this land." She sucked her teeth. "Maybe. Just don't farm right here in town. It ain't soil here, just rocks."

Finally some information that she could use!

"Better to settle somewhere a few miles out of town."

"Yes," said Yasmine.

"But not *too* far," she snapped, "or the heathens will get you!"

"Yes," said Yasmine.

"And not anywhere near them swamps or standing water. Those bugs be drawn to it like a bee to honey. And then, your baby there will be dead just like that." At this, the woman lowered her eyes, which Yasmine somehow interpreted to mean that she had lost some of her own here, at some point. Yasmine suddenly felt compassion for the woman.

"Thank you," she began, but the woman interrupted her again.

"Thank you for what? For showing you the way around hell?" She laughed, even more bitterly than before.

"Thank you for being born black? For white folks who make sure you ain't got nothing on two continents?"

Yasmine backed away from her, suddenly scared. Maybe this place had truly robbed the woman of her sanity.

The woman did not seem affected by Yasmine's reaction. "You think the dry season's bad? Wait till you see what comes next. Rain up to your ears, rain thrown down from the sky like bullets. Rain that will flood everything you built and ever tried to grow. Rain to bring water, water to bring the mosquitoes, and mosquitoes to bring death. I ain't no root woman or savage devil-worshipper, but I can see fear well enough. And you got plenty, girl."

Yasmine turned on her heel, giving the woman a half-hearted wave good-bye. She grimaced as she began walking away as fast as her legs could carry her.

"You want to thank me for something, thank me for reacquainting you with fear. That's the onliest thing that'll help you live here," the woman shouted after her. It was remarkable, but no one else on the road even stopped to stare. "Stay away from hope," she called. "That's the surest path to death."

When Yasmine got back to the communal house, she barely greeted the boys. It was all she could do to stumble through the door, hand Lani to Little George, and fall into a chair by the wall.

Big George regarded her curiously, through the corner of his eye. "You find anything good, Mama?"

She nodded absently, staring at the families gathered around her, some of them laughing, some of them resting, and most of them talking quietly with one another. *It's all the same to them, you know, whether we're holding spears or Bibles. Black is black is black.* Shaking her head, she hoped the woman's words would fall out of her ears. But the more she stared at the newly arrived and clearly unprepared men, women, and children, the more she could see the truth of the woman's words.

Turning away from his mother, Big George exchanged glances with Little George, who just shrugged and went on rocking his little sister in his arms.

The woman was right that this whole adventure had been masterminded by the whites, after all. Yasmine remembered the abolitionist meeting the Medgers had taken her to in Norfolk before they had left. A finely dressed speaker lectured to a full hall:

> "Who are the members of this 'benign' American Colonization Society, anyway? Why, slaveholders, plantation owners, and those who benefit most from their cruel and devilish economy. They know only too well that the ranks of freedmen are swelling, and that the example of our lives only shows what they know in the deepest places of their black hearts,

and what keeps them awake at night: that we are in every way equal men to them in skill, reason, and religion, and in fact, superior in our understanding and application of morality. They know that our brothers in bondage see this truth, as well—being equal to us in all parts save their freedom—and that their whole way of life should unravel were they to follow our similar paths. That is why they have embarked on this path of African colonization. It is not to provide us with better lives, and it is not to tame and bring the light of religion to our savage brothers and sisters across the Atlantic. No. It is only to eliminate what they view as their greatest threat to their livelihood. Us."

CHAPTER TWENTY-NINE

"HOW I SUPPOSED TO clear if I ain't got no plow, no ox?" Big George asked his mother one morning, the sweat from his brow dripping salt into his eyes. A cutlass dangled loosely from his palm, the remnants of freshly cut grasses and roots still on the blade.

The two older boys, who had worked in the fields back home, had similar responsibilities here. The only difference was there was no overseer to whip their hides, tell them to pick faster, move down the rows with more ease, or stop talking to each other. Yasmine clung to that distinction. Here in the motherland, they were in charge of their own destinies and their own field for the first time. And the children detested it.

They were in the middle of a massive slash-and-burn project, which would leave the ground charred and open. "This some savagery, Mama, working like this. It take us upward of a month to clear this whole area, and even then, we don't know if the corn and greens gonna come up here," said Little George. "This soil all wrong."

The longing in his voice was as sharp as the hunger pains that wracked them at night. The meager rations of millet and dried herring that the colonization society agent had given them when they left the communal house were almost gone. When she had time to think about what they would do once it was gone, Yasmine was filled with terror. Nuts and greens would not fill their bellies.

"I wanna go back to Master Scott's," said Big George. He slumped down into the ground. "I miss Penny and hoecakes. I miss bacon, and I miss church."

On the far edge of the field, Nolan played with a stick in the dirt, beside Lani. He was prancing around, yelling at her to pick up this imaginary pot, cut this onion, stir the stew. "Get to work, girl," he shouted. Lani appeared to be happy to be included, and diligently did as she was told.

Suddenly Yasmine realized that Nolan was imagining he was back in Virginia, like everyone else. She blinked, trying to get her bearings, trying to remember how to be a good mother to her children. Even time itself was different here—she noticed that in the second it took her to blink, her entire adulthood stretched out in her mind. Jumping the broom with James, her mother's shriek as she took her last breath and entered the kingdom of heaven, the agony of pushing each little body out of her. And then in the next instant, she was back. Back to a place where the sun was burning them to ash, back to her aching and impotent hands, back to freedom, and a four-acre plot of land that was made of clay and sand, but out of which was going to sprout plantains, beans, cassava, sweet potatoes, and American corn—even if she had to squeeze all the blood out of her body slowly to make them grow.

"Ain't no going back," Yasmine told them solemnly. She hoped they couldn't see that she was telling herself at the same time, hoping that she would start to believe it soon. "We dead to Master Scott, we dead to Penny, dead to everyone back on that godforsaken plantation. And we gonna be dead soon ourselves, if we don't get some of these seeds in the ground." She struggled to get a hold of her words and the emotion behind them, to convey a sense of control to her children—a belief that they were in God's hands now and that He had not forsaken any country or any people, no matter how remote. *Build up the body of Christ*, the preacher had said. And that was exactly what she intended to do. "Ain't nothing here for us that we don't make ourselves. That the price of freedom."

Little George began to cry, which hadn't happened since they left the other shore. It surprised both of them. For the most part, he appeared to be content in his new life, chasing chameleons and spying on colonists and heathens alike. Still, there was something soft in his gut; a dull ache for home that she worried would never leave him. "But we was more free back in Virginia—"

Before she even knew what she was doing, Yasmine

reached up and slapped him. The sharp snap of it was as final as the sound of the whip on their bare backs, and it startled them all. But she could not let them venture down that road, not even a little. It was one thing to visit home in dreams and quite another to express that longing in waking life. It was dangerous: Before too long, the need to go back would consume the dreamer. None of them could afford that now. "Boy," she said quietly. "Don't never let me hear you say them words again."

Little George gathered his knobby knees to his chest. He put his head on his knees and began rocking back and forth, sniffing. His big brother put his hand on his shoulder and glared at his mother.

You all can hate me, Yasmine thought, *as long as we make it. They ain't understand, but they ain't have to. God do.* "Now get up offa them miserable behinds, and get back to clearing this field, both of you. I don't care how it get done. Just see that it does. I wanna see *our* vegetables, from *our* field, in *our* new home steady growin', get it?"

The two boys nodded, neither one meeting her glance.

Yasmine felt her stomach roll over, because she knew what she needed to do. She had been able to protect Nolan from fieldwork at Master Scott's by making him Mrs. Barnes "special helper" in the kitchen. That was another dream she couldn't afford now.

She strode over to the other side of the field, where he was humming quietly to himself, laughing at something

Lani had just said. "Nolan," she said, and her voice star-tled him. He jumped up quickly and brushed off his pants. She handed him her cutlass silently. He looked at her in confusion, clearly wanting to say something but decid-ing against it. The instrument weighed down his small six-year-old arm, and Yasmine's hand flew to cover her mouth to contain a scream.

"Mama?" Lani asked cautiously. When Yasmine didn't answer, she toddled over to her mother and held out her arms, her gesture to be picked up.

Yasmine's eyes never left Nolan's. "You got to work," she said evenly.

Nolan blinked at her slowly, taking in the words.

"Go with your brothers," she said, trying not to look at his soft brown palms. "You the only men here now, and you got to provide for us womenfolk."

Nolan smiled at that, which made Yasmine smile, in turn. She thought that he would like that—he always wanted to think of himself as a Little Man, so helpful to his brothers and family.

"Mama!" Lani yelled, angry and impatient. She swat-ted Yasmine's hip with both hands. Still, Yasmine ignored her. Something had changed between them of late, since Lani abruptly decided to stop nursing. Of all her children, Lani had nursed the longest, and the gentle but firm tug at her nipple had been a calming and steady fact of life these past two and a half years. Now there was only pain in her breasts. Still, Yasmine had to admit that she was ready to be done. She was exhausted and had nothing left to give the girl.

"Ain't no men *anywhere* here, Mama? In the whole land?" Nolan asked, looking up from his cutlass. "What about the heathens? The ones by the woods outside of town? The ones took us ashore, when we first came?" He turned around and scanned the horizon, searching for a human figure hiding somewhere in the bush.

"No," she told Nolan firmly. "They ain't real men. They . . ." She struggled to find the words. "They heathens what don't know right from wrong, reason from insanity. You the only man here. You and your brothers."

Nolan looked shocked, but also proud. He puffed up his chest and gripped the cutlass handle with intention. "Well," he said. "Let me get to helping." And then he turned away from her and walked over to Little George and Big George, who were bent over, hacking the dry, dense brush.

"Mama, no!" Lani cried, tears streaming down her face now. Yasmine knew that in a few seconds, things would degenerate down into a full-blown tantrum. But right now, she was not interested in that. Right now, she wanted to watch her youngest boy walk away from her, his shoulders seeming to grow wider and more imposing with each step. She sighed. As Yasmine watched Nolan, she recognized her own self-determined gait in his, the way he walked on this new earth as if he owned it, and she was surprised to realize that it scared her.

★

CHAPTER THIRTY

IN THE END, IT took even longer than Little George predicted to clear the field, in part because Yasmine spent the next three days in their shack, burning with fever. The children feared the African illness that had already claimed so many of the colonists, but Yasmine's aching breasts told her otherwise. "I got milk sickness," she told Big George. She pulled him close so she could see his eyes. "You and your brothers and sister got to keep working that field. You make this our land, you hear me?"

He did hear her. For three days, Big George led his siblings out to work their land while their mother sweated and dreamed.

Sometimes, the wildness called to her children, and she was powerless to pull them back to her. In her dreams, she could only watch.

Little George sat, watching men walk to and fro carry-ing wood or tools or munitions and the women gathered in the streets discussing domestic issues and trying to feel normal. He spied the shifting length of a chameleon tumbling down a tree branch off the side of the road. In a single motion, he was in the road, almost knocking over a man carrying two shotguns from the munitions locker and speeding into the bush. Lani, stumbled behind him, eager to keep up with her big brother.

"Be calm in your haste, boy," the man called after him. "Else you gonna find yourself dead in the street before you grown!"

Little George spotted a small opening between the hanging vines of the mangrove tree that the chameleon was racing past and hid in it as quietly as possible. All the children knew chameleons were sensitive beasts, and the slightest rustle or sound could send them scurrying. Luckily Little George was light on his feet and could skillfully maneuver into spaces that his brothers could— or would—not. In a flash, Yasmine saw the secret he had told no one: his dream of becoming a great hunter in this country one day—perhaps the best that the colony had ever seen. He would hunt hippopotami, apes, even crocodiles, and would share all his spoils with everyone.

Little George lagged a slight distance, trying to spot the chameleon and anticipate its next move. "Stay here!" he hissed to Lani, who had finally caught up to him and was crouched beside him. She nodded vigorously, but Yasmine knew as well as Little George did that that did not necessarily mean she would do as she was told. Ah!

This girl hardheaded! Yasmine would complain at least five times a day.

Little George was poised behind a towering fern and ready to spring into motion when he heard a rustling in the grass ahead. He froze and maintained his position. To be so close and come home empty-handed! He could not allow it. The chameleon was directly on the other side of the tree, he sensed. This was his chance! Little George pounced.

Darkness would come, and with it her children, dragging one another back from the field. Someone fed Yasmine liquids and kept a steady stream of cold cloths on her forehead until finally she slept soundly.

It was no chameleon's tail Little George caught, but a hand. A black-black hand, attached to the arm of a girl about ten or eleven, her hair shorn to the scalp and various necklaces and shells hanging from her neck.

"Kuo!" Little George exclaimed.

He knew this creature!

The girl's skirt had been whipped about in the tussle, and she turned away from him for a moment to fix it.

He took the hint and looked down. Just then, Lani came thrashing through the underbrush toward them. "Jo Jo!" she yelled.

"I'm here!" he yelled back.

The black-black child waved her right fist at him and

turned to walk away, just as Lani reached them. She was triumphant, took her brother's hand, and would not let go. "Black-black," she said, pointing at the girl. "Black-black" had been Lani's first words only a month or so earlier.

The girl looked from Little George to Lani and then held out her hands. Without hesitation, Lani took the girl's hand, and in a moment George took the other. "Black-black," Lani said again.

Fever held Yasmine tight through the next day. Again, she felt water on her lips and gagged at an offered bit of food, the smell of palm oil overwhelming and threatening to bring up her stomach. She heard sounds that had the timbre of soothing words, but she could make no sense of the words themselves. Soon she slept and dreamed again.

The black-black child led Lani and Little George deeper into the bush. They pushed through a curtain of trees and saw, curiously, a bright red door. They had finally found it!

"Humph," Little George said, and he had walked up to the door and knocked on it three times.

Lani still held the black-black child's hand and bounced on the balls of her feet in anticipation.

The door flew open, and a short, middle-aged black woman with a small and worn piece of cloth wrapped around her stood before them. She had a kind face and warm eyes. She spoke as though to welcome the three children, and they seemed to understand, but Yasmine could not.

The woman stepped aside, and through the door they could see a clearing filled with huts made of what looked to be mud. Dried palm fronds served as roofs, and there were no doors. Women kneeled over fires, stirring soups and adding leaves and spices, while a group of men sat around talking and chewing kola nuts.

A small child, who looked like he had not only been playing in the dirt but eating it as well, ran up to Lani and began pulling at her leg. Lani screamed and tried to shake him off, without success.

The boy responded by jabbering something rapid in his language to Kuo, who responded with a series of harsh words that shut him up. The boy let go of Lani's leg, which sent her stumbling to the ground. Then he frowned as if he were going to cry and turned back to Little George, opening his palms toward him in supplication.

Finally a woman who seemed to be a little younger than Yasmine looked up from the soup she was seasoning and shouted at the boy. Her cornrows shone in the sunlight, as did her black-black skin, which glistened with sweat. The suppleness of the natives' skin was a subject that the Wrights had discussed on more than one occasion, as their skin and those of the other settlers seemed to be constantly drying and cracking. Little George wondered if they had a secret or if they were simply born that way in this land.

A group of men stood together by one of the other huts, talking animatedly about something. Like the women, they wore nothing on their torsos and covered their private parts with a cloth.

One man, spitting kola nut pieces, approached the three of them and laid one wide hand on Kuo's shoulder and the other on Little George's. The man's tone was amiable, and he laughed a few times while a flurry of strange words tumbled out of his mouth, mostly directed at Kuo. Kuo interrupted the man a few times and gestured at Little George. Then the man awkwardly patted each of them on the back, saluted to Little George, and walked away.

Again, Kuo took Little George's right hand and Lani's left and led them to a circle of about five women and two children squatting around a bowl.

Kuo squatted beside the others and gestured for him and Lani to do so, as well. A greenish-yellow glob sat in the center of the bowl, and the women and children reached in and took handfuls to eat.

Little George groaned. But he allowed himself to be pulled down anyway. Lani, already so close to the ground, squatted easily next to him.

Kuo reached her hand in and scooped up a glob of whatever it was. She seemed to be showing them how to eat it.

Yasmine could see Little George's reluctance in his expression, but Lani dug in immediately and without reservation, grabbing a clump of the mixture in her small palm. Then she brought it to her open mouth and shoved in as much as she could reasonably fit, the rest falling down the front of the worn little dress. George shook his head, but after a moment he too reached his hand in the bowl and took a very small amount of the goo in his hand. He put the strange food in his mouth and began to chew.

Little George nodded at Kuo, who by this time had reached for another mouthful of the soup. "It's not bad," he said. "Not bad at all, really."

It was like they understood him, because the women smiled and gestured for him and Lani to take more.

Lani grinned and grabbed another handful in her other fist.

Little George reached his hand into the bowl and collected a bigger scoop this time. All unease was gone from his face, and Yasmine watched as her children ate their fill.

After they finished, Kuo walked them away from the others, toward a spot in a clearing where they were alone. The whole village's eyes were still on them, of course, but they could sit down for a moment, a few feet apart. It was the hottest part of the day, and, with his full stomach, Little George began to feel drowsy in the sunlight. His baby sister staggered up from the now-empty pot, and came and curled up in his lap.

Kuo gestured to his neck and turned up her hand questioningly. Little George felt his face flush. He touched the space where the magical pouch she gave him had hung from twine around his neck. The place from which

Yasmine had ripped it. He looked down apologetically.

Kuo pulled out something shiny from behind her skirt. It was a pouch—but finer than the first one—made of what looked like leopard skin and fashioned with a metal clasp at the top.

He gasped.

Kuo laughed. She made a series of gestures with her hands that he didn't understand and then placed the extraordinary object in his hand. When she looked back up at him, her eyes were shining that same bright way. Yasmine knew what her son was feeling better than he did. He would kiss the black-black girl if he knew how.

In his lap, Lani had begun to snore contentedly.

"Yours," Kuo said, the word not fitting in her mouth quite right, but discernible to Yasmine as a thunderclap.

Little George closed the pouch in his hand. "Mine."

"I'm so tired," she called out to James, who was still not there. "And so fearful."

She could see him, seated on a small stool he had carved for himself, just out of her reach. He looked older, lines on his face deepening. He shook his head at her, smiling.

"Well, what that mean?" she demanded. "You never say anything that help me find my way anymore. You never there for me to lean on."

He was hazy, but he was still there with her, looking

her steady in the eyes, unblinking. "Just relax, Ma. You gonna feel better soon, I promise," he said.

Her brow furrowed. Why was he calling her that? "What? I'm your wife, James, not your damn mama! After all we been through, you don't know who I is?"

Small, rough hands placing a cold cloth on her forehead. "It's gonna be okay, Ma. We here."

Yasmine breathed in deeply, and then realized she was awake. She'd thought that her eyes were open before, but now, as she pried them open with much effort, she realized that had only been a dream. Little George leaned over her, worry weighing his otherwise youthful face. Lani was beside him like always, holding fast to his pant leg. In the corner, Big George and Nolan were hunched over a Bible, Nolan scribbling words in the dust as his oldest brother pointed them out.

"My babies," she whispered. Then she smiled at Little George, though she found it exhausting.

"Mama," Little George said excitedly, worry evaporating from his face. "You're back!" He turned to his brothers and said, "She's back! I think she's okay now."

The heat of the afternoon wafted through the small window her pallet was pushed up against, and made Yasmine sigh. It had also created small beads of sweat on her forehead and above her lips. She vaguely wondered what day it was and how long she had been so out of it. Little George handed her a cup of water and she leaned up to take a sip. She was surprised by how good it tasted and kept drinking until it was gone. Nolan and Big George had come over by this point, examining her anxiously.

"She look good. She look good," Big George said.

Nolan took hold of her clammy hand for a moment and then set it down. She tried to squeeze his hand back but found she was still too weak.

Yasmine lay back down and gingerly touched a breast under her blanket. With a start she realized that they were no longer filled with too much milk, that they no longer ached. It appeared that her children were right, she was well on her way to healing. She frowned, however. "Where is she?" Yasmine scanned the room, looking for any trace of the black-black girl.

"Who?" Big George asked. "Where is who?" He looked to his siblings in confusion.

Yasmine sat up once more, this time pulling her legs up in an effort to begin standing up. "The village girl. The heathen one that you love," she told Little George, who looked more confused than ever. "The one what gave you the charm." She tried to push herself up with her palms, but it was futile. She was still too weak and fell back down again.

"No one here but us, Ma," Big George said, gesturing around the tiny room they called their house. "Has been the whole time you was ill."

Yasmine blinked in confusion, remembering the strange food they had eaten together in the dusk of the village, and the elusive smile that had so enchanted her second child. How could she just have disappeared? "I know she's here," she said. "Even if she still hiding."

"You still tired, Ma," Little George told her. There was no mistaking the tenderness in his voice. "You need to rest."

She wanted to tell him she knew all about it, that the charm was still there, exerting its power on all of them. Its black magic sucking all the light out of the room. But she found she could no longer keep her eyes open. The exertions of consciousness and wakefulness had taken their toll. No matter what her mind and heart wanted, her body would not comply. She retreated, grudgingly, to the haven of sleep once again.

"Just let her rest," was the last thing she heard. "She be well soon enough."

CHAPTER THIRTY-ONE

1829, Monrovia, Liberia

IN THE FOURTEENTH MONTH after their arrival, Little George, who had waited what seemed like hours for his mother's breathing to become deep and even, roused his older brother from sleep.

"What?" Big George hissed, brushing off his brother's prodding hand.

Little George glared at his brother and pointed over the pallet Lani and Nolan shared toward the mound curled up on the floor that was their mother. The last thing they needed was Mama listening in. Ever since that fever that nearly took her, Little George felt like she watched him even more than before. A moment like this, where her eyes weren't on him, was too precious to waste.

"They's fixing to fight, then?" he whispered.

Big George hurrumphed. "Who you talking 'bout now?"

Little George sucked his teeth. It was one thing to be forbidden to go to the meeting. To be denied the details of it by his own brother was too much. "You know who!" he hissed. "The menfolk, of course."

Big George sighed deeply, then sat up. "Man can't get no good sleep even in his own house," he lamented.

Little George punched his brother's arm.

Big George recoiled, holding his bicep. "Why you do that now?" he demanded.

Little George shushed him again, more forcefully this time. "You tryna get us both in trouble?"

Big George rubbed his eyes. "Actually, I just trying to sleep. Strange thing to do in the dead of night, ain't it?"

Little George shook off his brother's sarcasm and continued to press. "What you know about the attacks? By the savages? I heard they getting ready for something big."

Big George frowned. "I ain't about to—"

"Jo Jo?" a small voice said beside them. Lani sat straight up, blinking slowly at each of them. She smiled. "Jo Jo." Her baby name for both of them.

Little George scowled at his brother. "Now see what you done."

"What *I* did? Now look here—"

But Big George was cut short by the sturdy palm of a toddler caressing his face. Lani had plunked herself down in Little George's lap, but had reached over to touch the short beard Big George was growing. It fascinated her.

240

"Jo Jo bird," she said, in that angelic little voice that never failed to disarm him.

"Jo Jo *beard*," he said, moving her hand around his cheeks.

Little George grew impatient. It seemed that ever since Big George had become old enough to attend meetings with the other men, he'd grown distant from his younger brother. "I know the governor tried talking reason into them dark, dark brains." He crossed his arms. "And I know some a them brutes dead set on raiding villages and stealing their enemies to sell into slavery—say we got no rights here. Say this *their* land we on, even though Governor and them negotiated fair and square for it. Jack Banks tell me so."

Big George hurrumphed again. "Well, if Jack Banks tell you so much, what you need me for?"

Lani sat quietly, turning her head to face whoever was talking. She pulled Little George's arms around her tightly. Little George looked at his brother pleadingly.

Big George sighed and finally relented. "Jack Banks ain't wrong. They sure is fixing for something. But so is we. We ready for whatever may come to pass."

"What that mean?"

Big George met his gaze, unblinking. "It mean we got extra men and weapons ready." He pulled at the ends of Lani's short ringlets. She giggled in delight. "We killed two savages in skirmishes, and wounded two. They wounded two of ours. When the governor try to talk to the village

241

chief about it, he just do one of these," Big George sat up regally and waved his hand. Then, mocking the accent and demeanor of the chief's translator, he said, "'They are a rebel faction. They do not speak for us, or any Bassa on these lands. The white man gave them guns, taught them how to use them, and paid them handsomely for bringing enemies to take across the water.'" Big George shook his head in disgust. "That village chief's even more scared than we are. Like Mama always say, we the only men in this jungle."

When Big George looked over at his brother again, Little George was leaning forward in anticipation. "Do Mama know all this?"

Big George laughed. "Of course she know. Mama know everything go on in this sad little outpost. She the one burst into the meeting all uninvited, righteous with anger 'cause 'who are they to think they run things 'cause they just men,' and all other kinda nonsense."

"*What?*" Little George blurted out, incredulous.

Big George laughed again, getting caught up in the energy of the story. "Yep. Useless old Sam Longsten tried to stop her from coming in and you know what she do? *Put a knife to his chest.*"

"What?" Little George hissed.

Big George nodded. "Oh yes. She *your* mama now, Brother. Longsten tell her no women allowed, and you know what she tell him?"

Little George shook his head, completely mesmerized

by the story. He stole a glance at Mama, to make sure she was still sleeping. Her eyes were pressed shut, her breathing still deep and regular.

"'I think you need to see what a woman can do. I don't see no kind of proper 'preciation in you,' she say, all cold-blooded and dark-like. Sound like she got some kind of devil in her."

"No, she did not," Little George said, eyes as big as saucers.

"Oh, she sure did, Brother. It was like she been practicing those words for some time, just waiting to say 'em." Big George shook his head. "Forget about them savages; I'm sure she got at least one Christian man plotting to kill all of us right about now."

Little George could feel the steady up and down of Lani's rib cage in his arms, hear the small staccato of her snoring. "So . . . ?"

Big George just blinked.

"So what you do?" Little George demanded.

"What I do? What you think I do, Brother? I took the knife from her, gentle-like, the best way I could before somebody see what she done. On the way out, I tell Longsten 'I sorry, but my mama ain't well these days. This life done turned her on herself.'"

"He believe you?"

Big George shrugged. "Didn't have much choice. Either that or admit a woman got the best of him. No man likely to do that."

Little George cocked his head, contemplating all Big George had told him. It was too much. It was all too much.

"We gotta get to sleep now," Big George told him, pulling his blanket around his shoulders. "Dawn be here before you know it, and Mama be at our backs, yelling why we moving so slow in that damn field."

Little George nodded. He carefully lifted up his sleeping sister, and set her down on her quilt. Only a few minutes later, his older brother was unconscious too, but despite his own overwhelming exhaustion, it was a long time before Little George could let go of wondering if there were any men at all in this jungle.

★

CHAPTER THIRTY-TWO

NOT EVEN TWO MONTHS later, Little George was dead.

In the middle of a scorching, humid afternoon, his gangly and feverish twelve-year-old body let out its final breath. The rest of the family was in the field, frantically trying to harvest the cassava and corn crop, when Little George breathed his last. But for the rest of his life, Nolan couldn't help but link the moment of his older brother's death with the moment that same afternoon when Lani inexplicably dropped the harvest basket her brother had made for her from palm fronds and sat down, crying inconsolably.

Little George was the child who was to be the compensation for the death of Yasmine and James's first George, who as a baby seemed to be forever ill and perpetually on the brink of death. Little George was born when this five-year-old brother was locked in a four-month-long coma, expected to die at any minute, and his auspicious birth, it was believed in family lore, had magically "cured" his brother of his ailments forever and brought him out of his coma a week later. Little George, who had never been ill a day in his life, had in the end expired before his elder, succumbing to the African fever, which had by that point killed over a third of the settlers and which many said was carried in the bodies of mosquitoes, "insects born of Satan."

But Yasmine did not believe it. Her whole body shuddered, and she grabbed Little George desperately, rocking his too warm, sticky body in her arms. "No!" she screamed, but it was the sound of a feral animal more than a word. A guttural protest to what had to be. What already was, but which a mother could never bear. "No," she said more softly this time. "No . . . no . . ." She continued rocking him back and forth, back and forth. He was the strongest of them all, her George, so how had he succumbed to something as commonplace as African fever? Oh, she knew.

"Where is it? Where's that godforsaken pouch!" she screamed at her three remaining children.

There was no comprehension in their silent faces, only shock, fear, and exhaustion.

"The black-black bitch. She did this," Yasmine continued. "You brought her into this house!"

She raved like this for some time before Big George managed to get her settled on her pallet so that inevitable bone-crushing weariness could find her. Even then, she choked out a final sob. "You have forsaken us, dear Lord," she whispered.

Five days later, as they were lowering Little George into the ground in a small wooden casket, Yasmine promised him, wherever he was, that now no more harm could come to him. That the savages could no longer ply their dark magic on their vulnerable, unsuspecting bodies. That, thanks to the Lord, she could now see the spells they had destroyed him with, but that on her life, she would make sure that no harm came to the rest of his siblings. *I am sorry I let you down, Son. You gave your life to birth a new black civilization. But they so cursed, all they could think to do was kill.* She broke down in sobs so heavy that they caused many at the service to look away in embarrassment. Big George held his mother tight, praying all the while that his brother's eternal soul could rise up in this blighted ground.

Years later, Nolan would recall how Yasmine often said it was during this period that her mind would not work right. She would be going along, tilling the fields, pulling cassava from the unyielding earth, and she would see a gecko on a tree branch or a monkey higher up near its top, and tell herself to remember to tell Little George when she got back to the cabin, because he was in the process of amassing a vast catalogue of all the vegetation and animal life in the area and could surely establish a vantage point from which to observe them here too. She would be constructing the whole conversation in her head, how she would say, *The monkey's fur was thicker and darker than those others we seen. Don't know, but it coulda been another type.* She would anticipate the way he would nod solemnly as he always did when he was thoroughly engrossed in a topic, *Could be, Ma. Could be.* It wasn't until she had pulled the cassava root from the ground and was inspecting the leaves that her mind realized the conversation it was constructing could never happen, would never happen, because her son was dead now, had been dead for months, and would be forevermore. "My mind was broken then," she would say. "*Broken.*"

CHAPTER THIRTY-THREE

1830, Monrovia, Liberia

TRY AS HE MIGHT, Big George could never quite get used to the rainy season the way his sister could. The rest of them would be hovering, shivering in the doorway of the tiny cabin, as the water pummeled the roof and trees and turned the ground to mud; and Lani would be out there right in the middle of it, dancing to some song only she could hear, sticking her tongue out to catch drops. George found the way that the rain bombarded them, in sheets of periodic swells of torrential downpour that came at the oddest moments, and then cleared for a moment before resuming—or, alternately, the ongoing slam of water that seemed to go on forever, flooding the streets and waterways for months on end—to be insulting. He couldn't help but take it personally, the essential *wrongness* of the way that the thing known as rain was delivered in Africa. Rain was supposed to be manageable, to come in storms that visited occasionally and then left.

It was not supposed to last for weeks on end, and it was not supposed to appear out of nowhere and overtake a land and the people who were trying to tame it. And it certainly was not supposed to interfere with the normal daily work of farming, tending to the animals and general life of the colony. And yet, every May to October, that is exactly what happened. They were confined to the small space of the cabin for days and weeks, watching the dull theater of rain and the wind that carried it whip palm fronds and tree branches to and fro, and the fields devolve into a pond for mosquitoes to gather and breed in. Big George found it downright offensive, the rainy season in this country, and because of this felt the need to challenge it whenever he could. Succumbing to its force seemed weak to him and the opposite of what they had come here to do. Which was why he jumped at the chance to join the expedition that Gov was leading into the bush.

"It ain't a good idea," Yasmine told him one night, before the dying embers of a small fire they stoked in the cabin. Nolan and Lani lay splayed out on the ground beside them, unconscious and snoring blissfully in that way that only children can, free of the burdens of men. "There a reason the savages don't do nothing in this weather."

Big George sucked the last marrow from the bones of a slim goat they had killed a few days before. "Yeah," he said. "They be lazy."

Yasmine licked a few specks of yam from her fingers.

"No, that ain't what I mean." She wiped her hands on her apron and cleared her throat. "They understand something about this land and the way it be that we can't really. They not out in the rain 'cause they seen what the rain can do, and they respect that. Plus, they know the season of sun's comin' soon enough." She tapped her son's arm lightly, almost playfully.

After Little George had gone, it seemed to Big George that Yasmine had softened somewhat toward him and his siblings, like she had decided to enjoy her remaining children, not just fear for them all the time. "Seem like we the onliest ones can't accept the way things be here. Always tryna make everything like it was somewhere else." She shook her head. "That's why we ain't hardly got no crops."

Big George threw his goat bones aimlessly out the small window beside them. A modest pile of bones and scraps from meals past was growing there. "You the last person I'da thunk would say we got something to learn from them criminals."

Yasmine winced. "I ain't saying—"

Big George looked his mother right in the eyes. "But you is, Ma."

Yasmine frowned and looked away. "I worry I done wrong, bringing you here," she said. "I worry that this place making you—making us—different. Meaner. Smaller, somehow."

It was the truest thing she had said to him in months,

but it was like Big George hadn't heard her at all. "Look," he said, "Gov say they planning something. Another raid on the munitions locker maybe, a direct attack on the colony, maybe. Bassa men been trading with the Kru been trading with the British for guns and ammo and powder and knives and God knows what else."

Yasmine sucked her teeth. "Watch your tongue, boy."

Big George shook off her admonition as he would a fly and continued his analysis. "Slave trade may be illegal, but you and I both know as long as it make money, they always be demand for more captives to steal and take back on them there ships. Now, I ain't fixin' to let that happen to me and mines, after all we been through."

The children stirred beside them. Nolan swung at an invisible mosquito.

Big George took his mother's hand and gently guided her glance back to his. "They comin' for us, Mama. One way or another. You can be sure of that. They not just sitting there in the rain, eating they goat meat and yam like sitting ducks. Naw. They preparing an army to get rid of us, wipe us out. Gov sent out scouts three days back, and they came back, reported that they seen them savages getting they guns and spears ready for something big, looked like."

Lani stirred and mumbled in her sleep. Yasmine put a finger to her lips and glared at George. They were quiet for a moment.

"How you know it us they comin' for?" Yasmine

hissed. "Just as likely they comin' for them Kpelle or Gio. Or maybe they finally ready to deal with them Kru and Mandingo they hate so much. You don't know."

He squeezed her hand and prayed for the words to soothe his frail mother's heart. He had been dreading telling her, but now there was no way around it. He had waited too long; they were leaving tonight. "Gov always know, Ma. Always." He took a deep breath. "That's why I going with him tonight. We gotta surprise 'em, 'fore they come for us."

Yasmine blinked and was quiet for a moment. "You ain't going," she said as evenly as possible. "You ain't."

Big George gathered his gun from its standing place in the corner, as well as his pouch of supplies, ammo, and powder. "I prayed, Mama," he said. "I asked Him to protect me, protect us." He looked down at her, her whole body taut on the floor where they had been sitting. Big George smiled. "He told me I was righteous. That I would win."

She shook her head. "God don't—"

He silenced her by picking her up in a huge embrace. "He say I gonna win," he said. Then louder: "He say I gonna *win*, Mama!"

Gov's expedition did win; Big George had been right. The group of five men had indeed located the same Bassa faction that caused so much trouble so many months before, engaged in a plot with some men from a Dei village to not only raid the colony's munitions locker, but to then use its weapons to capture as many of the colonists as possible.

Almost three full days after Big George left the small cabin and ventured into the muddy, wet world outside it with the expedition, they marched back into the colony, bloodied, weary, but victorious. Because they acted swiftly, the colonists had had the element of surprise and were able to come at the insurgents while they slept. Each man told how he had killed one, two, even three of the savages while they slept, unaware—except for Big George, who through his cunning, strength, and superior fighting skills, had been able to kill seven. "We never would have been able to overpower them without him," the governor told Yasmine gravely, as the rain hammered both their skins to numbness. "He was truly a patriot. A hero. You should be very proud." He clasped a massive, scarred hand on her shoulder. He brought her beside a tree with leaves enough to partially shelter them and told her that Big George had fallen at the river. After suffering so many losses at George's hand, the savages' leader—known to be an exceptionally skilled warrior in villages throughout the area—chased George out of their encampment, pursuing him for miles until he cornered him by the bank of the river. "None of us were there, so we don't know exactly what happened," Gov told a weeping Yasmine. "We only saw . . . after."

Lani, who loved the rain and had never seen her mother cry, came out of the cabin and carefully took her hand.

The governor tried to embrace Yasmine, but she stepped away from him before he could manage it.

"What did you see?" she whispered.

The rain seemed endless. It pounded his pale face and bulbous features, making him look even more distasteful than she found him. Lani held on tighter, the harder the rain fell.

The governor shook his head. "We saw...his body..."

Yasmine found her voice again. "Tell me what you seen, exactly."

The man looked at her, still not fully grasping her words. "Your son's dead, ma'am. That's what we saw." He reached out to her again, but she took another step back.

She stared back at him. "I need you to describe him. How he looked. What they done to him. Where he is now."

He recoiled visibly. "But you can't want to know—"

"But I do," she said. "I do."

Lani looked up through the rain at her mother's face, which seemed very old suddenly.

The governor scowled. "There's no reason—"

"He's my son," Yasmine said, emotionless. "What you done with him?"

He shook his head. "Ma'am, I see you're upset. Hell,

who wouldn't be? The savages done killed your eldest boy. One of the kindest, most devoted, best fighters we got in the whole colony. There's none like Big George. Never will be again. That's God's truth."

He looked like a thick, tired tree that the wind could upend if it blew hard enough. Yasmine wished it would. She really wished it would.

"They sever his head from his body? They cut him into bits with a cutlass?"

The governor shook his head again. "What kind of…?" Then he pointed at Lani. "With your little daughter here too, you want to talk like this? Yeah, I been warned about you. Plenty of people say you ain't no natural woman. Being so close to George, I always defended you. But now I can see they were on to something." He tapped his head. "Something maybe ain't quite right up there in that head of yours. Yeah, I'm real sorry for your loss. Real, real sorry, in fact. George was my best friend, my best man here at the colony. Gonna miss him something fierce, myself. But he died defending those he loved. Can't you find a way to take some solace in that, at least?"

"Shut up!" Yasmine screamed, dropping Lani's hand so she could cover her own eyes. "Shut up! Shut up! Shut up!" Lani felt her mother completely lose control of herself. Her boys were dead. *Dead. Dead. Dead. Dead. Dead. Dead. Dead. Dead.* Rotting in the ground. Never coming back.

People were running toward them now, gathering by

the commotion. Lani tried to hug her desperately. "I need to see the body," Yasmine told the governor when she opened her eyes again. Her tone was even, emotionless again. "Where the body?" She took a step toward him.

The governor took a step away from Yasmine and Lani. Something in his eyes—Lani saw it was fear—let her know there was more to the story. "He isn't . . ." He shook his head.

"What?" she screamed, again losing her composure.

He jumped, this man, this great general of the colony, at the sound.

Lani finally succeeded and encircled her tiny arms as far around Yasmine as they would go.

"The savage cut him up and fed all the pieces down the river," said the governor. "The only thing he left was the head, so we knew it was him."

Lani felt for a moment that her mother was becoming the rain itself, the water collecting everywhere around her, flooding her pores and blinding her eyes. Yasmine could gather herself with force and slam into an object to break it, as she had seen water do even to stone. But she could also dissolve. She could let herself disappear, become another drop of water entirely, assume its weight, its consistency, its route. Yasmine fell down then. Down into the mud. And even though her mother still had Nolan and her, Lani saw in Yasmine's eyes the desire not just to die but to be annihilated. To cease to exist, to think, to remember anymore. For everything that was Yasmine

Wright to wander away from itself and find another form to take. It would be better to be a log or a rock in a river, slowly whittled away by the steady current of water. Far, far better.

CHAPTER THIRTY-FOUR

1845, Monrovia, Liberia

DUSK WAS ROLLING IN on what Lani supposed was the longest day of her life. The clouds thinned across the horizon, and the sky was turning a shade of blue that reminded her of the large vats of indigo some of the women in the village stirred with long sticks slowly, waiting for it to gain strength enough to hold color on fabric. The breeze from the ocean had become cooler now, urging her to pull her shawl tighter across her narrow shoulders. She scanned the path to town for any trace of Gartee, but could see nothing yet. Her right foot tapped against the ground nervously, a habit her mother was fond of telling her was both annoying and unladylike. Lani smiled at the thought: quite a charge from the woman known across all quarters of the colony as Mr. Wright. Her mother, head of the most prosperous farms in Monrovia, second to Governor Whitman, and ace marksman in the troops, would seem on the surface to put no stock in common notions of ladylike behavior. But Yasmine Wright was nothing if not complicated. Lani sighed. For once, she wished she didn't know this so well; it would be easier to go on like they had been and pretend that what was happening was not.

Finally the sound of footfalls on the grasses came closer and closer. Lani sat up—he had finally returned from the village with news from the elders. They would finally set a date and finally be free from all this sneaking around. But as the footsteps neared, she realized that they were too deliberate, too heavy to be Gartee's, who like so many Bassa men, walked like his feet and the ground were two halves of the same whole. Nolan, on the other hand, walked like he owned the place. Now a successful trader, interpreter, and negotiator who was widely favored to be the governor's successor, he effectively *did* own it.

"Good evening, Sister," Nolan called across the path to her. He had come from a lengthy set of talks with a Grebo paramount chief, who presided in a district a week's walk from Monrovia. He and the governor's people were attempting to obtain more land for the settlement, as well as trade in various goods.

"Good evening," Lani said evenly, once her brother had reached her. "How the journey?"

He sat down heavily on the rock beside her, throwing his suitcase into the dust. Normally he would insist on sitting on a proper chair inside and having one of the small girls or boys bring him water, rice, and soup immediately after such a long journey. But it wasn't often that he found his sister alone and unoccupied like this, and he wanted to talk to her.

"Fine," he said, wiping his brow with a handkerchief. This damned country was so humid, a man had barely bathed before he found himself drenched in sweat and dirt again. "We got half the land for the settlement. I think the chief can see reason in it. I think it won't be long before he gives us the rest, either."

Lani laughed. "Who wouldn't see reason, when reason got rifles and spears and friends from every ship comes to port from America and Europe behind 'em?"

Nolan frowned and made himself laugh. His baby sister had always been contrary growing up—favoring salt over sugar, pepper soup over the American chicken soup their mother labored over for so many hours. But he had assumed she would grow out of it, like so many other young girls, as she came closer to womanhood. She hadn't.

"What you doin' out here, anyway?" he asked, thinking it best to change the subject. A mosquito buzzed in front of his eye, and he swatted it away. "You gonna get eaten alive."

Lani shrugged. The mosquitoes never bothered her as they bothered Nolan and their mother. Sure, she got bitten but never like they did, and by some miracle she had never come down with the fever. "Beautiful night. Thought I'd take in some air."

He nodded. Their mother probably wanted her to

visit with her in the sitting room, but her contrary daughter had declined. Those two were always at each other's throats lately.

They sat there for a moment, he catching his breath from the long trip, she peering intently at something in the distance. Nolan followed her gaze and saw something maybe a half mile away from them making its way toward them. It was small and black, but moving swiftly across the terrain. He sighed. He should have known.

"Why do you hang on him so? You know nothing good can come of it," he said in a small voice. "You know Mama ain't never gonna allow whatever it is you two dreamin' of."

Gartee had come to them from his village when he was five, to help out with the fetching of water, cleaning and maintenance of the house, caring of the livestock. It was rapidly becoming the custom here to have at least one small boy and small girl from the bush come and stay in your house and help out, in exchange for providing them with the gifts of civilization: education and the Word of the Lord. Not to mention regular meals and a decent roof over their heads. Nolan was of the same mind as most of his fellow Congo people—the name the local tribal men had given them: The natives were getting the far better deal in the arrangement.

Lani scowled. "I grown now, Brother," she said, still peering at Gartee so far away. "Time for allowing and forbidding and punishing's long gone." She turned to him, smiling sincerely now. "Now's the time for acceptance.

And happiness for what's to be, and what already is." Then she took off down the path, her gait light and swift at the thought of Gartee's embrace.

"Lani, wait!" Nolan yelled after her, but it was already too late, she was gone. He wasn't stupid; he had seen them together when they thought they were alone, could discern the meaning of the Bassa they spoke rapidly to conceal its meaning from his mother and the rest of the Congo peers she kept company with. He just never thought she would actually do it—give up everything to live like an animal in the bush with a savage. He wanted to tell her to fornicate with him if she must, but let him marry some other unfortunate beast. He knew, though, that she wouldn't hear him, so the words had lodged in his throat for months now.

Lani lifted her skirts and walked as fast as her legs would take her. She couldn't help it—when she was a minute's walk from Gartee, she broke into a run to meet him.

"Aha!" he exclaimed, as she jumped up and wrapped her arms around him. "Little Swallow, you have found me at last."

She laughed, delighted at the sound of his name for her from his mouth.

He spun her around. "And I couldn't be happier." He nestled his nose in her hair and breathed in its clean, flowery scent. She was fond of putting pepper flowers in her hair, and the smell of the small, white, star-shaped plants always rubbed off on her.

She pulled away and eyed him anxiously. "What did they say?"

He wanted to tease her, keep it from her a little longer to draw out this small moment of power he had over her, the power of knowing something she didn't, something so important it would irrevocably change their lives forever. But taking in those huge, imploring eyes, he just couldn't do it. "They said we should come immediately," he said, smiling. "They said we shall be wed within the month."

Lani squealed with delight and threw her arms around him all over again.

"What kind of woman is this?" his parents and elders would say if they saw them so brazen like this, but they were completely alone now, and so he didn't care. He allowed himself to plant kisses all along her forehead, this forehead he had seen so many times and resented so often while they were growing up, but which he now loved as no other forehead he could imagine. Off in the distance, Nolan watched, shaking with anger, and then finally turned away to walk back to the house.

Yasmine and Nolan sat impatiently at the table in the dining room, waiting for Dechontee, their new house girl, to place the lunch of rice and cassava leaf in front of them. Wlojii, their house girl of many years, was leaving them to marry a young man in her village, so she had been training Dechontee faithfully these last few weeks. The twelve-year-old girl was not a quick study, however, and had a sullen disposition on top of it.

"I swear, this whole house 'bout to go to ruin," Yasmine said to Nolan, seated across from her. "All the help got an opinion 'bout everything, and they in love with they laziness."

Nolan sipped on his palm wine, half listening to his mother. He had heard the speech countless times before.

Dechontee finally shuffled out of the kitchen with the food. Once she had put the platter on the table, she carefully lifted the bowl of soup and brought it toward her mistress. Unfortunately, she moved a bit too abruptly, and some of it spilled over onto the finely stitched tablecloth that had come from Boston last month.

Yasmine slapped the girl's hands, incensed. "Stupid wench!" she hissed. "You too much like the ape to learn *simple* thing!"

Like so many of these natives, Dechontee's face registered no response to the words or the slap. "Sorry, Ma," she said, as she worked to scoop up the spill with a rag from her lappa.

Yasmine frowned and then laughed ruefully.

Nolan raised an eyebrow, wondering exactly what his mother was thinking.

"No, I the one who sorry," she told the girl. "Can't get no good work from your kind no way."

The girl picked up her platter and left the room as slowly as she had come in, apparently unaffected by Yasmine's outburst.

"You could show the girl a little mercy, Ma," Nolan said after she was gone. "Ain't no way a body can learn what's being screamed at."

Yasmine eyed him coolly, then shrugged. "We both of us know they ain't tryna learn from us anyway, son. Look at Gartee, all those years we tried so hard to teach him how to roast a goat proper, and look at this here mess." She gestured down at the oily, lumpy brown soup in front of her. "And if he think he can just take my baby with him, back into the bush, I ain't taught him nothing."

Nolan took a large gulp of his wine. He couldn't imagine the house without Lani in it; hated to think of himself alone here with the few help they had left, with his increasingly vitriolic mother.

"Sometimes, it feel like this whole country just a dream to me—and a bad one at that," Yasmine said bitterly, pushing the bowls of food away. She pulled on a strand of curly gray hair that had somehow escaped her hand that morning and tucked it back into the tight bun at the top of her head. "Ain't no way to make things go the way they oughta. Ain't no way to make things right. We all just gotta make peace with what bits we given and let go how we thought things was gonna be." She sighed, resting her hand, now flecked with liver spots, on her only living son's shoulder.

Nolan glared at her. "You mean we gotta let Lani go away into the bush with that . . . boy?" He spit out the last word like spoiled meat. "That traitor?" He shook his head angrily. "I can't believe she wants it."

Yasmine peered at him carefully. "Wants what, honey?"

Nolan's face was getting redder by the minute, puffed up by images of his sister committing foul acts with Gartee, probably for years, right under their noses. "Wants to soil her womanhood with that . . . savage," he sneered. "Wants to live like a beast in them huts, mosquitoes and ants crawling all over them, no proper schooling for the chullins, Godless, hopeless. How could she want that, Ma? How could she possibly want that? You think he tricked her or something? Put one a them juju spells on her?"

Yasmine grimaced. She leaned her thin, wiry frame against his thick, muscled one and then led him into the sitting room. They sat down in chairs the best carpenter in Monrovia had made for them some years back, in exchange for a parcel of land Nolan obtained for him from a Bassa chief nearby. Nolan felt Yasmine looking into his eyes, the light brown eyes of the boy who had grown into such a fine, competent young man—a man she could count on for everything from planning new encampments, to organizing survey expeditions into the bush. Yes, Nolan knew he had grown into a man his father would be proud of. If she could take pride in nothing else she had accomplished in this wretched land, it was this.

"What I think," she said slowly, "is that a woman's heart be as open as the night sky, 'fore she learn better. And your sister one of those been born with the openest hearts of all. It why everyone love her so—highborn, lowborn, American, savage, and everything in between. It why she always seemed to know their pain and their joy." She smiled, and Nolan imagined she was remembering something like the image that flashed in his own mind, one of Lani teaching the children in town their ABCs at the schoolhouse in the mornings, then walking down to two, sometimes three villages in the afternoons to do the same with the savage children. Sometimes he wondered where this beautiful, generous, trusting young woman had come from.

"You right that Gartee took advantage of that openness, that goodness your sister got." Yasmine sighed. "But the truth is, she let him do it. And now she gonna hafta pay the price. She gonna hafta choose."

Lani had walked with Gartee to the tiny room he shared with two small boys and their head carpenter and said good night, when she heard a door close on the floor above them. Then, footfalls across the floor, and waiting at the top of the stairs. She knew it was her mother, who she had thus far been able to avoid in their spacious grounds since Gartee had returned with the good news. But she could see that her time was up now, that her mother had decided they must talk. And once Yasmine Wright decided something, there was no turning away from it.

Lani shuffled down the hall to the foot of the stairs, dreading the unpleasantness that was about to unfold. Her mother, all sinews and hard lines as she finished her fifth decade, stood regally at the top of the staircase, her embroidered white robe wrapped around her like some kind of king's coat. She had let her hair down, and Lani reflected that she should do it more often, as the gray and white ringlets that framed her face took away some of the harshness that seemed to have dug in deep since Big George died. Lani had been three then, but Nolan told her plenty of times how beautiful their mother had been before she lost two children in one year, before her dream of a new start for the family had ended so abruptly. Before she had come to succeed beyond their wildest dreams in the colony, farming and livestock operations overshadowing all others. *She was even happy sometimes, 'fore they passed*, Nolan had whispered to her once when he was a teenager and she a child. She couldn't imagine it, couldn't remember a time when she had seen her mother smile. And now, here she was, about to break her mother's heart again. The worst part was, she couldn't even seem to make herself feel bad about it, either. Her feelings for her mother had dulled so much through the years that she sometimes secretly wondered if she loved her at all.

"You marry that boy, that's it. We all done," Yasmine called down to her, piercing the quiet of the night. She never was one to bother with greetings. What use were they, when there was a point to be made? "Don't you never come back to this house, you hear? And don't you never expect nothing from me and Nolan. Be like you dead to us. In the end, you come here to be just another *savage.*"

Lani looked up at her mother and was grateful that she felt something, even though the feeling itself hurt. And the feeling was twofold: sorrow and pity. How sad her mother had become, how devoted to her hatred of those she blamed for the deaths of her beloved sons. Almost every family she knew had lost someone to the African fever or the constant battle for land and power and resources. In fact, many families like them had lost more than one. Lani supposed that her mother's abiding grief wouldn't allow her to see this truth: that her loss was not unique, that loss defined what it meant to be on this land.

"Mama," she said softly. "I been dead to you for years."

They set out before dawn the very next day, the sounds of the dark forest swirling in their eardrums like whispers. Lani packed three of her dresses, two shirts and skirts, a few handkerchiefs, two bars of soap, her three favorite novels that Nolan had managed to find for her, and the fine Sunday shoes her mother had bought from a British merchant some time ago into her suitcase. She had been to the village enough to know that she wouldn't need much there, and what she didn't bring, Gartee and his family would either make or provide. As for Gartee, he had only the small pouch he had always carried with him when he traveled from the house to Giakpee and back again, and a machete in his right hand. In all the years he had been with them, he had not brought one more thing into the house, careful as he was instructed to be around the Congo people. Of course, he now knew that he was leaving with the most valuable part of the house itself—his wife-to-be. When Gartee had realized what was happening to them, that he and Lani had somehow stumbled into a connection, a reservoir of feeling much larger than each of them, his first response had been terror. Terror at his lack of control of feelings or Lani's. Terror at the prospect of bringing a white woman into his home, his family, and his line. But what made his gut clench in the wee hours of the night was the thought of how Yasmine would react. He had seen, firsthand, what the madame of the house was capable of doing in the name of preserving her Congo family and way of life. But the very idea of living life away from Lani, the curly-haired nymph who charmed whoever she encountered, the unabashedly sweet white woman whose Bassa had grown as clear as anyone's in the village after all those years of conversing with him and the other house boys and girls out of the earshot of her mother—Gartee could not imagine it. So many times during their midnight trysts in a meadow with high grasses a half hour's run from the house, he had told her that they had to end it, that it would never work, that her mother would force her to choose in the end: him or her family, and that this was no way for someone to live. And every time, she had watched him while he wrestled with what she knew he had to get out because he loved her, listening patiently, hands folded in her lap, eyes glistening. And then when he was done, anguished and alone in the decision, she reached out her hand and traced the outline of his jaw from his temple to his neck. His whole body woke up then, electrified, and he had no choice but to touch her. And he knew she was right: He had no choice but to love her. And Mrs. Wright, he knew, would have no choice but to hate him for it. Lani shrugged when he brought this up. People often mistook Lani for an ordinary woman when they met her, because of her reticence and good manners. But what they missed was her resolve, which could not be moved once it had settled. Gartee had seen Lani's mother rail against her for seeking out to consort with "those savages" during the harvest festival, confiscate her beloved books in order to punish her for not agreeing to let various Congo men she found distasteful call on her. Lani always sat calmly while these storms raged before her, as if watching a play she had no real interest in. This, of course, seemed to enrage her mother more. So that in the end, no one could say who had the stronger will: Mrs. Wright or her tenaciously kind daughter.

Gartee took her hand now and squeezed it, a gesture that was so foreign to him and his people because it was seen as a sign of weakness to show such affection publicly to a woman. She would be his first wife, and he knew, somehow, that she would do well in the village, that she would never look back, because she felt like she never belonged in this sad Congo house anyway, that they would create their own family of beautiful, bright children.

"Time to go," he said to her in Bassa, and she squared her shoulders and nodded.

He took her suitcase and started walking, and she followed behind him. It would be a long journey to Giakpee, but they would take it one day at a time and arrive there within a week, together.

They had only made it down the first turn of the path to the house when Nolan ran out, half dressed and wild, his right hand held fast in a fist.

Lani turned around, confused. In the end, her last living sibling had sided with their mother, as he always did. She wasn't surprised but couldn't help be disappointed.

"Take it," Nolan said when he reached them, huffing and puffing from his exertions. "I buried it after Little George died, 'cause I knew he would want us to have it." He opened his clenched right hand to reveal the small pouch with a brass clasp that some natives had given him not long before he died. The years had done their work, and the animal leather of the pouch was frayed and broken, the shine of the brass long gone. Yasmine had spoken of the trinket just a few times in Lani's life, how her beloved son had been murdered by "the devil's magic," and how they had to watch the help and everything they brought into the house so carefully so that history would not repeat itself.

"What . . . ?" Lani's voice died out before she finished the sentence because she didn't know what she wanted to say. She had no memories of either of her older brothers, although they were central figures in family lore by now. Every time she heard the story of Little George's passing in particular, however, she felt a deep and inexplicable grief that flooded her senses—like the violent remembrance of events she couldn't have witnessed in the first place. She had never been able to explain why she felt so keenly the loss of someone she had only known as a baby.

Nolan looked back at the house fearfully. Then, he hugged his sister, crushing her small bones against his sturdy torso. Lani allowed herself to be hugged by him, although she did not hug him back. He pulled her away after a moment, held her at arm's length to look at her.

"I'm sorry," he said, his voice breaking. "So sorry," he said, and this time he moved his eyes from Lani's to Gartee's, and all three of them knew that in that second at least, he was speaking to him too. Then he turned and began to walk back to the house, slowly, his head down.

There were so many things Lani wanted to say or do, but in the end she simply closed her fingers around the trinket and took her soon-to-be-husband's other hand. He squeezed it, and then they took their first steps on the long journey home.

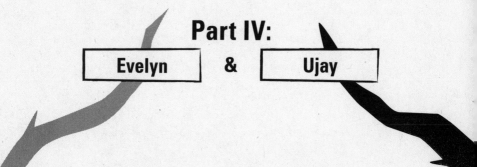

Part IV:

Evelyn & **Ujay**

You cannot carry out fundamental change
without a certain amount of madness.

—Thomas Sankara

★

CHAPTER THIRTY-FIVE

April 6, 1980, Sinkor Area, Monrovia, Liberia

IT ONLY A DREAM!

Evelyn sat bolt upright in bed, clutching at the wet cotton sheets. Her chest was tight enough to constrict her breathing, and sweat burned her eyes. She wanted to scream, but it was the middle of the afternoon, and her mother was likely in the kitchen right off the hallway from her bedroom. So she closed her eyes and bit down on her bottom lip, until she felt the rush of salty blood on her tongue. Only then did the terror in her gut begin to subside, and the sound of gunfire ringing in her ears give way to the steady *tick* of the ancient clock in the foyer.

"Hey, ma," her mother said from the doorway. "What happen, my daughter?" She stood with a dishrag and a cup she had almost finished drying in her hands.

Evelyn sighed. Her mother had always had a preternatural sense about her three daughters.

"Uh-huh. It only...," Evelyn said, trying not to flinch

under the sharp glare of the sunlight streaming in the window, "a bad dream." She could almost believe it herself.

Saybah Kollie stared at her oldest, most intelligent, and least marriageable daughter. "Palm butter with cassava wasn't fine-oh" she said, referring to lunch. "Must have given you indigestion."

Evelyn looked down at her hands, so that her mother would not see her frown. "Yeah, Ma." Her mother had told her many times that she should not eat the way she did if she wanted to find a husband, and that lying down after eating only made the food stick to her already too-large thighs, hips, and stomach. The Old Ma stood at the doorway for another second. Evelyn could feel how much she wanted to ask about the dream. Finally she turned away and walked purposefully back to the kitchen.

Evelyn was still working up the courage to actually push out the retort that seemed to be permanently lodged in her throat: *I don't want a husband, Old Ma.* But the next thought came right behind it: *Maybe what coming will make me dry from all the worry-menh,* Evelyn thought, smiling wryly. *Maybe the Old Ma will end up happy with me after all.* Then she remembered Mr. Buchanan being dragged from the house next door in the dead of night, screaming in his skivvies that he was innocent of any and all crimes of which he might be accused. That was more than two months ago, and the word in the neighborhood was that the rebels had taken him to an undisclosed location outside the city. Evelyn shook her head. Buchanan's daughter, Elizabeth, was her best friend and a fellow first-year at the University of Liberia. Since her father's kidnapping, Elizabeth had trouble getting out of bed each morning and was on the verge of flunking her courses this semester. With all the rumors and all the trouble, Evelyn was having an equally hard time concentrating and wasn't far behind her on this path of shame.

She had always had a wry sense of humor—which had gotten her into plenty of trouble throughout her life—but even Evelyn had to admit that there was little about the situation that was funny. She wiped her dripping brow with the back of her hand. No, her personal joke about becoming dry at the expense of the nation wasn't funny. But she hoped, at the very least, that the movie tonight would be. It was too exhausting not to laugh for months and months.

Love Brewed in an African Pot was showing at the Relda, and Evelyn and Elizabeth were determined to go see it that night. That was why Evelyn had laid down in the first place—to be fresh for the increasingly rare night on the town that the two had been planning for weeks. They had gone down to Broad Street and each purchased a new dress, just in from America. Elizabeth's was made of a delicate and rich red chiffon, and gathered at the waist, showing off her figure, while Evelyn's was a simple peach cotton that swirled like an open flower when she turned suddenly. These would have been extravagant purchases a year ago, but now, they were positively decadent. However, each of them had confessed to the other that they could not remember the last time they had bought something for themselves, something that made them feel beautiful, like anything could happen, that the world was filled with nothing else but pregnant possibility.

Placing her feet flat on the carpet, Evelyn began to walk, very slowly, toward the bathroom. Her head was still a bit dizzy, and she was vaguely nauseous, but she had the feeling that both would pass as soon as she could step into the shower.

You cannot walk this line forever, my dear. You will soon have to take a side—and each will have a very steep price-menh. She blinked, and tried to wipe Ujay's brash voice from her mind. *You chastise us for using violence, but you know in your heart it the only way change gonna come to this country-oh. What did one hundred fifty years of nonviolent protest and silence get us? Nothing. Nowhere. They still own us-oh. People like you, indigenous and privileged, gonna tip the balance to justice, small-small. You know this, Evie. That why you keep coming to our meetings. That why you prepare and carry the prisoners' food.* Evelyn shook her head violently and covered her ears. "Enough!" she yelled. It was bad enough to have to be in a room with Ujay's prodding in real life—the last thing she needed was to bring it home with her to her dreams.

"Eeh-menh!" Evelyn said under her breath. Her mother would be there in an instant, asking if everything was all right. This time, there would be no stopping the questions about her dreams. Evelyn leaned out the bathroom door and called, "I fine. Only, I slipped." Then she tore her clothes off, turned the shower up to full-blast, and let the cold water overwhelm all of her senses.

The night was cool, so both young women wore shawls around their shoulders. They also each carried identical white leather purses that Mr. Buchanan had brought back from his most recent trip to France. They walked slowly toward the blazing red lights of the Relda, almost not wanting to reach it too quickly. They both knew that the night would end too soon, and that tomorrow would be upon them well before they had even begun to prepare for it.

"They surround him then?" Elizabeth asked, leaning into her friend.

Evelyn nodded, the dream becoming all too visceral again. "He didn't see them coming and was overwhelmed-menh."

Elizabeth peered at her in horror. "Eeh-menh! What they do to him?"

Evelyn looked away from her, at the cars making their way leisurely down the boulevard. She did not want to say, but she knew she would feel better once she did.

"They gutted him," she said evenly. They were at the steps of the Relda and faced each other.

"Oh!" Elizabeth exclaimed, then clasped her hand over her mouth. "They did not-menh!"

Evelyn sighed. "They did-menh." She started up the steps slowly. The wind picked up for an instant and billowed her skirts around her.

Elizabeth regained her composure and quickly ran up the steps to meet her. She grabbed Evelyn's arm. "And what did you do-oh?"

Evelyn turned to her incredulously. "What you mean, what I do? I wasn't there."

Elizabeth backed away from her. "But you *were* there. It your dream-menh!"

"Right," Evelyn said, opening her purse to find her money. "It my dream, and I wasn't there-oh."

Elizabeth's brow furrowed. "But how you watching it if you not there? I don't understand. The dreamer always part of the dream"

"Not this time-oh," Evelyn said. She paid the attendant for a ticket. After Elizabeth was done paying, she said quietly, "To watch the president be murdered by his own men, our own army-menh. I had no body—only eyes and ears."

Elizabeth frowned. She looked down at her shoes, then back up at Evelyn. "What your mother say-ya?"

Evelyn shrugged. "I didn't tell her."

Elizabeth opened the door and walked through it. "Oh."

Evelyn followed. "But she knows. I know she knows-menh."

Once they were in the foyer, the night disappeared behind them, on the other side of the glass. The elegant red carpet of the theater pushed back on their pumps purposefully with each step, and they felt like they were gliding forward, in their Western dresses and lotioned limbs.

CHAPTER THIRTY-SIX

April 7, 1980, West Point Area, Monrovia, Liberia

IT WASN'T SO MUCH that he hated them. It was more like he hated what had happened to him. And the worst part was, he wasn't even sure if he could blame it all on them anymore. He could admit now that writing and distributing the anti-Tolbert poem was not the smartest move he'd made in his nineteen years. As a trained Progressive Alliance of Liberia activist, he knew very well what it meant to spend your political capital—to throw it like a bomb into the insatiable mouth of the Congo people, and watch it do its work. And then to feel the consequences. Still, Ujay Flomo smiled. His dream of a university education might have been snatched away, but his dream of a just society? They couldn't take that from him any more than they could take his name. The more they tried, the more vigorously he and PAL and everyone in the movement would resist. *As one Comrade drops, another takes his place-oh.* Yes, that was the way of it.

They didn't even see the wave until it was upon them.

"But what use is democracy if you cannot participate-oh?"

Ujay groaned now and rolled over on his lumpy, dirty mattress, pulling his wrists over his ears.

"Eeh-menh! Now you expelled, all those political aspirations falling away, small-small," she had told him at the meeting the other day. "That beautiful justice you fighting for so hard, that one you say worth an ocean of blood and another of fear, that one will not allow you to serve those you represent. You will never be a senator now, and the people of West Point will never benefit from the strength of your leadership." Her usually steady voice was almost shaking at this point, and her delicately coiffed bob was slightly askew. He knew what he should be feeling at that moment should have been anger, but instead, all he felt was an acute urge to touch her face, and move the delinquent hair behind her ear. "What will you do when all this is over-oh?" she asked him. "*What will you do-menh?*"

His breath had caught in his throat then, and he broke his gaze with her. "Nothing is ever over, Evie," he said. He knew she hated being called that—it was what her mother called her—so he had delighted in almost exclusively calling her "Evie" since they had met years ago, as children. He watched her wince and resisted the urge to pinch her. If she only knew how hard he had to work every second he was around her not to touch her.

"*That*," she said, her mouth in a thin, pinched line, "is bullshit." He couldn't help it then—he burst out laughing, which of course made her even angrier. He finally got control of himself, and said, "Careful, Evie. What would your mother say-ya? You'll never get a husband that way."

She was livid now. "I not getting no husband," she said and stomped off.

But Ujay knew she would; whatever the two of them had become recently, he knew she would. She was a product of her place, family, and stature, after all. Her class always married—up, if possible; never down.

He stretched out now and made a conscious decision to wipe Evelyn from his mind. Nothing good could come from thinking of her, he had learned that long ago. No, better to consider the rumors circulating all over the city that George, Oscar, Dika, and the others might be executed next week, to mark the occasion of the first anniversary of the Rice Riots. Wilson had told him about it a few days ago, and the thought of it made him want to break something. The trouble was, there was nothing around to break—his family owned little of value, and everything that was valuable was already broken.

"They want to make an example of them-menh," Wilson had told him, leaning over their water glasses at the student center. "They feel the same energy on the streets that we do-oh—the exhaustion with their easy brutality. They know they have to do something to quell it, and they think that something is right in their compound."

Wilson was Kpelle, from Bong County, and head of the Student Unification Party, which had gained strength and power over the past five years, as more indigenous students came to school in Monrovia. Students from the city had dominated all aspects of university life for decades, but with the current political climate, they were finally seeing their limited perspectives challenged. A skillful speaker, Wilson was able to bring together Kru, Grebo, Krahn, and Geh, clans that had never before seen a common goal: to have a place at the table at the seat of the republic.

"Their compound is connected to our compound," Ujay said, taking a sip from his glass. "If they try anything, more blood will be spilt-menh. And this time, the blood will not only be ours." He looked around the student center, at the men and women laughing and teasing one another, and he was struck with an intense longing throughout his entire body just to rest—to be easy. But then, in the next moment, his breathing seized up in his chest, and he knew that he could never rest until he had seen it, the entire thing, through.

Wilson's hand slamming down on the tabletop woke him from his reverie. Suddenly Wilson's finger was in Ujay's face. "Blood is blood," he said. "And we all Liberian-oh."

The intensity of Wilson's glance was getting to be too much for even Ujay to stand, so he broke from it for a moment to look at the DJ, who was switching out James Brown for the new Earth, Wind & Fire LP. Ujay knew a complicated political debate was moments away, and he simply didn't have the energy. "These people . . . They not people-menh. I don't know what they are. They come here over a century ago, to escape from slavery, they say, to find a new land, a home to be free, and what they do-ya? They act as if no one here already, as if we have no culture, no civilization, no religion, no humanity-oh." He laughed again bitterly. "No, no. The Congo people know no other way of rule than brutality. All they know how to do is kill—whether slowly, by the deadening poverty we endure, or quickly, by force-menh." Ujay felt the familiar hotness behind his eyes and swallowed quickly, telling himself to calm down. That was all he needed, to cry in front of Wilson. "And that is why," he concluded, "the only solution is indigenous rule-oh."

Wilson shook his head slowly. "The only solution, eh?" He took another sip of water. "And John and Mary, Cecilia and Josiah? What about all the Congo people try-ing to help us-oh? Shall we kill them too?" Wilson's voice was rising, and Ujay motioned for him to quiet down. Who knew who was in the student center right then? This was a time when no one was safe—especially those who were stupid enough to think they were.

"For God's sake-menh!" Ujay hissed. "I not saying we

should kill anyone—least of all our friends." Ujay grinned at Wilson mischievously. "Or lovers."

Wilson's eyes flashed in alarm.

Ujay held up his hand. "It okay-ya," he said. "I not gonna say a thing."

Wilson scowled. "You just did-menh."

Ujay shrugged. "Love is love, my friend."

Wilson leaned into him, seeing an opening. "Oh ya? So, what revolution, then?"

Let's groove tonight, the speakers thrummed. *Share the spice of life.* A woman's peal of laughter shot out from a corner. Ujay shrugged.

"Revolution the opposite of love for you, Ujay," Wilson continued, all the fire evaporating from his features. He just looked sad now. "And that why I don't trust you-menh."

CHAPTER THIRTY-SEVEN

April 7, 1980, Army Barracks, Monrovia, Liberia

"IT MY DREAM, and I wasn't there-oh."

Garnahweh heard the dull thud of his boots against the concrete sidewalk and wondered if he might be lucky enough to be the only one in his unit's quarters. The others were out at the bar, sharing pints of Star beer and stories about their women—or the women they would have, as soon as the change that was coming finally came to this godforsaken country. Since he had joined the army after his eighteenth birthday a little more than a year ago, Garnahweh himself was surprised by how little interest he had in either women or beer—subjects which seemed to provoke an endless amount of discussion and argument among his peers. On the whole, he was far more concerned about the meager harvest his family had collected back home in the village and about Janjay, his six-year-old niece, who had been designated his charge after his sister died from the curse last year. If Garnahweh didn't yet have a wife and daughter of his own to protect, he took his duty to his niece seriously.

Garnahweh shivered and pulled his rough cotton hat over his ears. The day had been sunny and dry, but when night came, he always found that he was not able to keep warm under the thin, scratchy blankets they were issued. He would not dare ask for another blanket, however. Such an admission—of having "thin blood"—would raise suspicion about not only his ability to execute the demanding requirements of a soldier, but about his very manhood.

The unit's quarters were about twelve feet wide by twenty feet long, with four sets of bunks squeezed into the sides and one in the center. Threadbare sheets strapped perhaps half of the bunk beds—a futile effort by some of the men, who, like Garnahweh, were desperately trying to create some semblance of home, of "progress." The walls were blank, except for the peeling white paint that was dulled by dirt in some places and marred by boot prints in others. The floor was cold, packed dirt, which should have been swept clean every morning, but which was not, because all the men considered this to be women's and girls' work, and none of the newly made men in the unit would risk the insinuation that they were suited for such things. There were times when no one else was around, however, when Garnahweh had been tempted to pick up the broom of palm fronds himself and sweep the area clean. If there was one thing he could not abide by, it was dirt. The only thing that was almost as bad as that was disorder.

He strode over to his bunk and flopped down on it with a sigh. When would they finally come for him? He closed his eyes, imagining himself sitting behind the large desk of the Minister of Agriculture. Garnahweh had glimpsed it only once, on an errand to pick up a classified envelope for Master Sargent Samuel K. Doe. The desk was made of a deep, rich maple, no doubt crafted in Europe. But the fat man behind the desk, the man whose name Garnahweh had not even bothered to learn because he would not be in the position for much longer, this man did not seem to even understand, much less appreciate, the beauty before him. You could not even see the desktop, since numerous papers were flung across it in disarray. It was a wonder, Garnahweh thought, taking the envelope from the man's limp and clammy hands, that anything got done in the Agricultural Ministry, given the state of things. It had taken all of Garnahweh's strength, all of his soldier's training, to keep his face impassive when a feeling of nausea invaded his gut. The simple truth was— this fat Congo man, like so many others who populated the halls of the executive mansion—disgusted him. They, like most Congos, might have grown rich off their laziness and power, but they had also become old, obsolete— effeminate, almost. They had forgotten what an honest day's work felt like, they had begun to believe the image of themselves that they perpetuated, because they made sure it was in everyone's line of sight. He could never tell Master Sergeant Doe or any of his superiors this, but Garnahweh almost felt sorry for the Congos. What was a man if he wasn't a man anymore? He shook his head on his bunk now. Garnahweh had heard whispers that Congo men could no longer satisfy their women, could not even plant their seed in them, which was why so many young Congo women were looking for Bassa, Vai, Gola, Krahn, and Kru boyfriends lately. This must have been the final humiliation for their men.

He eyed his gun, hanging on his bedpost, and reached for it. They were required to clean their AK-47's every week, but Garnahweh preferred to clean it every day. These were times when no one knew when a gun, or any kind of force, might be required. After President Tolbert had detained the demonstrators, Master Sergeant Doe said that it would be anytime now that they would make their move, and they should be ready. Garnahweh removed the gun's magazine and set it on the mattress. He moved the safety lever, pulled back the bolt carrier, and ejected a round from the chamber. He pushed the bolt carrier forward and then pressed the rear end receiver cover. He unrolled his brushes from the scrap of cloth where he stored them and lost himself in the work of making his weapon perfectly clean.

Garnahweh knew that he could take down and clean a gun better than any educated Congo man could even dream of doing. He smiled, disengaging the front receiver *cover from the rear sight housing slot. His teachers in primary school—in truth, the only school he'd known—had always said that he had a gift for identifying plants, and even helping them grow. Especially the really important ones, like cassava. No, Garnahweh saw no reason why he would not be the logical choice for the new Minister of Agriculture. He expertly lifted the rod and spring backward from the bolt carrier, and set the rod beside the magazine, on the mattress. An image of himself behind the beautiful maple desk, two neat stacks of papers on either side of him. Garnahweh's smile deepened as he welcomed the dream. There was no doubt about it: He was the man most fit for the job.*

CHAPTER THIRTY-EIGHT

April 11, 1980, Monrovia, Liberia

AFTER TIPPING A PAIR of baby scorpions from his shoes, Ujay put them on and stepped through the front doorway of his house. It was six in the morning, but West Point was already bustling. The street hawkers leaned from their kiosks, beckoning him with palm oil, cool bagged water, rice and soup, soap, bread, transistor radios, and everything in between.

"How the morning-oh?" Old Man Togbah asked him, his toothy smile on full display. He was the neighborhood mechanic and could fix anything. Ujay often reflected that he would have been a top army engineer, if he were born Congo.

"The morning fine-oh." Ujay smiled—a gesture that never failed to surprise him with its ease.

Old Man Togbah nodded vigorously and handed Ujay the sugarcane stalk he had been munching on. "Fresh, fresh from the bush," he said. "So sweet!"

Ujay took the stalk from the man and chomped down. Thick, sugary juice washed down his throat. Closing his eyes, he could almost believe he was back in Buchanan, where he had lived as a young child, in Grand Bassa County. There, the forest had carpeted his every step, and baboons and monkeys had been his playmates. His father had made them move to Monrovia when he was ten, believing that there would be far more opportunities for work here. Instead, all he had found were crowded slums and more questionable orders from Congo boss men. Ujay scowled. Even the fresh cane couldn't cover the reek of the open sewer, the smell of dawn in West Point.

"Fat girl be looking for you. Nice, fat girl-oh," Old Man Togbah continued.

Ujay laughed. He and Evelyn had agreed to meet at Mama Lulu's for tea this morning. She had sounded elusive at school the other day, saying that she had to speak with him.

"Why you keep such fine women from me-menh? How you manage so many wives and deputies-oh, and your old man here still empty-handed?" He turned his palm upward. "You always be talking, 'We must share this, share that. Unify together to fight the Congo,' but why you not share your fine ladies, then?"

Still laughing, Ujay pulled Old Man Togbah's elbow and moved them both in the direction of the tea shop. "Maybe if you let go the kola nut for one minute, your teeth not blacken and rot out, and the fine, fine, fat women be kissing you everywhere-oh," he said.

"Eh-menh!" Old Man Togbah said, swatting Ujay's arm. "Why you pain me so-ya?"

It irritated Ujay to hear to hear the old man exaggerate his success with women. In truth, Ujay'd never been to bed with anyone but Evelyn—and that only recently. He wished the old fool would find something else to rant about.

Ahead Ujay could now see Evelyn sitting at a small table in the tea shop, sipping a cup of something. He would never tell a living soul, but he collected images like this into a fantasy of sorts, in which he and Evelyn were married and woke up each morning to things like tea together, conversations of what the new day held, and, of course, morning sex. Ujay took another bite of the sugarcane stalk. It was sweet, but he knew that Evelyn was so much sweeter.

"Why you try to keep an old man lonely?" Old Man Togbah continued. "My bed cold-oh!"

They were almost to the tea shop, but Evelyn still hadn't seen him. Maybe if he snuck around the back, he could surprise her.

"Boy, you don't even listen to an old man complain no more," said Old Man Togbah. He stopped in his tracks and smacked his hand on his thin trousers. "Ha! You thinking about taking a bite out of the fat girl, I see it in your eyes-menh!" He pointed at Ujay, his voice rising.

"You not fooling an old man. I know what fever rises below."

Ujay turned toward Old Man Togbah to shush him. He could not be quieted, of course, and Ujay's plea only made him laugh louder. "Oh! The boy going to get him a second breakfast-oh!" he hollered.

Evelyn turned then and stared right at him. "Ujay Flomo! Why you sneaking up on me?"

She was wearing a purple skirt, which hugged her thick hips and would hug her full buttocks when she stood. She had tied a bright green scarf around her head, and he swore that it picked up tiny jade specks in her eyes. Ujay's testicles ached.

"What?" she asked him. "What I got on my face-oh? Tea already?"

He shook his head; she really had no idea how beautiful she was. "No, nothing. Nothing, honey. You fine-oh." He pulled out a chair and sat down across from her, pretending not to see Old Man Togbah gesticulating wildly at him out of the corner of his eye.

Evelyn eyed him suspiciously. " 'Honey'?" she asked. "How I become your honey-menh?"

Ujay's face flushed red. The word came out before he'd had time to edit it. The best thing to do was change the subject. "How the body?"

"The body fine-oh," Evelyn answered. She stirred her tea. "And the tea too. They know how to make it in West Point."

Ujay signaled to the waitress. "That one thing they have over Sinkhor, eh?" He laughed at his own joke.

Evelyn's face clouded for a moment, digesting the dig at her class, but then let it go. "It too early in the morning for that-oh." She reached over and grabbed his forearm. "Let us simply have breakfast for once. Enjoy each other's company."

Ujay looked up at her sharply. Enjoy each other's company? Where was Evelyn Kollie, and what had God done with her?

She sighed. "Yes, I'm trying to make nice-oh. You haven't noticed, this country falling apart at the seams." Lowering her voice, she peered at him sideways. "You might have heard people say war coming."

He coughed. There were those who had mentioned such a thing at recent PAL meetings, but it was always in hushed tones and under cover of night. Certain things could not be spoken in daylight. He was about to tell her so when he saw her wipe a tear from the corner of her eye.

"I just need certain people to know they are important to me-oh." She took a deep breath, and then swallowed. "Whatever happens."

What was she talking about? His brow furrowed, and he leaned into her. "Evie," he began, "is something going on-ya?"

"It not what is going on-menh," she said. "It what I have seen-oh." The tears were falling freely now, although she was trying to conceal them with her hanky.

His hand rose, almost of its own accord, to touch her cheek. He was amazed; she didn't even flinch. The tears kept on falling. He felt like they were maybe in a dream—one of those he had as sleep engulfed him every night—and he didn't want the spell to be broken. He did want her to stop crying, though. "What you see?" He whispered. If they were alone, he would have kissed her.

She covered her mouth with her hand and began to sob. "I cannot say-oh."

His thumb rubbed her cheek—the skin was so soft! "Tell me," he said. "You can trust me-oh." He wished she could love him.

"I have always trusted you," she said, sniffling.

This surprised him. He studied her long eyelashes, her strong nose. He believed her.

"In my dream the other night . . . I saw death," she said. "I saw Tolbert killed." She wiped away more tears.

Ujay looked at her, uncomprehending. "Killed?"

Evelyn nodded, exhausted from her confession. "By a group of men in army fatigues. They came late in the night, after he fell asleep working-oh. They . . . cut him . . ." Her voice trailed to a whisper, and the tears started up again.

Ujay had never seen Evelyn like this—couldn't have imagined it. How many times had he fantasized about what it might be like to see her when she was not in complete control? Even the handful of times they'd made love had been in her bed, on her terms. But now that the moment of weakness was really here, he wanted it to end.

He couldn't stand to see her like this. It brought him back to their first time, after he'd climaxed. He'd expected that when he had finally been with a woman, whatever it was inside him that created this inescapable longing might finally let him have some peace and quiet. Instead, he found only a new reserve of worry, a new depth of exhaustion.

Skipping on sandals made from old tires, Old Man Togbah came right up to the table and leaned in between them. The thin odor of palm wine hung in the air. "This man want to bed you-oh," he said, as if he were announcing the coming of a storm.

In the lengthening moment afterward, Evelyn pulled her hand from Ujay's arm, and her eyes, which had been so clear the instant before, regained their usual glassy armor.

"Togbah!" Ujay cried. "Leave us, now, you old beast!"

Pulling her purse strap tightly around her shoulder, Evelyn stood up. "I have to go," she said icily.

"Sorry, sorry," Old Man Togbah said—more to Ujay than Evelyn. "I only meant to say that you should be his wife-oh."

Evelyn turned away from both of them and strode down the stairs, toward the taxi stop.

Ujay leapt up and ran after her. "Pay him no mind— he just a crazy old papi."

Evelyn kept on walking.

He took hold of her arm and faced her. "Take this," he said, grasping the worn brass clasp around his neck.

His grandfather Togar had given him it when he was a boy, had told him that it was a good-luck charm, and that it had gotten him out of many dangerous situations. The old man said it had been in their family for some time but would not elaborate.

As he pulled the thin chain over his head, Evelyn shook her head. "I can't—"

Ujay placed it carefully in her palm. "Take it-oh," he said more firmly.

Evelyn sighed, and he saw the tears fill up in her eyes again. "All right," she whispered. She closed her fingers around the tiny brass clasp, met his glance one last time, and then strode away. She took exactly thirty-three steps before she rounded the corner and was out of sight. He lifted his hand up to his neck and felt the hollow of his clavicle, where the charm used to be.

CHAPTER THIRTY-NINE

April 12, 1980, Monrovia, Liberia

"I HAD NO BODY—only eyes and ears."

Blessing expertly navigated the throngs of hawkers who swarmed the cars stopped in traffic, trying to reach the Big Man who anxiously snapped his fingers at her, hissing. He had bought her bags of groundnuts before, although she was sure he would not remember her. Why would he, when she was just another anonymous small girl on the street? The Big Man leaned out of the window of his shiny black BMW. Perspiration dotted his brow, and he wiped it with a hanky. After a moment, he grabbed a bag from the center of her plate, and then gave her a twenty-five-cent piece. Blessing dug around in her lappa for the change, as the line of cars inched forward. She had only been out here for an hour this morning, since five, and already she was tired. It would be a long day. Her task was to walk from Broad Street down to Old Road, back and forth, until she sold all the groundnuts.

She sometimes finished in the late morning, but more often by the early afternoon. Then she would head back to her uncle's house and give all the money to her aunt.

She had been living with her uncle and his family in town for three months now, but she still couldn't seem to get used to it. Surveying their thirteen children, and the impossible task of feeding them all at their small village in Bomi County, Blessing's parents had decided it would be better for her to stay with her father's younger brother, an assistant to the postmaster general. You work small-small, he pay your school fees-oh, her father had said. Make yourself useful in the house. Get educated-ya? Learn Congo people ways. Get yourself a future-menh, her father told her one evening. But she hadn't heard anything about school since she had come to her uncle's house, as her days were filled with a steady stream of hawking groundnuts, preparing food for the family, cleaning the house, and doing the wash. The promise of school was becoming dimmer to her with each passing day.

"Eh-menh!" the Big Man snapped, hissing in her face. "Where my money-oh?"

Blessing frowned, her line of thought severed. She shoved a five-cent piece she had found in her lappa into the man's hand, and he harrumphed a kind of acknowledgment. Then he shooed her away, as one might a fly, and his car shot forward toward the junction.

A sigh escaped her lips, and Blessing imagined what would happen if she refused to put the plate of groundnuts back on her head again, and instead began walking the long journey back to her village by foot. It would take days, and she didn't really know the way. She had no money, except the few coins she had managed to come by through selling this morning. And if by some miracle she actually managed to reach home, her parents would just send her right back here, convinced as all country people were that life would be better in every way in the city, and that whoever was caring for their children was doing so lovingly and responsibly. No one would believe a lowly girl-child.

"Cold water!" a boy of about five yelled beside her, and she winced. A wooden case of water bags and ice balanced on his head, steadied by his tiny arms.

"Water, yes!" a woman in an African suit yelled farther up the road.

The small boy grinned at her and then scampered toward her.

Blessing grimaced, then got her plate of groundnuts back on top of her head.

After about an hour she had passed the University of Liberia campus, and was maybe halfway to where she had picked up the groundnuts in the dark of morning, downtown. She had sold another ten packs by this time, which wasn't what she had hoped for, but wasn't bad either. As she passed onto Camp Johnson Road, the Ministry of Internal Affairs loomed large on her left. Taxis packed with civil servants heading into work sped past her, as did the huge jeeps and trucks of NGO workers. She turned a few times to see if anyone inside might be hailing her for groundnuts, but saw only clouds of exhaust. About twenty minutes later, she found herself staring at the back of the massive executive mansion just as a band of soldiers began crossing the lawn, toward the back doors. Their crouched, youthful bodies were tense and their guns gleamed surprisingly, as though they'd just been lovingly cleaned and polished.

The plate on top of Blessing's head fell to the ground, the sound of plastic on pavement clanging loud in her ears.

Garnahweh grimaced, signaling to the men behind him to flank left. Their sources on the inside said that Tolbert had worked late as usual and dragged himself into bed a few hours before. His security detail was playing draughts downstairs. Most of them were sympathetic to the struggle anyway and would support the rising new country even if they would not pull the trigger themselves. They knew it was time. Had known it was time for years now. The only thing left to do was commit the act once and for all, the violent sacrifice ushering in an unprecedented era of peace and prosperity for the real people who had built this country and suffered silently for it for generations: the indigenous. The only thing Garnahweh could do was become the man he was always meant to be.

He crept stealthily, hugging the edge of the hallway, ears attuned to every sound, every movement. Garnah-weh wiped the sweat from his eyes as they rounded the corner to the bedchamber. He shook his head; the miscreant hadn't even bothered to shut the door and lay sprawled across the bed, half dressed and snoring, his paunch hanging out from a too-short undershirt. The old man does not deserve to govern, *Garnahweh thought.* He cannot even manage his own body-menh.

As he tiptoed forward, Tolbert's figure came into focus. He was curled up in almost a fetal position, except his left leg was stretched out completely. Garnahweh wondered how a man—one of such power, particularly— could allow himself the luxury of such vulnerability. He wasn't a baby, after all, and sleeping in such a way only invited others to see his weakness. You could see it in the easy rise and fall of his chest, in the spittle that ran down his chin, that at some basic and primal level the man didn't believe the world held any real dangers for him. That his whole life—perhaps even before birth, when his mother carried him—he had known he was safe from any real harm. Garnahweh chuckled. This was the real danger of being a Congo man: You were fooled into believing you could cheat death. That you could sleep in your bed—the most powerful man in the whole of Liberia— and be utterly and completely shielded from harm. That no one would cut you down when you were defenseless. Garnahweh took two more steps until he was face-to-face with the man he imagined for months in his dreams, the barrel of his gun just touching the quivering left nostril. The eyes fluttered beneath the lids, and Garnahweh allowed himself to wonder for a moment if Tolbert was perhaps lost in some strange dreamworld of his own, or if some part of him knew that this was the moment of his undoing, his death. "Do it-menh!" the man behind him hissed. Garnahweh bit his lip, and as the blood rushed into his mouth, he pulled the trigger. He thought of his niece, Janjay, then of his family back in the village, and how they would one day sing songs of this moment, the moment when he found the strength to release them and their countrymen from their blinding, crushing poverty. The moment when their collective dream of a free and truly democratic country came into focus.

★

CHAPTER FORTY

EVELYN FILLED THE TEAPOT with water from the tap, then placed it on the stove top. No one could start their morning without tea and some small piece of bread with butter or jam. She hummed to herself while she grabbed two plastic cups from the shelf. The Old Ma would say that she shouldn't worry herself, that Poady, their small girl, would prepare breakfast for them. But Evelyn found that preparing the water, stirring the tea, cutting the bread, actually calmed her as she woke up and began her day. It was a ritual of sorts, one which had soothed her since she was a very young girl. And after last night's dreams, she needed soothing. At least this morning, unlike the last few, she was not overcome with nausea.

She saw a trio of mangoes on the counter and realized that Poady had already been to the market. Evelyn smiled and grabbed one to cut; the mango would be sweet with bread and tea. Poady was a good girl.

In a few moments breakfast was ready, and Evelyn placed it in the center of the kitchen table. She set a place for herself, a place for the Old Ma, and a place for Poady (even though she knew the Old Ma wouldn't approve; this was the new Liberia President Tolbert was inelegantly inching them toward, and it would require all of them to make adjustments). The teapot tooted as steam rose from the top. Evelyn had just turned off the burner and grabbed the pot when Poady burst through the doorway, breathless, clutching the *Observer*. Evelyn jumped and dropped the metal pot on the floor, sending scalding hot water all over.

"He dead! He dead!" Poady shouted, thrusting the paper and its big, lurid headline at her. MURDERED! It read. "They killed him in his sleep!"

Evelyn watched her arm slowly move across the expanse of water she had spilled on the floor to meet Poady's and take the dreadful paper. SOLDIERS ASSUME COMMAND; DOE SAYS COUP NECESSARY TO RESTORE ORDER, she read in the subheadline. Bile rose in her throat, and then the vomiting began.

CHAPTER FORTY-ONE

April 23, 1980, Monrovia, Liberia

"THE DREAMER ALWAYS PART of the dream-oh."

"Not this time-oh."

Once more he was in her bed, and she had wrapped him in her arms and her legs. Held his eyes with her own. Surrounded him with him inside her. So he would see that she was real and give up the dream. "It is not the only beautiful thing in the world," she whispered in his ear. The wind rattled the window she'd closed tightly and his eyes strayed. "Here." She brought his hand to her belly. "Here." They were naked but for Ujay's clasp lying between her breasts. "Here." She held her hand over his on her stomach, trying to make him know.

Again the wind rattled the glass, and this time the latch didn't hold. Suddenly there was so much shouting and the sound of gunfire and where was Ujay? Where was she? Where was the baby?

Beneath a coarse cotton cap, the young soldier watched the young woman in the purple skirt run across the road to where the melee between the protesters, drivers, and passengers was unfolding. The ruckus they were making grew louder with each passing moment, as more young people joined the fray. Even as the crowd of rioters grew, though, the young soldier found he couldn't take his eyes from the girl in purple. Yes, she was one of these new educated women who thought herself above the common man, a soldier with no prospects or reason. They, who thought themselves above the obligations of womanhood. Their selfishness and determination to be men would bring shame down on their family and community. It was even rumored that many of them weren't even women at all—that they didn't actually possess womanly parts. The soldier lowered his AK-47 from his shoulder and crouched down on one knee, following the progress of the melee through the front sight. When things started getting disorderly, the soldier found it helpful to examine whatever was happening through his front sight. It helped him focus. His gun, always impeccably cleaned and ready, gave a certain clarity to the world.

He saw a middle-aged man with a Bible beating a young man over the head with it. Looking down the barrel of the gun, he saw two young men pick up the stools that were blocking the road and throw them to the side. Smoke seemed to be everywhere, a hazy cloud spreading out faster than the eye could follow. The soldier saw small boys hawking water drop their cheap plastic bowls and pull out guns and clubs and pieces of cut glass to kill the Congo people. He saw the boys, years later, as men, marching in perfect formation to the national anthem. The soldier watched the bodies of his people—hundreds and thousands of dead country people—rise up out of the ground and salute him. Beside him, the sinewy, growing body of his young niece appeared suddenly, and she kissed him affectionately on the cheek. The soldier saw the young woman in the purple skirt insert herself between a taxi driver and a student screaming at each other, pleading with both of them. And then he saw the young woman falling sideways onto the ground, as if a powerful invisible force had plowed into her. The sound of the gunshot rang in his ears, and with a start he realized that his bullet had been that force.

Farther up the street, Ujay saw the students gathering and milling about, no doubt preparing whatever program they had in mind for the new purveyors of democracy in Liberia. The packed bus pulled to the side in order to let him and a few other passengers off in front of the executive mansion. Its ancient brakes exhaled in relief, as Ujay muscled through the arms and legs, torsos and heads blocking his way to the exit. It had been a long ride from West Point, with too many people and far too many stops. But it would be worth it, if only to see her.

He wiped his palms on his freshly ironed suit pants. They were always sweaty when he was nervous.

He quickened his pace and peered ahead. There was some kind of commotion going on, with plenty of angry shouting and moving, agitated bodies. He couldn't see what was happening exactly but could sense that it was rapidly getting out of hand. He broke into a slow jog, scanning the crowd for any sign of Evelyn. He knew that she would be there and wanted to surprise her. He hadn't liked the way their last conversation had ended on the phone, with her answering in that passive way she did when she had given up on someone. She was the last person he ever wanted to give up on him. Although he didn't like to admit it, he needed her too much for that.

Finally he saw her, once again the purple skirt that hugged her in all the right places—her hips, her thighs, her buttocks. She was trying to keep two young men from throwing punches at each other, her long outstretched arms the only thing between them. He was maybe two car lengths away from her when it happened: Something struck her, and she fell heavily to the ground. The two men she had been handling looked perplexed and were so shocked that they stopped yelling immediately and crouched down beside her. Ujay's stomach lurched, and he broke into a full sprint. *Evie. Evie. Evie. Evie. Evie. Evie.* Everything else inside his brain went blank, save that one simple word.

By the time he reached her, the blood had encircled

her completely, collecting into an ever-widening pool. Ujay's knees buckled beneath him, and he collapsed on top of her. He couldn't stop saying her name, but she never answered him.

★

CHAPTER FORTY-TWO

1998, Gomoa Buduburam Refugee Camp, Outside Accra, Ghana

THE NIGHT FELL COOL on Ujay's arms as he rocked his young son to sleep on the porch. The boy had just awakened from a nightmare, crying out for his father. Now that the boy was in his arms, Ujay knew it wouldn't be long before he succumbed again to the lure of sleep. This was his favorite part of being a father: the physical closeness between him and the child. The way it inexplicably, magically translated into emotional closeness. The boy nuzzled into his father's chest, sighing contentedly.

"Bad dream-oh?" Fanewu asked from the doorway of their tiny concrete house.

Ujay jumped. He had been so focused on Kollie, he hadn't even heard her come in the back from fetching water.

Fanewu put a thin, gentle hand on his arm. She was the sixth child in a large Loma family and had grown up in the village cooking, cleaning, caring for the children younger than she. In fact, caring for others was Fanewu's pride and joy. And besides that, she was seven years his junior and beautiful. She would have been the perfect wife, had he loved her.

"Oh," Ujay said. He snuggled the boy into his chest. "I thought you were going to do the wash-oh." The last thing he wanted to appear to be was a useless husband, only good for doing womanly things like rocking babies. But when it came down to it, that actually *was* all he and the other men at the Gomoa Buduburam Refugee Camp were good for. There was no work, and no prospects for work. They were all guests of the UNHCR and the Ghanaian government, until and if Liberia stopped unraveling from its civil war. As soon as things stabilized, Ujay was set to return with the family to Bigazi, in Lofa County, the place where he was born and the place he had decided they would call home. In the eighteen years since the coup, Ujay had gotten his masters in sociology and had begun to teach and write at the University of Liberia in Monrovia. But he no longer believed in the state's ability to educate the masses, the idea that had lit him up in his youth. No, if Liberia's slow descent into chaos had shown him anything, it was that education was no buffer to man's blind ambition for power. That, and the devastating limits of violence to bring about fundamental social change were the major lessons he carried with him on his exodus to Ghana. In the end, Evie had been right about everything.

Fanewu laughed, showing her brilliant white teeth.

With her hair plaited tightly against her scalp and her high, regal cheekbones she really was a beauty. "Angel going to wake up with night terrors any minute now too. You mind looking to her after you done with him, while I get the wash?"

Ujay grimaced. He knew she hadn't meant it that way at all, but her response felt like an affront to him. Like an insult. "Glad you finally found the time to keep us clean-oh," he sneered. "That mountain of dirty clothes in there about to run us out of this shack." As soon as the words were out of his mouth, he regretted them. He knew they were not fair, were cruel actually, given how hard Fanewu worked to keep the household afloat. In addition to all her housekeeping and family duties, she also sold small bags of water at a kiosk beside the house, to bring in the tiny little bit of money they did have. But somehow, Ujay simply could not help himself around his wife. It wasn't her fault they were stuck indefinitely in this godforsaken camp and country that didn't want them. Nor was it her fault that Liberia had been taken over by madmen who gleefully massacred thousands in the name of "freedom" and "democracy." And it certainly wasn't her fault that the love of his life had died in his arms, on a plain, dirty road in the capital. None of this was Fanewu's fault, yet he behaved as if it was. Ujay shook his head angrily, wishing he were another man—a man who could be the husband that Fanewu deserved.

Fanewu sighed.

She might have been trying to avoid a fight by not

responding to him, but her restraint drove him crazy. He wanted her to argue with him, and argue fiercely. He wanted her to denounce him, to recite the litany of things he had done to malign her, but she would not. She would never. Instead, she leaned over and took the boy from his arms—gently as ever—and kissed his head lovingly. "Little Kollie," she whispered. "You brought your father-ya. You resemble so much." She smiled at Ujay, and it was a peace offering, a way to let go of their mini-spat.

But he shivered in the night air, without the little bundle that had warmed his whole being only moments before. *Can't she see I want my son? Doesn't she know that he is the only thing that makes me feel alive here?* He fingered the trinket that they had pulled off Evie's cold, dead body. It had been in his family for generations, and he sometimes wondered how many now-dead fingers had once clasped it as he did now, what their dreams and sorrows had been, if they ever wondered, as he did, if they really had a country to call home.

"Good night," he said icily, signaling to her to leave him.

"Good night," she said softly, and walked back inside.

After a moment he went inside to comfort four-year-old Angel, who woke up every night from the same bad dream. Then he came back out on the porch and sat there for hours, watching the sun rise. Wondering if his own history was just a dream-loop folding back on itself over and over again, in endless variation and repetition, always in search of a place to rest.

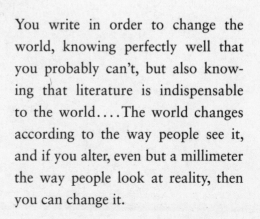

Part V:

Angel

Felicia

Kollie

Ujay

Fanewu

You write in order to change the world, knowing perfectly well that you probably can't, but also knowing that literature is indispensable to the world....The world changes according to the way people see it, and if you alter, even but a millimeter the way people look at reality, then you can change it.

—James Baldwin

★

CHAPTER FORTY-THREE

THE CLASP IS NOT here, around my neck.

It does not sit in the hollow of my clavicle. It never has. It has not been delicately handled and hidden and passed down through generations, an easy legacy that can be seen, held, and quantified. If there is a clasp to bind up all your hopes and dreams for the human spirit, I have never seen it. Not with my eyes open.

Yes, there were such trinkets in the colonial period and in the forced labor period and even in the heyday of the Tubman years and beyond. But I never saw any of them outside a museum case. I created the clasp in order to tell the story, nothing more.

Ten years on, Kollie—our black diamond—back but never actually really *here* the way he was before, the way we need him to be; Ma finally divorced from Papi, as she should have done years ago; and I still don't know. I don't know anything except this: The truth is fluid and fungible and untrustworthy and won't abide by any one telling. And sometimes, in inventing the truth, we can discover something deeper. We can find our place in the story, because that, at least, is one thing we can make for ourselves. A story. No matter how busted our family, how lost our history.

If you were me and your older brother had been exiled to a country he only remembered as a waking nightmare, and if he came back so changed and so silent and damaged that you could count on one hand the number of complete conversations you had with him in the years he's been back, you would have done the same. If words were the only tools at your disposal to make sense of a lineage in two countries that never seemed to align or intersect in ways that made you feel like anything but a perpetual foreigner in either place, you too would have spent the last three years trapped in a small room behind a computer screen, desperately punching out an invented history. You too would have dug up every scrap and half story that might or might not have basis in historical or family fact and carefully assembled it with other pieces and bits collected from your life, your research, or the collective unconscious, to create what one of my creative writing professors might call *a fictional canvas of fact*. You too would have shamelessly stolen most parts of your brother's story and thrown it on the page. You too would

have spent months in research libraries and on data-
bases, gathering every article and every book you could
get your hands on that detailed the colonial experience
for those first African American settlers in Liberia. You
would have even flown to Monrovia, hired a car to drive
you to Grand Bassa County, and walked on your own
two feet to interview the few men still alive who had lived
through the horrors of forced labor in the 1920s and
somehow survived with their families and dignity mostly
intact. And you would have dragged your reluctant but
supportive black American girlfriend along with you, because without her, you weren't sure you'd ever find your
way back. Instead of years of therapy, you would find
solace and comfort, and most of all meaning, in a manu-
factured family narrative. More than that: an invented
national narrative spanning two continents, one ocean,
and so many forgotten bodies. I decided to make whole
in story what, in point of fact, will always be broken in
reality. Wholeness and story can be a *choice*. It can be
decided upon; it can be conjured into being. It can be as
tough as an old pair of hand-me-down boots and as sweet
as a stolen mango. It can shimmer like a Friday-night-on-
the-town dress. If one doesn't have a coherent and unified
country or family or story to call home, one may simply
grab the facts she can and dream them up. What are facts
if not the soil from which our dreams grow?

———

If you insist on The Facts alone, however (in the conventional sense in which I know you mean the word), what I will tell you is this: Kollie lives in Des Moines, Iowa, now and works as an insurance adjuster. After he returned from those five miserable years in Liberia, he went off to college at the University of South Dakota. He did very well there. He even played soccer. So, from my parents' point of view, sending him away was right and justified. From my point of view, and Kollie's, however (although we have never talked about it), it was an unmitigated disaster. (The story you were expecting after Papi left Kollie at the airport? Whatever it was you imagined? It happened too. If not to Kollie, then to someone else.) He wrote me while he was there, begging me for money, to find a way to get him back home, to appeal to the Old Ma and Papi to buy him a ticket back. He wrote that the relatives there were not feeding him regularly—not because they didn't want to, but because like most other Liberians, they simply didn't have the money. He said he had no clothes that were not old and ripped, and that he had to walk more than three miles every day to get to school. I still have the letter where he tried to explain how the other students treated him, gleefully bullying the strange and uppity American kid. *They call me fucking "White Boy" here, Sis. White Boy! Me, darker than most of them, me, child of Bigazi. They gather round me in a circle if I'm not paying attention or if I'm not quick enough, and beat on me to try to give them American dollars that I don't have.*

I got into so many fights with my parents during this time, screaming at them over and over again about how they had abandoned their son, that he would die there, that they would never forgive themselves. At first, they tried to reason with me and explained quietly why this was the best thing for everyone involved, until, at last, they just shrugged me off and would only say in a very tired voice, "He will be back." Once, during a particularly bad fight, my father told me: "He can be mad-menh. He can even hate us-oh. But he will be alive."

When Kollie was almost twenty-two, they brought him back. He was bigger, bulkier, talked even less than he did as a teenager, and mostly wanted nothing to do with me, my parents, or our entire extended Liberian family. His anger was palpable, as was his grief, and with everything he'd been through, I felt compelled to respect them both. My parents just kept saying—still keep saying—"It will take time for him to adjust-oh. Give him time and space." To which I wanted to respond, "Why would he want to readjust to the two of you? To our fucked-up family?" But I don't.

"Time and space." I have traveled both now in these pages. I have found many things, but nothing like peace, nothing like rest for bone-deep weariness.

Other facts that may be of interest to you: My father tells half stories of his great-grandfather Togar once in a while.

He occasionally drops scraps about Giakpee, the small but prosperous village in Grand Bassa County, where this Togar was apparently a person of some significance in his time. Papi has said nothing about him working on the Congo people's plantations—that was a historical phenomenon I stumbled upon in my research and found appalling. Of course, Liberians don't really talk about it—so much of their (or is it "our"? I never know) history is not written anyway. And the last thing people who have experienced trauma want is to relive it over and over again by narrating it. I found two older gentlemen who had some experience on Congo plantations and building roads and such who would talk to me a little bit about it while I was in country two years ago, but honestly, they couldn't tell me that much. Or maybe it was also that I couldn't *hear* that much of what they were saying, my Liberian English has fallen off so.

Do I have relatives who immigrated to Liberia in the colonial period and helped build the country and colony? Who became "Congo People"? Who went from being niggers fearing the lash to white people wielding it? Maybe. Probably. I don't know. Certainly no one in our family has stories from that far back. But I was thinking, *imagining* what it must have been like for those African Americans who dreamed of true freedom and equality, and who thought that they might actually get it from making a new life in Liberia. How the United States abandoned them (or is it us?) so many times throughout history, and so how, of course, they would be eager to believe any kind of fiction an organization like the American Colonization Society would feed them about starting new and being champions of their own destinies. How they ended up reproducing in many ways, the unjust and violent conditions they were fleeing in America—this time on someone else, the indigenous. How we Liberians—both indigenous and Americo-Liberians—have never really reconciled that. How *I* have never really reconciled that. And how that might be something for me to think about, as I am eight months away from marrying an African American and the love of my life.

There is no closure in this story. No circle. Only an ever-turning spiral—characters, themes, and questions folding in on themselves over and over again. Time passes, oceans are crossed; circumstances change, or they do not. One continent is exchanged for another, but still the spiral does not become a circle. No, spirals rise and they fall. Sometimes it's hard to know which.

And yes, you read that right. A wedding. Evidently I've placed my bet on rising.

My mother will talk to me a little bit about Felicia, will acknowledge that we live together, and plan to make a life together. She has even helped me plan some elements of the wedding and service. *It fit you so fine-oh*, the Old Ma, Fanewu, said when I first tried on the dress Felicia and I eventually chose for the wedding. Even now, if I close my eyes, I can feel my mother's damp palm on the small of my back, tugging on the zipper gently, smoothing an imperceptible wrinkle. Her fingers tidying, fussing, and quietly loving the body of the daughter she'd carried to a moment she never dreamed of. *And Felicia will love you in this*, she said softly, and I could see the incipient smile she was trying to hide. The joy that not even her sterile blue scrubs could blunt. Her hand finally moving to grab mine while we looked at me, all white and regal, in the dress shop's huge mirror, big enough for both of us. *My beautiful daughter. Now a beautiful bride.*

I am twenty-six years old and only in these last few years have I finally come to something resembling an appreciation of my black-African-queer-woman's body. I have seen it—in mirrors, in other people's eyes, in this book—as a site of so many painful battles for myself and for my mother. And yet our bodies endure. More than that: They possess reserves of tenderness I didn't think possible until that mirror showed me a flash of it.

Our bodies enclose the twisted threads of history— passed flesh to flesh, from parent to child, conqueror to conquered, lover to beloved.

But my father . . . I wonder if he will ever come around. And I don't know—Felicia would kill me if she heard me say this—but maybe he has endured enough forced journeys on this spiral that it is unreasonable for me to expect him to take the turn that brings him face-to-face with his daughter's love of a woman. All I know is my father is my father, he has always been opaque to me and probably always will be. We have never really understood each other. He wanted me to be a nurse and would not pay for my undergraduate degree in English. He still says I will never be able to make it as a writer, even though I got a full ride to graduate school, and several publishers have expressed interest in this manuscript. (And honestly I haven't decided if I'm going to publish it yet—which drives both Felicia and my agent crazy—but it's not their decision to make. I didn't write it to get it published. I wrote it as a conjuring act. I am a magician, and my spells are words. They are not coins or even pages for other eyes to consume.)

Sociological tracts and books litter my father's bedroom, close at hand for him, but hidden away from his few visitors. In Liberia, he had a master's degree in sociology. But, though he is no stranger to hard, humbling work, he will not make the effort to re-earn the degree here. I feel like some part of him gave up and died in the process of leaving the refugee camps of Ghana and coming here. Like there was some vivacious, challenging, energetic part of him that Kollie and I never got. Because all that ended with the war and the violence the coup unleashed. That's why I invented Evelyn. Because all my life, I have imagined in some shadowy part of my mind and heart that my father lost someone close to him, someone he loved deeply, and in doing so, lost his own dream too. Which is why he is so intent on the rest of us letting go of ours before they really start. At least now I know that he believes these losses are a kindness.

This room has that peculiar quality of two-in-the-morning-with-only-a-laptop-screen-for-illumination darkness that I've come to know very well. It has been too long now, so many hours I have sat here with you, typing, drawing the magic thread of story from one fragment of fact to the next. Trying to bring them all—all my people—here, into this basic studio apartment with peach walls and scarred wood floors. Trying to see the whole spiral at once. So many days, so many months. Years even.

On the other side of the room, Felicia snores softly, sleeping lightly as she always does on these nights when I can't sleep and must write. Her chest rises and falls underneath the down comforter Papi gave me for college, her body forming an expectant hollow for mine. Though it is hard leaving her to follow the path of the spiral, she encourages me. She came to this city from Chicago for school. "I stayed in the frigid Great White North for your crazy ass," she has said more than a few times. When this work leads me to despair and discouragement, I ask her to tell me about when she was a kid on the South Side, before she knew me. This is already a well-worn ritual in our still-young relationship, and she quickly obliges me with a story of the barber who gave her fades and made her look fly, cutting late at night or early in the morning so her mama wouldn't stop her from tending to her maleness, and she could avoid the kids on the block who'd call her a dyke. Or, she will cajole me with a story of Uncle Nene, who told all the mamas and the papas he was taking the children to Bible study, when they ended up at Wilson's Stop 'N Shop or the playground half the time.

"Why would you ever leave such a place to come here?" I ask. And her answer always brings me around again.

I am smiling now, my reader, my friend, as I close this file. I am done, weary after all the near misses and endless longing to be so much more than we are now, to be further around these relentless turns toward freedom. I too want a moment's peace and quiet. But I am not resigned. I am not apathetic. I am not finished. No, I am in love. Undaunted and in love. Sliding in beside her, I slip my arm around the doughy center of her stomach, and she squeezes me, now us, back. I giggle into her neck, and she sighs in her sleep. I wish you could see us.

—*Angel Yasmine Flomo*
September 3, 2018
Powderhorn Park, Minneapolis

AUTHOR'S NOTE

When I stepped into the Gomoa Buduburam Refugee Camp just outside of Accra, Ghana, in 1998, I had no idea that it would change the trajectory of both my life and my writing. I was twenty-three years old, on a year-long research fellowship in West Africa, searching out connections between African Americans and continental Africans. The knowledge and history I stumbled onto talking to the Liberian refugees at Gomoa Buduburam would haunt me for years to come, and later compel me to struggle through the many drafts, voices, and narrative threads that finally became *Dream Country*.

The first thread I picked up was simple enough. I was befuddled when I saw what I thought was the American flag strung up on a pole in the middle of the makeshift camp. "No, that's our flag," my steadfast hosts informed me. "The flag of Liberia." When I began to argue with them, they told me to look closer and then asked me why I had never heard the history of their country.

They wanted to know why *I* didn't know that Liberia had been colonized by "your own people," freed American slaves. I remember a feeling of pressure in my skull at this revelation, which I still fought them on, impossible to my steeped-in-mainstream-American-narratives brain as it was. I truly could not fathom how it was that I had missed this story completely, as central as it was to the ongoing African–African American encounter. That it was also a quintessentially American story of reinvention, re-creation, and colonization did not escape me either.

What did it mean that African Americans who had known bondage set out to fashion a more perfect union across the sea, not where they had come from, but where their ancestors had called home? How had they managed to shape a country with the indigenous who already lived there? And how and why had it all fallen apart so completely? How was Liberia, the dream of those formerly enslaved people and the land that native Africans had loved and nurtured for generations, ruined by the spilt blood of its people, a country cleaved and utterly broken by civil war?

I sat down with a woman who told me she had given birth to three children, although she only carried the smallest, her baby, on her back. The rebels had killed the other two, after they raped her and burned down her house. Then they went next door, raped her mother, killed her father, and burned down their house too. I did not know what to do with the numbness I felt while hearing this story, the way the woman who told it both recalled it as banal fact and then recoiled in horror at the memory.

When I returned to the States from my trip, I searched out every piece of information I could find about Liberia—in books, articles, and people. I was incredulous and dismayed to discover that, for the most part, the freed blacks who came to Liberia in the nineteenth century re-created the very conditions of oppression they fled in America. Indeed, these "Americo-Liberians" as they came to be called by some, and "Congo people" by others, really did create a *colony* in Liberia, in every sense of the word. The government they established recognized their class as citizens at the expense of the indigenous Africans on whose land they settled, and funneled almost all of the resources of the interior to the capital. In this way, 95 percent of Liberia languished for generations, fomenting the resentment that catalyzed the violent uprisings and coup of 1980. I could not understand how people who by all indications *should* have known better, *didn't*. The role of the American Colonization Society as the anti-black colonization vehicle in all of this certainly complicated matters, as did European and American imperial meddling on the continent throughout the late-nineteenth and twentieth centuries, but those facts didn't absolve Americo-Liberians for their role in more than 130 years of indigenous domination.

For years I struggled with the relationship of those black American settlers to the indigenous Africans they oppressed in Liberia. How might I explore it in fiction? Did I even have the writing chops to do so? More important, did I have *the right* to represent this subject matter in a novel, given my black Americanness? In the meantime, I wrote a whole other book, called *See No Color,* that began to address my own complicated place in the context of American blackness. The fact is, however, that some stories you choose, and others choose you. *Dream Country* was surely the latter—it wouldn't let me go, hard as I tried. So, in 2008, ten years after my first trip to West Africa, I decided to return. This time I would venture to Liberia and interview everyday people, politicians, community leaders, professors, and everyone in between about the run up to the 1980 coup that plunged the country into its disastrous fifteen-year civil war.

A young Liberian college student I met in Monrovia introduced me to numerous contacts while I was there, and helped me navigate the nation's institutions and broken infrastructure. And in so doing, we also fell in love. Eventually we had kids, married, and later divorced. Our children, Boisey and Marwein, embody all the promise and contradictions of their shared black American–Liberian heritage, growing up here in America but part-time in their dad's house, which is distinctly Liberian. So *Dream Country* is for them, so that they may see their cross-cultural identities as enmeshed in the larger, ongoing, spiraling history of the African–African American encounter. And so that they may come to see that in many important ways, the African American story cannot be told without also telling the Liberian one. And that, in key ways, Liberians are forever connected to African Americans, for better and worse.

Dream Country is for all those Liberian and Somali boys in Minnesota and elsewhere, who, like Kollie, get "sent back home," because their immigrant parents believe this to be the only way to save their lives in an educational system that at best cannot accommodate them, at worst destroys them. It is for all those disaffected, forgotten, powerful young men whose stories have not yet been told. And for those like Angel, who love them, but don't know what to do.

Dream Country is for all those on the continent and in the diaspora who feel they have no home, due to the relentless violence of colonialism and enduring systems of white supremacy. It is for women of African descent who still, to this day, are not fully seen, included, or valued in their families or communities as the black diamonds they are. It is for anyone anywhere who has tried to make themselves whole through small pieces of a larger story they could cobble together. It is for everything we have forgotten, and what we dream.

—Shannon Gibney
Minneapolis, Minnesota 2018

SELECTED FURTHER READING

Clegg, Claude Andrew. *The Price of Liberty: African Americans and the Making of Liberia*. Chapel Hill: University of North Carolina Press, 2004.

Cooper, Helene. *The House at Sugar Beach: In Search of a Lost African Childhood*. New York: Simon & Schuster, 2009.

Gbowee, Leymah. *Mighty Be Our Powers: How Sisterhood, Prayer, and Sex Changed a Nation at War*. New York: Beast Books, 2011.

Hartman, Saidiya V. *Lose Your Mother: A Journey Along the Atlantic Slave Route*. New York: Farrar, Straus and Giroux, 2007.

Johnson, Charles Spurgeon. *Bitter Canaan: The Story of the Negro Republic*. New Brunswick, NJ: Transaction Publishers, 1987.

Shaw, Elma. *Redemption Road: The Quest for Peace and Justice in Liberia*. Monrovia: Cotton Tree Press, 2008.

Walker, David, and Peter P. Hinks. *David Walker's Appeal to the Coloured Citizens of the World*. University Park: Pennsylvania State Univ. Press, 2000.

Wiley, Bell Irvin, ed. *Slaves No More: Letters from Liberia, 1833–1869*. Lexington: University Press of Kentucky, 1980.

Wilkerson, Isabel. *The Warmth of Other Suns: The Story of America's Epic Migration*. New York: Vintage Books, 2011.

SELECTED VIDEO

Firestone and the Warlord. PBS Frontline, 2014.

Liberia: America's Stepchild. Grain Coast Productions, 2002.

Pray the Devil Back to Hell. Balcony Releasing, 2008.

A SELECTED TIMELINE OF
MAJOR EVENTS IN LIBERIAN HISTORY

1816—The American Colonization Society (ACS) is founded in Washington D.C. Present at the founding meeting are future presidents James Monroe and Andrew Jackson, *The Star-Spangled Banner* author Francis Scott Key, two future secretaries of state, and the nephew of President George Washington.

1822—The ACS works with freed slaves and free blacks to organize their return to Africa. After landing in Cape Mesurado, the initial group of colonists names their first settlement Monrovia, in honor of President James Monroe.

1824—Colonists decide to call their new country Liberia.

1847—Using the United States Constitution as a model, colonists create a constitution for Liberia, thus making it the only independent state on the African continent at the time. More than ten thousand colonists reside there.

1897–1930—Known as "the Forced Labor Period," this era in Liberia is marked by government officials colluding with the military and American and European business interests to recruit indigenous "boys" for labor—by any means necessary. Many of these de facto slaves are sent to plantations on Fernando Pó, the European name for Bioko, an island off the coast of West Africa.

1971—William Tolbert, Jr., becomes president of Liberia, after the death of President William Tubman. Like every other Liberian president up to this time, he is Americo-Liberian, or a descendant of the colonists.

1980—Following a year of protests by various activists and political groups, Tolbert is assassinated during a military coup organized by Master Sergeant Samuel Doe. Only four members of Tolbert's cabinet escape execution in the days that follow. Doe's faction suspends the constitution and assumes control.

1985—Mired in allegations of voter fraud, Doe wins the presidential election.

1989—Charles Taylor and the National Patriotic Front of Liberia (NPFL) start rebellions that further destabilize the country and lead to civil war.

1989–1996—The First Liberian Civil War, in which more than 200,000 Liberians lose their lives and more than a million others become refugees. The war is notable for the involvement of child soldiers, many of whom are led by the notorious warlord, Joshua Milton Blahyi, known as General Butt Naked.

1990—The United Nations High Commission on Refugees opens the Gomoa Buduburam Refugee Camp, near Accra, Ghana. More than twelve thousand Liberian refugees seek safety there.

1997—In a climate of widespread voter intimidation, Charles Taylor is elected president.

1999–2003—The Second Liberian Civil War, in which rebel groups attempt to overthrow Charles Taylor's government. More than 250,000 are killed between both civil wars.

2006—Ellen Johnson Sirleaf, one of the four who survived the Tolbert coup in 1986, is elected president of Liberia and begins the long and ongoing process of rebuilding the postwar nation. She is the first woman president in Africa.

2017—George Weah is elected president. It is the first democratic transfer of power in Liberia since 1944.

ACKNOWLEDGMENTS

Although writing is an activity that takes place in a solitary room with a solitary human, the truth is that all novels are the collective work of many individuals, institutions, communities, and resources, over many years. *Dream Country* is not only not exceptional in this way, but is actually an outlier in that it took the extraordinary effort and support of numerous people and organizations, over a period of twenty years to bring it to fruition. This is no small feat, and I am so grateful to everyone for their contributions.

To Carnegie Mellon University, and the Alumni Study/ Travel Award stewards who saw fit to give a wide-eyed twenty-two-year-old graduate a fellowship to travel to Ghana for a year to study relationships between continental Africans and African Americans and write short stories on this very broad topic so many years ago, thank you. The seeds of that journey are what grew into this book.

Thanks also to the McKnight Foundation and the Loft Literary Center, whose generous funding made possible the time and space needed to complete key portions of the manuscript.

To my parents, Jim and Sue Gibney, who stood behind me and helped me plan and execute every trip and process every return, and who have never faltered in their support of their daughter's strange writing vocation and wanderlust, your constancy and love are the rock that has always steadied me.

Candid interviews with Samuel Brown in South

Dakota and Clarence Nah in Monrovia gave me a deeper understanding of the experiences—and therefore the psychology—of young men like Kollie. Thank you for the immense gift of trusting me with your stories.

Books, including Claude Clegg's *The Price of Liberty: African Americans and the Making of Liberia*; Bell Irvin Wiley's *Slaves No More: Letters from Liberia, 1833–1869*; and Charles Johnson's *Bitter Canaan: The Story of the Negro Republic*, provided essential historical background for the second, third, and fourth parts of the novel.

Sensitivity readers Joy Dolo Anfinson and Nyemadi Dunbar offered much needed objective eyes to the manuscript at a key time in its development. Thank you so much.

Thanks also to Jon and Megan for being an exceptional uncle and aunt to my children, so I could work.

Thanks to my badass agent, Tina Dubois, for fighting for me and the manuscript. You have made me a believer in the odd world of agents—something I never thought I'd be able to say.

Thanks to everyone at Dutton and Penguin Young Readers—Julie Strauss-Gabel, Anna Booth, Melissa Faulner, Natalie Vielkind, Anne Heausler, Rosanne Lauer, Katie Quinn, Lindsey Andrews, Kelley Brady, and Deborah Kaplan—for being so amazing and invested in *Dream Country*, from impeccable copyediting, to visionary designing, and everything in between.

Thank you to Edel Rodriguez for his transcendent jacket illustration.

Thank you to Chaun Webster for creating a brilliant discussion guide.

Thanks to Bobbi Chase Wilding, Dagny Hanner, and Karen Hausdoerffer, for hanging in there with me all this time, and to the V-Vault Ladies Taiyon Coleman, Kathleen DeVore, Shalini Gupta, and Valerie Deus for getting me through a very rocky two years.

Greta Palm, Lori Young-Williams, Bao Phi, Sun Yung Shin, Juliana Hu Pegues, Sarah Park Dahlen, Ben Gibney, and so many others, know how much I appreciate how you hold me up when it's called for, and throw down when necessary.

Boisey and Marwein, you didn't have a choice, but all the time you gave up with Mama for this manuscript meant so much, and will one day be paid back in full. I promise.

Andrew Karre, we have done it once again: Created a book out of thin air, it seems. Your care, professionalism, vision, and commitment to excellence pulled the best version of *Dream Country* possible from my consciousness, into the editorial process, and now into the world. I could not imagine a better editor. Thank you, a million times, thank you.

DREAM COUNTRY DISCUSSION GUIDE

Ruptures

"For me, the rupture was the story."
—Saidiya Hartman, *Lose Your Mother:
A Journey Along the Atlantic Slave Route*

*"Then he came back out on the porch and sat there for hours,
watching the sun rise. Wondering if his own history was just a
dream-loop folding back on itself over and over again, in endless
variation and repetition, always in search of a place to rest."*
—Dream Country (page 321)

**Dream Country weaves together several stories and repeatedly
confronts the trauma of enslavement, colonialism, and war on two
continents. The resulting narrative tapestry is not linear and is frequently and violently ruptured. In many ways, the author refuses to
allow the story "a place to rest," perhaps due in part to how these
difficult historical traumas lay right beneath the surface for Kollie
and Ujay, Fanewu and Angel, Eddie and Clark.**

1. In what ways does the author "rupture" the story and attempt to
   recover histories in this book?

2. From the beginning of the book, we see various examples of
   a hostility living right beneath the surface of almost every
   interaction between African Americans and Liberians. Discuss
   what reasons you see for this.

3. Education comes up often in this novel, both as a primary
   instrument for carving the way "out" of global second-class
   citizenship and also as a site of violence. How is education
   experienced by Angel? Kollie? Clark?

4. There is a very difficult scene in the book's beginning where Kollie
   witnesses the school security guard, Eddie, assault Clark. In that

moment, Kollie feels stuck and unable to interrupt the violence. After Eddie leaves Clark, Kollie attempts to comfort him but fails, and Clark, in a fragile state, threatens Kollie, demanding that he never say anything about the incident. Discuss what connections these kinds of violent experiences have to silence. Why do you think, in this moment, Kollie and Clark were unable to find a way to be tender with and comfort each other? Do you see parallel moments elsewhere in the book in other places and times?

5. Throughout *Dream Country*, Ujay is hardened to Fanewu, Angel, and Kollie. Why do you think this family was so distant from one another?

6. Part III tells the story of Yasmine Wright and her family, beginning on an early nineteenth-century plantation in Virginia. Yasmine, like many enslaved, formerly enslaved, and other "free" black people in North America, looks for a better life for herself and her children, one where they will not always have to go through the back door. Describe the role that the American Colonization Society (ACS) played in many African Americans departure to "settle" Liberia. How did this create a rupture between African Americans and indigenous Liberians and reproduce the master-and-enslaved that the Wrights fled in Virginia?

7. Yasmine begins Part III as an unambiguously black woman, but by the end of her story, Lani, Yasmine's youngest child, is described by an indigenous Liberian as an "unabashedly sweet white woman." Discuss how the book presents "whiteness" and "blackness." What causes a person to be perceived as "white" or "black" in each of the sections?

8. Discuss the American Colonization Society's interpretation and practice of Christianity. Did this interpretation view the indigenous people of what would be Liberia as fully human? Did Yasmine adopt the same view of Liberians? How does Yasmine's character develop in her view of the indigenous people of Liberia in practice over time?

Dreams

"We are the ones on the plantation speaking and singing to each other in code, to let others know our intent—such art and artfulness precede what sets us free, and more often than not, are the code by which that freedom is achieved. If we cannot first imagine freedom, we cannot achieve it. Freedom, like fiction and all art, is a process in which the dream of freedom is only the first part."
—*Kevin Young*, The Grey Album:
On the Blackness of Blackness

"…I have imagined in some shadowy part of my mind and heart that my father lost someone close to him, someone he loved deeply, and in doing so, lost his own dream too. Which is why he is so intent on the rest of us letting go of ours before they really start. At least now I know that he believes these losses are a kindness."
—Dream Country (pages 333–335)

This novel is aptly titled *Dream Country*, as it is a mosaic of stories highlighting self-recreation and intense longing for elsewhere. This elsewhere is an imagined territory—a dream—that is sometimes spoken of, other times kept hidden away, safe from war or the auction block. Wherever the dream lives, the fact remains: "if we cannot first imagine freedom, we cannot achieve it."

1. Take a moment to think about the various hope and dreams parents in this novel have for their children. Discuss the ways these worked out or didn't and why.

2. *Dream Country* moves backward and forward again and again. Why do you think the author chose to structure the novel in this way?

3. In Part II of the book, Togar remembers in a dream his young wife explaining why she left the home she loved to live with him in his village: *"Because it is not the only beautiful thing in the world, my husband."* This line is implicitly echoed again by

Felicia, Angel's fiancée, when she answers Angel's question about why she left Chicago. Discuss the ways that dreams of love help characters throughout the book overcome, if only momentarily, the ruptures in their lives.

4. At the end of the book, Angel writes about her father, saying that she believed "he lost someone close to him, someone he loved deeply, and in doing so lost his own dream too. Which is why he is so intent on the rest of us letting go of ours before they really start." Discuss how the dashed dreams of parents can become unfair expectations or imposed life-paths for their children.

5. The book's title is *Dream Country*, and the characters in the novel cling to imagined or dreamlike territories in their minds: Yasmine of an Africa free of the ghosts of slavery, Ujay of a liberated Liberia and then later of any place free of all the terrors of the Liberian civil war, Kollie of his club in the suburbs. In what ways do these imagined territories weave together? In what ways do they collide?

6. Angel, at the end of the novel, seems to be the fulfillment of many of the various dreams. In the closing paragraphs she speaks of how "Our bodies enclose the twisted threads of history—passed flesh to flesh, from parent to child, conqueror to conquered, love to beloved." Discuss the twisted threads in this book's five generations. How do they come to culminate in Angel?

DREAM COUNTRIES: A CONVERSATION

Andrew Karre © 2018

Shannon Gibney (left) and Kao Kalia Yang, November 2018

The following is an excerpt of a conversation between Shannon Gibney and Kao Kalia Yang. Yang is a teacher, activist, speaker, and author of two award-winning memoirs, *The Latehomecomer* and *The Song Poet*. She's also author of *A Map Into the World*, a book for young readers. Yang's work addresses her experiences as a refugee and immigrant and the experiences of the Hmong diaspora, since Hmong people began arriving in the United States in the late 1970s. Gibney and Yang spoke on November 2, 2018, at a café near the site of the Swede Hollow neighborhood of St. Paul, Minnesota. Founded by Swedish immigrants in the mid-nineteenth century on what was historically Dakota and Ojibwa land before Minnesota became a state, Swede Hollow was home to successive waves of immigrants from Sweden, Poland, Italy, and Mexico until 1956, when the city forcibly removed the remaining residents and burned all the homes to the ground.

The Page Is a Dream Country

KAO KALIA YANG: The heart of all your work is this question you ask very beautifully in the Angel section of *Dream Country*: "If one doesn't have a coherent and unified country or family or story to call home, one may simply grab the facts she can and dream them up. What are facts if not the soil from which our dreams grow?" Where is your dream country? Where is the place where Shannon Gibney is a citizen unquestionably?

SHANNON GIBNEY: I think my dream country is someplace where I can just be. Where there's no foreground or background that I have to answer for and to, and there are no breaks or cracks that I have to account for, I guess. I think that my whole experience of being a mixed black, transracially adopted woman artist in America has felt like this exercise having to justify my experience. First, I have to understand it, right? But then also to justify why I'm not black enough to the black kids or why I'm bringing up these annoying race issues in the context of my white family and white social spaces. I think that is part of the reason why I was drawn to the story *Dream Country* investigates, the stories of these African-descended folks crisscrossing the Atlantic in the context of this brutal regime of white supremacy and kind of connecting but not really connecting. Because that's been my experience.

One of my best friends read the book—someone I've known since I was six—and she started crying when she was talking to me about it. She mentioned the Saidiya Hartman epigraph ["For me, the rupture was the story."] and my friend told me "for me, that's the through line of all your work—*Dream Country* and *See No Color*. The ruptures are the places that define who you are."

KKY: These are themes of your life and they're going to be the themes of your work. But what I find so interesting about your response to the question about your dream country is that it is a present space, divorced from the before and the after, and for me, as a writer, such a space is of course the page. But you use the white, blank space of the page to go into these big problems of the world—the things that you don't want to have to justify—and yet you meet them on the page. You and I both know there are writers in the world who do use that same space to dream, to imagine freely. To escape. But you, in the guise of fiction—in that vehicle, that ship—sail into rocky waters.

SG: I feel like I was born in rocky waters.

KKY: I think you were.

SG: And you're writing similarly, right?

KKY: Right. Not to escape.

SG: You can't escape.

KKY: But escape should be tempting. Is it tempting? In your heart, is there a space, a time, a place where you imagine you can write divorced from this present reality, the reality of the world you were born into?

SG: No.

KKY: You don't ever want to write about the leaves shimmering in the autumn sun?

SG: That is a truth, right? My characters will experience the leaves shimmering in the autumn sun, but that's going to be in the context of this larger world we live in, always.

KKY: There are so many characters in *Dream Country*. Is there one who has truly released him or herself? No. Nobody escapes. Every single one of your characters from the most minor—like the girl with groundnuts—to Kollie. Nobody escapes.

SG: No.

KKY: And I have to ask you, because I'm asking myself: why don't we ever escape? We who go on the page that is open, where there is no requirement that we justify. And yet.

SG: I think this gets down to the question of why people write. We've talked in the past about our experiences in graduate school, but one of the reasons why I had such a rough time was because I assumed—

KKY: We both did.

SG: —that my fellow writers came to writing for the same reason I did. And it's not true. People write for very different reasons. For me writing has always been a place—the page has always been a place—where I can see where I've been, I can see what I think, what I believe. A lot of times I don't know what I think about an issue until I start writing about it. But also, the writing that I've always responded to—James Baldwin, who I've loved since I was sixteen—

KKY: Because he's so damn smart! Because he whips every white person who attempts to attack him.

SG: *Yes!* He doesn't look away. It's like that Nikki Finney quote: "My job as a poet is to not look away." There's a freedom in embracing the way things are. There's a freedom in no exit, in acknowledging that this is how it is. So what do we do with that? What I'm arguing is that admitting there's no escape through artistic practice, *that's* the true freedom. Because we can sit and linger and really dig into what that means. My dharma teacher has this phrase, "the problem with the mind is we get trapped by what we know."

KKY: Do you feel safe on the page?

SG: Yes. That's what I'm trying to say. That's freedom for me.

KKY: It is Angel's dream country, the page. You make her a writer. You position her in Powderhorn Park, and I'm thinking, "Shannon knows that neighborhood. Shannon is a writer. Shannon spent all these hours." If the page is our dream country, if above and beyond our citizenships in America or Liberia or Thailand or Laos, we are citizens of the page . . . You and I talk about the responsibility we feel to encounter reality in our work—

SG: Yes.

KKY: And so what would be the most beautiful dream? Of this place,

America? If our dreams are an encounter with reality, and our reality is Donald Trump's America, with everything that's happening at the border with children and families—all the legislation. . . . Are we living in a nightmare? In your nightmare, in my nightmare?

SG: Yes. And at the same time, we've been here before. And that's also part of the project of *Dream Country*: to show that these layers of history—as Angel says at the end—are a spiral. And so this whole thing about the menace of the freed black population in Yasmine's section, this thing that the American Colonization Society members—these white, slave-owning elites—are articulating in front of Yasmine? The language might sound different than it does now, but it comes from the same impulse, from the same concern with objectifying black, brown, and indigenous bodies. Concern about capital over humanity. Concern about the flow of bodies across borders. That's a quintessentially American experience, what happens to Yasmine. And now that *Dream Country* is out in the world, the Yasmine section has been the section that's moved the most people and disturbed the most people. People are deeply troubled by that section, and think that's because it is a layered, complicated, and nevertheless devastating critique of the American project, which is what we're living through right now.

KKY: Which is white supremacy realized. You make Yasmine—a sympathetic black woman—into a white plantation owner by the end of that section. You turn her into that slapping hand we all recoil from.

SG: It's horrifying.

KKY: It is, but it's completely believable. This is what happens. The reality you present is a very dim one, my dear. You show us we've been here before.

SG: But there are people throughout history who recognize that every moment is an opportunity, and as human beings we're always in process. I feel like what your question is getting at is, does it have to be this way? No. Angel says no and I say no. It does not have to be this way. But this book and the work you're doing and I'm doing and other writers are doing to use the imaginative dream country and not look away, that is the only thing that can really save us.

KKY: How many generations does it take?

SG: I don't know.

KKY: You and I are writing down these histories—hundreds of years of histories, unwritten, neglected. My little brother Maxwell has this line, "We're like the empty spaces in a sentence. To be a Hmong boy is to be an empty space." Hmong boys like Max need us to make sense of the world, but there's nothing to read. I think this is also true in many ways of the African American space. How have we been cared for in the dream countries of other people's imaginations?

Does It Take a Woman?

KKY: This is a selfish question (but it also isn't): does it take a woman?

SG: [Laughs.]

KKY: Angel's a good character but I didn't think the book was going to end with her. It was Kollie's story. He's the one who is physically sent back to Liberia. But we don't come back to him. You do a writerly trick. Why? Does it take a woman?

SG: I think the book, insofar as it's a critique of white supremacy and racism, I hope that people also see that it's a critique of patriarchy and conventional gender roles and the damage that sexism can do. White supremacy has been so successful in large part because of these regimes of patriarchy that it gets coupled with.

KKY: When did you know it was going to end with Angel?

SG: Not until very late. I realized that the story is about large societal questions—racism, sexism, etc.—but it's also about the transformative and ultimately healing power of storytelling. At the end of the day, Angel is a storyteller and a healer.

A Process of Discovery

KKY: Literature, whether we want it to or not, educates both the heart and the mind. You are in that way a very intellectual writer. You teach.

SG: The book was a process of discovery for me in writing it, and I hope it's process of discovery for readers. But you know, Toni Morrison asks this question in *Playing in the Dark: Whiteness and the Literary Imagination*, a question which I think is still open for debate: given the white American colonial project, which is a bloody, racially violent one, we have to ask: is it possible for American writers to imagine discovery, to imagine encountering difference in a way that is not about domination? I don't think I answer this question. I don't know if there is an answer, but I think it's one of the fundamental questions of the book.

KKY: Thinking of myself, I was six years old when we came to America [from a refugee camp in Thailand, where Yang was born]. I knew A, B, and C, that was it. But I started writing in English fairly quickly. My first story was about a watermelon seed planted in the ground. And the watermelon knows as soon as she grows, she'll be eaten, so she tries not to grow. (This is from a six-and-a-half-year-old.) But she doesn't have hands or feet so she can't stop the growth and one day she's eaten. All she can do is send one wish at the moon: that the wind blow and all her seeds will be scattered and take life somewhere else. I am still a part of that wish, and you are, too.

Wakanda Forever

SG: Part of my trepidation in writing *Dream Country* was that most of what's written about Liberia has been written by non-Liberians. That is a colonial model. But, then, the conclusion I eventually came to is that the book is about these chasms between Africans and African Americans told through the lens of this specific historical example.

KKY: But even beyond that, you're speaking to the beating hearts of your children. You have a stake in the outcomes of the Angels and

Kollies of the world. They're your students, but also your own children. It isn't so clean as a colonial model.

SG: No, it's not. Even though I'm divorced, I'm forever a part of a Liberian family through my children—

KKY: Who for Halloween two days ago chose to return to the mythical dreamland of the dreamlands: Hollywood.

SG: Right! Wakanda forever. Both of them [wore *Black Panther* costumes]. Their father has been telling them recently about how their family is from Lofa County in the northwest of Liberia, and how there's a story from his family that they're descended from the last king of Lofa—Lofa was one of the last territories to become part of Liberia proper. And so my son now—he's almost nine—has been telling people he's a prince, an African prince. He's very proud of this. He was last there [Liberia] when he was four and half, but he remembers. And he wants to go back.